BACKFIRE

THE FIGHTING O'NEILS
BACKFIRE

WILLIAM W. JOHNSTONE
AND J.A. JOHNSTONE

PINNACLE BOOKS
Kensington Publishing Corp.
www.kensingtonbooks.com

PINNACLE BOOKS are published by

Kensington Publishing Corp.
119 West 40th Street
New York, NY 10018

First Printing: May 2023
ISBN-13: 978-0-7860-4964-6

10 9 8 7 6 5 4 3 2 1

Printed in the United States of America

CHAPTER 1

The day began strangely for rancher Sean O'Neil . . . and got stranger.

He and his brother Johnny had just finished breakfast when the Abe Patterson stage rattled to a halt outside the door and a man's voice yelled, "Howdy, the house."

Sean recognized that voice. He wiped off his mustache, tossed his napkin onto the table and stepped outside. The sun was just cresting the horizon and the morning had come in bright and clean.

Driver Buttons Muldoon and shotgun guard Red Ryan were up in the box, silhouetted against a crimson sky, and both looked serious, rare expressions for two usually smiling men.

"Howdy, Sean," Buttons said. He touched his hat to Johnny who stood behind his brother. "Champ."

"Been a while, Buttons," Johnny said.

"Me and Red are on the El Paso run, don't come down this way any longer," Buttons said.

"Well, you're here now, Buttons, and we got coffee on the stove," Sean said. "You and Red step down and have a cup."

"I'd admire to, Sean, but we got to be going."

"What's the big hurry? I don't see any passengers."

"Nor mail either. I'll cut to the chase, Sean. Have you seen the Tucker and Scott stage pass this way real recent?"

Sean shook his head no. "Can't say as I have, Buttons. The last time I saw it was oh, maybe a month ago when it brought someone visiting the Oaktree ranch this way. You looking for it?"

"Yeah, me and just about every stage line and lawman in West Texas. The Tucker and Scott stage was on a run from Abilene to San Angelo when it just up and disappeared."

"What do you mean, disappeared?" asked Sean.

"I mean gone, poof! Vanished off the face of the earth. Six passengers with Cowbell Creek Max Tillman in the driver's seat and Tom Welch riding messenger, a pair of experienced and gun-handy men. Tim Tucker has posted a thousand-dollar reward for finding it."

"You suspect road agents, Buttons?" Johnny O'Neil said.

"Maybe. But road agents wouldn't have taken the stage. There's no sign of it, or bodies either." Buttons sighed. "I guess we'll keep searching, though I'm not holding out much hope of finding it. How about you, Red?"

Red Ryan shook his head. "It don't look good. Sean, Eddie Burchett the Abilene drawfighter was on that stage. I don't think road agents would've tangled with him."

"Apaches maybe?" Johnny O'Neil said.

"Maybe. But Apaches travel light," Buttons said. "They wouldn't drag away a stage weighing more than two thousand pounds and then hide it someplace. They'd take the horses is all."

"It's darned spooky is what it is," Red said.

"That's a natural fact," Buttons said. "Red, do you recollect the Whiskey Creek ghost town that time?"

"How could I ever forget?" Red said.

"You have a story to tell, Buttons," Johnny said, his expression hopeful. Good yarns were hard to come by on the remote West Texas range.

"Maybe some other time, Champ," Buttons said.

"It ain't a long yarn," Red said. "Go on, tell it, since it concerns a stagecoach an' all."

"Our coach," Buttons said. "How it come up, me and Red had just started out with the Patterson stage line, when we ran into the biggest thunderstorm we ever did see, then or since. The heavens opened, the rain came down in sheets, and the lightning, well, them spikes were bad enough and close enough to curdle a man's blood."

"Where was this?" Johnny said, excited, warming to the tale.

"West of the Pecos, about twenty miles out from El Paso," Buttons said. "That's wild, open country, flat for the most part until we found ourselves in some kind of canyon that had no right to be there."

"Later we looked for that gulch but were never able to find it again," Red said. "All we saw was flat ground and a few scrubby trees, nothing else."

"No canyon," Johnny said.

"No canyon," Red said. "And no sign of a town, but I'll get to that directly."

"Well, the storm was so bad and the night so roaring and black, I lit the sidelamps and we kept on going," Buttons said, "hoping we'd find a place to shelter and where I could settle the team, since they were pretty worked up. The thing is, the deeper we drove into the canyon, the worse the storm got, thunder banging and them sizzling lightning flashes every minute, or so it seemed."

"Dangerous," Johnny said. "I mean you and Red perched so high in your seat."

Buttons said, "Yes, it was, Red and me, we was riding

a cyclone with the bridle off and right there I started to get really boogered."

"Now," Red said, "to make a long story short . . ."

"No, don't," Johnny said. "Take your time."

"Champ, we got a schedule to keep," Buttons said.

"Tell us how it all ended," Sean said. "I haven't heard a decent big windy in ages."

"Sean, it ain't a big windy, especially when it ended up with Buttons putting a bullet in a man," Red said.

"Well, I put a bullet into something that looked like a man," Buttons said. "We never did find a body."

"How did that happen?" Johnny said.

Buttons said, "The canyon got wider and in the distance the sky took on a red glow as though the brush was on fire. But nothing could burn in that downpour."

"Then we drove into a large clearing where . . . Sean, you're not going to believe this . . ."

"Try me," Sean said.

"It was a small town, but despite the rain every one of its buildings were on fire. But it was a fire like no other. It gave out no heat and even though the stores and houses burned, they were unharmed, as though it was . . ."

"A phantom fire," Johnny said.

"That's what it was, fiery structures in lashing rain. And then it happened . . ." Buttons continued the story. "Suddenly this skinny old coot with a long gray beard and a rifle in his hands, ran toward the stage and in a loud, screeching voice yelled, 'Get away from here or I'll kill you both.' Well, no one charges the Abe Paterson and Son Stage and Express Company with a gun in his hands, not so long as I am the driver."

Johnny's eyes were as round as coins. "What did you do?"

"Do? Why, I pulled my Colt and plugged him. He was there and then gone and although we searched those burning buildings all around us, we never found the body."

"Then you shot a ghost," Johnny said.

"Seems like. But spook or mortal, he shouldn't have charged the Patterson stage like he did. He was asking for trouble, and he found it."

Red said, "Later we were told that there was a settlement called Whiskey Flat, but it burned to ashes in 1867 and its entire population burned with it."

"Then, who was the old timer with the rifle?" Johnny said.

Red shrugged.

"Who knows? As I said, me and Buttons went back that way to take a look and found nothing, no canyon and no burned town."

"And no body."

Red shook his head. "No body."

"Buttons, do you think something like that happened to the Tucker and Scott stage?" Johnny said.

"It's possible, but I doubt it," Buttons said. "The Tucker and Scott stage vanished without a trace." He leaned over and slapped the side of the coach. "As you can see, we're still here."

"Stranger things have happened, I guess," Johnny said.

"You're right about that," Buttons said. "But not many." He looked over the side of the stage. "Champ, bang that door shut. It works itself open all the time."

Johnny did as Buttons asked, and the driver gathered up the team's reins. "Well, it was nice talking to you again, Sean and the Champ. Now we're headed north for El Paso and on the way, we'll see what we see."

"Which probably will be nothing," Red said.

"It sure is a mystery," Sean said. "But since Tim Tucker has posted the thousand-dollar reward for information leading to the return of the stage we'll keep our eyes open."

"Well, so long," Buttons said. He cracked his whip, and the stage lurched into motion. "Good luck."

"Yeah, you too, good luck," Sean said.

Under a dawning sky banded with red and jade, the sun coming up like a crucible of molten iron, Sean and Johnny watched the stage leave until it was shrouded by its own dust cloud. Maria Perez stepped out of the cabin, her weeks-old baby son in her arms. "We had visitors?" she said.

"The Patterson stage," Sean said.

"It seems a Tucker and Scott stage has gone missing and everybody's searching for it," Johnny said.

"Gone missing?" Maria said, her baby fussing, making little bird-chirp noises.

"Off the face of the earth on a run from Abilene to San Angelo," Johnny said. "There's no sign of it anywhere or its six passengers."

"Oh, how awful," Maria said. She hurriedly crossed herself.

"Now you better get inside," Johnny said. "You should be resting."

Named Billy for her dead lover, the baby seconded that suggestion by caterwauling up a storm, and Maria said, "He's hungry. I'll take him in and feed him."

"I hope so," Sean said, frowning. Unlike Johnny, he was not too keen on babies, especially crying ones.

After Maria stepped into the cabin, Sean looked to the south and said, "Rider coming in."

"At a gallop," Johnny said, suddenly concerned.

The rider who drew rein beside Sean was the new owner of the Oaktree ranch, the man named Dick Peterson who'd once ramrodded the spread. Sean had long ago formed a favorable opinion of the man, and nothing had happened since to change it. He was tall, muscular, and hard-bodied, with a long, narrow face and intelligent brown eyes that spoke more of poet than rancher. Like Sean, he sported the sweeping dragoon mustache then in fashion among Western men, and the well-worn Colt on his hip was down to earth enough, as was the Winchester booted under his left knee. Peterson, who looked to be in his early forties, touched the brim of his hat and when he spoke his voice was harsh and commanding.

"I've got news for you, Mr. O'Neil," he said.

"Call me Sean. Is your news good or bad?"

"I guess the answer to that is up to you," Peterson said.

"Then let me get at it."

The man leaned forward in the saddle, hands on the horn. "There's a wagon train camped on your range." He pointed to the west. "About two miles that way. Looks like it's been there for a couple of days." He smiled, showing small, but white teeth. "And call me Dick, since we're neighbors."

"Did you see it, Dick? How many wagons?"

"I didn't see them, but one of my hands did. He said twenty wagons and downright unfriendly folks."

"How unfriendly?"

"Unsociable enough that somebody took a pot at him that came close to parting his hair in the middle."

"I don't like the sound of that," Johnny said.

Peterson nodded and then said, "Good to see you again, Johnny. How's the leg holding up?"

"I still have a limp, but apart from that it's fine."

"Glad to hear it. Sean, I took the liberty of sending for Sheriff Beason. I told him to come here, since those pilgrims are on your range."

"Thank you for that," Sean said. "Light and set, Dick. We've coffee on the stove, and I think there's some of Maria's bear sign left."

"I'm much obliged," Peterson said. He swung out of the saddle, looped the reins to the hitching post and glanced at the sky where streaks of red and jade bled like watercolors into a background of faded blue. "Gonna be a hot one," he said.

"Seems like," Sean said.

CHAPTER 2

The people, pilgrims in their own minds, called him Micah, the great prophet who'd brought them all the way from Kansas to this remote spot on the map. Men, women, and children, they gathered around him, eager to hear Micah's sermon on the terrifying reckoning to come.

"As a traveling preacher, I was riding, not a stone's throw from Kansas City, that Sodom and Gomorrah of the plains, and I had a great vision that made me fall from my horse in terror," he said.

"Tell us, tell us," the pilgrims chanted, their usual eager response to Micah when he told of his divine insight into the intentions of God.

"As I lay stunned on the ground. I was suddenly surrounded by a dazzling light," Micah said. He was small, slender and wore a crimson robe, a symbol of his divinity. "Behold, my vision cleared, and I beheld an angel of the Lord, dressed all in silver armor, a mighty flaming sword grasped in his hands. Give me a hallelujah!"

The surrounding pilgrims in the wagon circle erupted into a chorus of hallelujahs and yelled, "Tell us again, prophet, about what the angel said."

"He said bless all who follow me to the promised land

for they are the chosen and will escape the terrible vengeance to come," Micah said. "He told me to speak to the people of Kansas, urge them to sell their farms and possessions and follow me to glory. And praise the Lord, that's what you, the faithful ones did!"

"Tell us of the anger of God and the fires to come," a woman called out.

"Oh, they will be terrible fires as the Lord punishes mankind for their iniquities," Micah said, his eyes glittering. Then, almost screaming, "From pole to pole, the earth will be ablaze and every living creature will suffer the flaming death of the unsaved!"

"Where will we be safe, prophet?" a man said.

"Here. Right here, within this wagon circle," Micah yelled, raising his arms. "As the fires rage around us, God will have cooling fountains rise from the earth you stand on, and He'll shower down sweetmeats to sustain you. And then . . ."

"Tell us, prophet," a woman said. "Tell us about the gateway to heaven."

"Yes, you will see a golden portal open amid the flames and you will ride your wagons into paradise. Glory hallelujah!"

Amid cheers, Micah raised his hands for silence.

He pointed behind him to where a large wooden box sat on a pedestal draped in a purple cloth. "As the fires rage, there is the offering of gold I will surrender to the Lord as a sacrifice. I must implore all of you that you don't keep back money or jewelry. Give what you have freely. Remember, generous donations to the Lord our God is your path to paradise."

Micah acknowledged the applause he received and then said, "Now it must be said that we will protect our wagon circle from any and all attempts by wicked men intent on doing us harm. The Lord's offering is a rare prize for the unworthy and we will protect it with our very lives if need be. Yea, our very lives!" A voice from the crowd called out, "Prophet, will the Lord help protect us from the evil ones you speak of?"

"Yes, he will. He told me in a vision that He will not allow his chosen ones to suffer. Hallelujah!"

After the answering cries from the crowd died down, Micah raised his arms, tilted back his head, and stared at the clear blue sky. After a while he said, "Yes, Lord, I understand, and I will do as you say." He lowered his head, and his gaze swept the crowd. "Now is the time to surrender any remaining monies or jewelry to the Lord. Do not hold back. Remember the time of destruction is nigh, and ye must enter the kingdom of heaven without a penny in your pockets. So says our God and so let it be done."

There were cheers from the assembled pilgrims as a woman made a show of handing Micah her wedding ring, and he in turn bowed his head in all humility.

CHAPTER 3

Johnny O'Neil noticed it, Sean didn't . . . the unexpected, lightning flash of love at first sight. It was as though Dick Peterson had seen a flourishing utopia and become entranced by the abundant beauty displayed before him.

Sean talked cattle prices and range conditions and, always interested in ranch business, Dick Peterson returned in kind, but he had eyes for only Maria Perez, and while Johnny noted this with a keen, amused interest, Sean seemed totally oblivious.

"More coffee, Mr. Peterson?" Maria said, the sooty pot poised above the man's cup.

"Please . . . and call me Dick. You make good coffee Miss Perez."

"Maria." The girl smiled and filled his cup.

"My cook makes lousy coffee, way too weak and full of grounds," Peterson said. "This is the best coffee I've had in a six month and maybe ever."

Johnny stirred the pot. "You need a wife, Dick," he said.

He saw Maria's cheekbones color, and Peterson seemed at a loss for words. But the moment passed when Sean glanced out the window and said, "Sheriff Beason is here."

Sean opened the door for the big-bellied lawman who stepped inside and immediately filled up the room. "Now what's going on here?" he said. He scowled at Sean and smiled at Johnny. "How are you, Mr. O'Neil?"

"Can't complain, sheriff," Johnny said.

"How's the leg?"

"I'm limping."

Beason smiled. "Then we won't see you in the boxing ring again, huh?"

"No, you won't. I was finished with that anyway," Johnny said. "I'm getting a mite too old for prizefighting."

"I know, and what a loss you are to the noble art. It's a pity, a great pity." Beason's attention swung back to Sean. "Mr. Peterson's hand told me you have a few renegade wagons on your land. Is that so?"

"It's so. And a few wagons is twenty wagons, and they don't look like they're planning on leaving anytime soon."

"Travelers, no doubt," Beason said. "On their way to pastures new. Did you approach them?"

"Not yet. Dick's man saw the wagons but stayed clear after they took a shot at him."

Peterson said, "Lem Rising is a top hand and handy with the iron, but he said there was something strange about those wagons that he couldn't quite put his finger on . . . something dangerous. He says a voice in his head warned him to light a shuck double quick."

"What was an Oaktree rider doing on O'Neil's range?" Beason said.

Peterson said, "Renegade, my Hereford bull, got loose again and Lem was bringing him in."

"I . . . see . . ." Beason said, as though what the rancher just told him was of immense importance and required some deep pondering. Finally, he sighed and said, "Long ride out here from Mustang Flat. Gives a man a thirst."

"Sheriff, can I get you a glass of water?" Maria said.

Bob Beason looked like he'd just been slapped. "Water? Young lady, West Texas water can kill a man quicker 'n' scat, and that's a natural fact."

Johnny said, "I think the sheriff would find whiskey more to his taste, Maria."

"A thoughtful suggestion, Mr. O'Neil, but no. Since I'm about my duties, I will not imbibe a drop."

"Put the bottle away, Maria," Johnny said.

"But . . ." Beason said, rising a forefinger.

Maria waited, the Old Crow bottle in her hand.

"On second thoughts, I'd better wet my whistle since I aim do a heap of talking to them pilgrims with the wagons. Miz Perez, not too much. Just three fingers will do nicely. No, make it four since you have such a little hand."

"Then drink up, Beason while I saddle a horse," Sean said. "How come you ain't heeled?"

"O'Neil, if I told you once, I've told you a hundred times, I don't hold with revolvers. I can't hit a darned . . . sorry Miz Perez . . . a danged thing with any of them. But I have a rifle on my hoss. It's all an honest man needs."

"Beason, as I recollect, you can't do much with a rifle either," Sean said.

"Well, what I perhaps lack in shooting skills, I make up for in smarts. That's what a lawman needs these days, brain before brawn."

"And you have plenty of brawn, sheriff," Johnny said, smiling, removing the sting.

"I say we both qualify in that department, Mr. O'Neil," Beason said.

"Indeed, we do," Johnny said.

"I'll get my horse," Sean said, rising from his chair. A tall young man, lean and, according to the ladies at least,

BACKFIRE   15

handsome, he wore dusty range clothes and a walnut
handled Colt holstered on his hip. He looked almost frail
next to Beason's vast bulk, but much more significant.

"Sean, saddle one for me," Johnny said.

Sean looked doubtful. "Are you sure you want to ride
with that leg of yours?"

"Sure, I'm sure. Saddle the Morgan mare for me. She
knows how to act like a lady."

"You can't beat a Morgan," Beason said. "It's an easy-
riding hoss."

Sean nodded. "Get ready then, Johnny. We'll leave
soon."

Dick Peterson rose, replaced his hat, and smiled at
Maria. "Dear lady, you've been a sweet distraction, and
I hope we can meet again real soon."

"That's very sweet," Maria said. "You're welcome anytime, if you don't mind the baby."

The big rancher's smile grew wider. "I love puppies,
kittlins, foals, and I've got a son of my own who's growing
like a weed."

"I'd like to meet him," Maria said. Her smile was shy,
surprising the heck out of Johnny.

"Why, Maria, has your heart turned to another so
soon?" he said, teasing.

"I didn't realize . . ." Peterson said. His cheeks pinked
and he gave Johnny a sheepish glance.

"I did," Johnny said. "Maria is a lovely woman, and she
is fierce, she makes her own choices." He winked, and
though his eyes sparkled, and his tone remained playful,
he felt a pang in his heart. Maria slapped him lightly on
the shoulder, but both Dick Peterson and Maria seemed to
be momentarily tongue-tied, leaving it to Sheriff Beason

to say, "Love in the air? Is that what it was? It brushed past me like a spring breeze."

Johnny grinned. "You're learning, sheriff?"

"Learning what, Mr. O'Neil?"

"How to be a human being, old man," Johnny said.

CHAPTER 4

The morning's candy-cane sky had faded to a uniform blue and the risen sun burned like a molten coin, rapidly heating up the vast, rolling grassland where Sean O'Neil's placid Herefords grazed.

Favoring his brother's game leg, Sean kept an easy, cantering pace that ate up distance, and the circled wagons came into sight after an hour of riding.

"Twenty wagons all right," sheriff Bob Beason said. "They look peaceful enough. Folks just passing through."

"They're on my range," Sean said, his face like stone.

"Quite so," Beason said. "They have no right to be there, even if they're just passing through."

"I'll move them on, don't worry about that," the sheriff added. "Now they're dealing with the law."

When they were a hundred yards from the wagons, Sheriff Bob Beason drew rein and bade the others do the same. "I'll take it from here," he said. He removed his star from his pocket, shined it up on his pants, and pinned it to his shirt. "If those pilgrims are squatters, they'll soon know what it's like to deal with a sworn officer of the law."

"Sheriff, you're not county," Dick Peterson said. "But don't tell them that."

"There hasn't been a county sheriff in a six-month since old Barker Phillips got took by the consumption," Beason said. "He was a good man was old Barker and after he died, I extended my jurisdiction beyond Mustang Flat until a new county sheriff is appointed. And let me tell you, that's good news for this part of Texas. Now you boys stay right here while me and the wagon master, whoever he is, get to cussin' and discussin'."

"Be careful, Beason," Sean said. "Remember, somebody among those wagons already took a shot at an Oaktree hand."

Beason pointed to the star on his chest. "See this, O'Neil, it's my armor, the law's shining breastplate. Those pilgrims wouldn't dare shoot at an officer of the law."

Bob Beason said a lot of things in his career that turned out wrong . . . and that last was one of them.

"Prophet, a rider is coming toward us," a towheaded boy said, tugging at Micah's sleeve. "He's got a star on his shirt."

Micah looked beyond the wagons and said, "I see him. He's a lawman of some kind. The Lord told me to avoid the breed." He glanced around the wagon circle and yelled, "Stranger coming in. Be on guard everyone."

As armed men surrounded him, Micah said. "Let your rifles do the talking, but don't shoot to kill. With the Lord's help we can scare the intruder away without bloodshed."

* * *

Sean watched as Sheriff Bob Beason approached the wagons, his right hand raised in a peace gesture. The big lawman drew rein and yelled, "Hello the wagons!"

Silence. Within the wagon circle the only movement was the shuffling of the oxen herd that had hauled the pilgrims there. Now Sean was closer, he smelled meat roasting and rightly deduced that one of his cows was turning on a spit.

As though he'd read Sean's mind, Peterson said, "One of yours or one of mine?"

"My guess is one of mine," Sean said. "It's my range."

"And now it becomes serious," Peterson said, his face grim. "Cattle rustling is a hanging offense."

"If they'll just move on, I'm willing to forget about the cow," Sean said.

"And if they don't?" Peterson said.

"I haven't studied on that yet," Sean said. "Maybe I'm afraid of the answer."

Beason rode closer to the wagon circle and called out again. "Now see here, I'm an officer of the law. Make an opening there to admit me, I'm coming inside."

That request was met with a fusillade of fire, both men and women shooting from behind a barricaded wagon. It seemed that none of the shots were intended to kill, though a bullet sent Beason's hat sailing off his head. And that was enough for him. He swung his horse around and galloped back to Sean and the others.

"They don't want to talk," the sheriff said. His eyes were as big as silver dollars, and he looked pale around the gills. "I lost my hat. Somebody shot my hat clear off my head."

"We saw," Sean said. "Stay here, Beason. I'll talk to them."

"While you're there, get my hat, huh?" the sheriff said.

Expecting a bullet at any second, Sean O'Neil rode toward the circled wagons. They were all ordinary farm wagons fitted with canvas covers, not the huge Conestogas that had proved too heavy for prairie use. The canvases were threadbare in places, mud and smoke stained, an indication that the pilgrims had traveled a fair piece to get to West Texas. From where? Sean guessed Kansas, judging by the farm wagons, but they could be from anywhere. When he was within hailing distance, a man yelled from the circle.

"Go away, you're not wanted here!"

Sean drew rein and said, "No, sir, you're not wanted here. Your wagons are on my land."

"No, this is not your land," the man said. "This is God's land, the land I now stand on. Hallelujah!"

"Show yourself, mister," Sean said. "We need to talk."

"Your kind talk with guns."

"And your kind cut loose plenty of gun talk your ownselves."

"The lawman was a threat. He alarmed my people."

"Mister, I'm all through talking to a wagon," Sean said. "Step out and show yourself."

"My name is Micah, and I know the Lord will protect me, as He protects all my people."

A few moments passed and a small, slight man dressed in a long, scarlet robe stepped out from between the wagons. He had a high forehead and long, thin, straggly hair that fell to his shoulders, skinny and sun-wrinkled. He looked to be about fifty years old, but could've been any age. He was supported, his gnarled hands resting on their shoulders, by two young girls in drab, brown skirts, and homespun shirts. They looked as though they'd just come off the farm and glared at Sean with open hostility.

"Why are you here on my range?" Sean said.

"Perhaps to save you from the wrath to come."

"What wrath are you talking about, old timer?"

"The wrath of the Lord. He chose this hallowed spot to be a haven for us who believe in the terrible day of judgement to come." He looked up at the denim blue sky and raised his arms. "Hallelujah!"

"Hallelujah!" the girls echoed in unison. Plain-looking children with the shining eyes of fanatics.

"Why on my ranch?" Sean said. He reckoned he was dealing with a lunatic. "Most of West Texas is open range, there's plenty of room to park wagons."

"Because just three days past, this is where God reached out his mighty hand and halted our wagons. 'Here, Micah,' he said. 'This is the place I've anointed for you.' My people had come a long way for that sacred moment, and this is where we will remain."

"How far have you traveled?"

"From the godless Kansas plains." He waved a hand behind him. "We are the chosen people whom the Lord led from that heathen place."

Sean shook his head. "I don't believe I hear myself saying this, but what does God intend to do?"

Micah raised his thin arms and yelled, "What has God chosen to do? Tell him my people. Be heard! Let your voices be raised to the heavens."

Then, from the throats of many people within the

wagon circle, as though they'd learned it by rote, came an almost savage cry of, "He will destroy this sinful world with fire and brimstone and the flaming swords of his avenging angels will spare none but the chosen souls within the wagon circle. Hallelujah!"

"Repent!" Micah called out to Sean. "Sell all you have and join us. The sands run quickly through the hourglass, and the time of the great annihilation is nigh."

Men, women, and children, about sixty in number, appeared from between the wagons and chanted, "Repent . . . repent . . . repent . . ."

Sean hollered above the din, "Mister, you've got until tomorrow to get off my range."

"We do not care about your threats," Micah yelled. "We will be here until the world is destroyed and your range is aglow with ashes."

"Until tomorrow," Sean said, knowing he'd lost the battle.

"Begone," Micah said. "Do not defile this sacred place with your vile presence any longer."

The men, all of them looked like farmers in their thirties and forties, carried rifles of various types and calibers. There would be no pistoleros among them, but Sean reckoned they could make those squirrel rifles bark and bite.

He swung his horse away, leaned out of the saddle at a run and retrieved Beason's holed hat and cantered to where Johnny, the sheriff, and Dick Peterson awaited him.

"Well?" Beason said, ramming his hat back on his head.

"They won't move," Sean said.

"Then we'll have to move them," Peterson said.

"How?" Sean said.

"I'll figure out a way to bring the full force of the law down on those pilgrims," Beason said. "Shooting at a peace officer is a serious offense."

"Do you have any kind of plan so far?" Sean asked, as his restive horse tossed its head at a fly and its bridle chimed.

"Not yet," Beason said.

"Be sure to tell us when you do," Sean said.

CHAPTER 5

Even in 1880s West Texas, news traveled quickly. And though Mustang Flat was a two-hour ride from Oaktree, it was one of Dick Peterson's hands who brought exciting tidings to the eager ears of the Crystal Palace saloon denizens, emphasizing just one word . . . *treasure*. And that was a pity, because Black John Hannah and his boys were only passing through, but all of a sudden, they decided to stay, at least for a spell.

Black John, named for the color of his hair, eyes, and dark heart, was hell on wheels with a Colt and so were his subordinate gunmen. It was said that when they met him in the street even Jesse and Frank tipped their hats to Black John, and Wes Hardin called him sir. A man who sported a large mustache that matched his heavy eyebrows, his good looks were enhanced but not diminished, at least according to the ladies, by scars on his left cheek, put there by the fingernails of a Deadwood whore who didn't live long enough to boast of it. When asked by a reporter from the *Fort Worth Weekly Gazette* how many men he'd killed, Black John answered, "Twenty-three white men to my certain knowledge, all in fair fight, and every one of those sons of the devil deserved killing."

That was not quite true. Hannah once gunnèd an unarmed drover in a dugout saloon on the Bozeman Trail over the favors of a fallen woman, and in an alley near Fifth and Allen he bushwhacked and shotgunned a Tombstone gambler by the name of Loco Lloyd Burns for the money in his wallet.

Withal, Black John was an almighty dangerous man who stepped lightly on either side of the law, at times a bounty hunter, bank robber, town sheriff, stagecoach messenger, and serving a six-month stint as a Texas Ranger. But his steady occupation was as a hired gun, and he brought his three named pistoleros and five additional ruffians to the negotiating table when fees were discussed.

Now Black John was drifting, but the word treasure made him sit up, take notice, and throw out an anchor.

"Hey, cowboy," he said, shoving a chair out from under the table. "Come set and have a drink with us."

Flattered to be noticed by such an obvious badman, the young drover said, "Don't mind if I do."

As the cowboy pushed off from the bar, Lucas Battles, the proprietor of the Crystal Place whispered, "Watch your step, Jake."

If Jake Grimshaw heard, he didn't let it faze him. He sat at Black John's table and picked up the whiskey the man poured for him.

"Name's John Hannah, pleased to meet you."

"Jake Grimshaw. Right pleased to meet you, Mr. Hannah."

He extended his hand, but Black John didn't take it. He never, ever, let another man clamp fingers on his gun hand. "How's the whiskey?" he said.

"A sight better than what I was drinking," Grimshaw said.

"Tell me about the treasure."

"I work for the Oaktree spread and heard about it from another hand," the young cowboy said.

"Go on, tell me."

"Well, sir, twenty pilgrim wagons down from Kansas, have parked themselves on Sean O'Neil's Running-S range."

"This O'Neil, is he anybody?"

"His ranch is small, smaller than Oaktree where I work, but he runs Herefords, him and his brother Johnny, a retired prizefighter."

"Do O'Neil and the pug know about the treasure?"

"I don't know. Maybe."

A careful man, Black John said, "Is O'Neil gun handy?"

"Well, I wasn't there, but there was trouble at Oaktree about a year ago and two hired drawfighters made it mighty uncomfortable for Sean and his brother."

"Uncomfortable? What do you mean?"

"They made threats. And then Sean got shot. Put him in bed for a spell."

"Who were the drawfighters?"

"One of them got shot. I don't know his name, but the other one was John D. Lowery."

That drew a reaction from Hannah's gunmen. They'd heard that name before. Lowery was a marquee drawfighter who'd gunned more than his share.

"What happened to Lowery?" Black John said.

"What I heard . . ."

"Go on, what did you hear?"

"I heard he put a couple of bullets into Johnny O'Neil, but Johnny took the hits and killed Lowery with his bare fists." Grimshaw made wide shoulders with his hands. "Johnny O'Neil is a big man and strong."

Hannah absorbed that and then said, "Tell me what you heard about the treasure."

Grimshaw coughed. "All this talking has made my throat dry."

Black John poured another drink and said, "Go on."

"Well, Sheriff Beason . . ."

"Who's he?"

"He's the law in Mustang Flat, but he doesn't do much."

"My kind of sheriff," Black John said. "Go on."

"Well, Sheriff Beason went back to Oaktree for lunch with Mr. Peterson." Grimshaw saw the question on Black John's face and said, "Mr. Peterson is my boss. He owns Oaktree, the spread next to the Sean O'Neil's Running-S."

"Tell me about him."

"Who?"

"Peterson."

"He ramrodded Oaktree and then after the owner, Mr. Kincaid, was killed in that trouble I told you about, he bought the place."

"Anything else?"

"Well, the talk is he was a Texas Ranger and is good with a gun."

"Have you seen him shoot?"

"No. I just heard he was good."

Hannah nodded and then said, "Go on. Talk about the treasure."

"Well, how it come up, Sheriff Beason was talking with Mr. Peterson and said there are twenty wagons and that means twenty families sold off their farms in Kansas to come to Texas. Then Sheriff Beason said, 'Where is the money?' Then my boss said, 'I'm convinced, and keep this under your hat, sheriff, that there's a treasure chest in that wagon circle and that's why they fight so darned hard to keep strangers away.'"

"The price of twenty Kansas farms adds up to a pile of cash all right," Black John said. "Who's in charge?"

"Of the wagons?"

"Yeah, of the wagons."

"He wears a red robe, and he calls himself Micah, and that's all I know about him."

"Micah? What kind of ten-dollar name is that?"

"I don't rightly know," Grimshaw said. "If you ask me, he must be three pickles short of a full barrel."

"Why are he and his rubes here on whatshisname's range?" Black John Hannah said.

"That's where it gets strange." The young cowboy nudged his glass closer to the bottle. "He told Mr. O'Neil that God is coming to destroy the earth with fire and brimstone and only them pilgrims within the wagon circle will be saved."

Amid the laughter of his gunmen, Hannah said, "And when will this big burn happen?"

Jake Grimshaw shrugged. "I don't know. Pretty soon, before their water runs out, I guess."

"So why travel with all that money if God is just gonna burn it up?"

"To buy their way into heaven or out of hell, maybe. I don't know."

Black John poured whiskey in the cowboy's glass and said, "What's your name again?"

"Jake, Mr. Hannah."

"That's half a name."

"Jake Grimshaw."

"Right then, Jake Grimshaw, drink up your whiskey and make tracks. Us grown men have some talking to do."

The cowboy downed his drink and then stood and said, "It was real nice talking with you, Mr. Hannah."

"Yeah, you too, now pull your picket pin and drift."

* * *

After Grimshaw left, Black John's gunmen settled their chairs around their boss and he said, "Well, what do we think, boys? Can we take those pilgrims?"

"Twenty wagons, boss," Con Ransom said. He was a tall man with a broken nose, ice-blue eyes that were piercing and intense, and the direct stare of a man who remembered faces. "That means twenty grown men and maybe some half-grown boys. We could be facing thirty guns at least."

"For God's sake, Con, they're sodbusters," Black John said, irritated. "There's eight of us. I reckon we can take on any number of sodbusters with squirrel rifles."

"Boss, I still think we'd be cutting it mighty fine," Ransom said.

"Bill, what do you think? You've gunned sodbusters before."

"Yeah, a bunch of nesters up in the Oklahoma Territory when I rode with Wild Bill Longley and them," Bill Stern said. He was as swarthy as a Comanche, but his eyes were green, reptilian, his thin hair pale, falling in slender, unruly strands from under his hat. He was fast on the draw and as vicious as a teased cougar. "Them nesters weren't much, like shooting fish in a barrel," he said. "But, hoo-wee, did we have us a time with their women."

Amid laughter, Black John said, "I'm not asking about women. I want to know if eight of us can outshoot a bunch of sodbusters and take their treasure."

"Of course, we can, boss." This from handsome Adam Curtis, a fast gun out of Bandera who'd studied for the priesthood and carried a rosary with iron beads in his pocket. "Once we get into the circle, we can cut the rubes down like wheat before a reaper." He smiled, showing large, white teeth. "Of course, getting into the circle is the problem."

"Maybe we can sweet talk our way inside," Black John said. "Say we want to join the saved or something equally stupid that the hayseeds will believe."

Curtis grinned. "Sounds good to me. I think maybe we got ourselves a plan."

"A start of one anyway," Hannah said. He smiled. "I want that darned treasure, boys." He shook his head. "I want it real bad."

CHAPTER 6

As Black John Hannah and his boys discussed the plan for the treasure heist, someone else was intently listening. A figure sat cloaked in shadows in a dusty corner of the Crystal Palace, quietly sipping Barbadian blackstrap rum, having told Battles to leave the bottle. If Black John and his boys happened to glance toward the corner, all they saw was shadows, although later a series of tragic events would see Adam Curtis proclaim he'd seen the very devil sitting there that night. As the clamoring excitement over the gold, and braying announcements about the whores and drink the men would spend it on began to dissipate, the gang drifted out of the saloon and off to their beds. Alone at last, the sinister shadows shifted to reveal a man who slinked to the bar so softly Battles nearly jumped out of his skin when the man cleared his throat to get his attention.

"Jesus, Mary, and Joseph! Ye scared the wits out of me!" Lucas Battles proclaimed, resting the broom he'd been using to its place against the wall. Battles chuckled at his own fright, but it seemed suddenly that the saloon was very dark and seething with ghosts, and the wind picked up so that the saloon doors began banging on their hinges.

"I need to send a telegram, barkeep, right away. So sorry to inconvenience you at this hour." The man grinned, showing bright white teeth, his face shrouded in darkness by his tilted down hat covered by a thick black cloak. "The witching hour they call it," he said, as the chimes on the grandfather clock began to proclaim it twelve o'clock in the morning.

"Magic happens, you should make a wish."

Although the stranger's voice was silky and soothing, something in his tone set Battles' hair to standing on end. The man was menacing, and Lucas Battles was not a man easily menaced. Although he was, most certainly, a man who would encourage any customer to spend their wages in his fine establishment by staying open to any hour, not tonight—no he badly wanted this eerie stranger gone so he could lock up those incessantly banging doors—where had that wind come from?—and go home to light all the lamps and take a sleeping draught.

He forced his voice to sound chipper.

"Surely love to help, sir, but I don't send wires. You'll either need to see if Luke Lawson is still awake over to the mercantile or maybe rouse the night clerk at the inn. Luke is probably your best bet and he charges less, too." Battles left the bar and peered out the door across to the mercantile, "Looks like the old boy's still open, if you hurry."

He desperately hoped this man would hurry, as the longer the stranger stayed and stared at him the more boogered Lucas felt. "Anyway. Looks like you've finished up, and it's time I lock up and close this establishment. You understand, I'm sure, wife at home sure gets worried!"

Battles was near to rambling with nerves and bit his

tongue to stop it from betraying his fear, but his skin was covered in gooseflesh all the same.

"Oh, I understand." The bright white grin again. This time it sent a shiver down Battles' spine. From within his cloak the stranger produced a double eagle coin, "For the rum and your troubles."

Luke protested, but the man brushed him off, "I always take care of my friends, you're my friend now, right Lucas?"

The man returned to his table, downing the last of his rum in one gulp. Battles noticed he wore an elaborate ruby signet ring that sparkled in the dim light as he tipped the bottle back and replaced it gently on the table. At last, Battles walked the man to the still banging doors to see him off. The stranger dissolved into the murky gloom of the street and seemed to disappear. Lucas Battles fought with the unruly doors, and made quick work of his barkeep duties before fleeing the Crystal Palace as though the devil were after his hide.

Luke Lawson heard the midnight bells of the bank clock and sighed. Another late night but such was the burden of a conscientious business man. His store was attached to the family home where he knew his wife and sons would have already taken to their beds. Ah well, Luke thought, a few more years of this and someday I'll build them a proper mansion with servants, and hire a shop-keeper or two that'll hold down the fort whenever I want a day off. Plus, I've earned enough to surprise Alice with one of those back-east fashions she's always mooning over, just in time for her birthday.

It was those cheerful thoughts that filled his head as he checked over his new shipments, readying a display for the morning rush. The bang of the mercantile door opening gave him a start. He would have sworn he'd locked it up. "Howdy, welcome to Lawson & Sons. Made me jump, sir," Lawson said. "I'm usually in bed by now but some days the work seems endless." Lawson watched the man approaching and instantly felt ill at ease. The door must have caught in the wind and continued banging back and forth as the stranger moved toward him with unhurried strides. The normally gregarious Lawson felt a bit off-kilter when he said, "Don't think I've seen you around town. Anything I can help you find?"

The man ran his hand across bolts of calico and took mild interest in a display of buttons before saying, "I was told you would be kind enough to send a wire for me at this late hour so as not to wake the innkeeper. Your friend Mr. Battles also informs me your rate is far cheaper. A penny saved is a penny earned, all that." The man grinned perfectly white teeth, yet his face was covered in shadow from the black cloak he kept pulled over his wide-brimmed hat. On his right hand the man wore a distinct signet ring. Tooled iron crosses held a red stone that sparkled like ruby, and for a moment Lawson found it hard to look away.

Recovering quickly from the unease he was feeling, Lawson said, "Oh sure, I can send a telegram for you, cost you maybe two dollars, depending on how many words."

The stranger had stopped admiring the sewing supplies and was peering over a small collection of jewelry and combs and ladies' potions and notions displayed in their glass case. "What's it like to have a wife, Luke?" The man's voice was plaintive, and a surprised Lawson answered, "Why, it's the most wonderful thing in the world, Mr. . . . . I'm sorry but I didn't catch your name."

The man grinned again, and Lawson found it sinister and looked away.

"I didn't give it. Now about this telegram, Luke, shall we get to it?"

Luke Lawson hurriedly sent the telegram and relieved that the business was done, saw that the man had made no attempt toward leaving.

"Sorry, Luke, just one more thing before I go and leave you to check on Alice. This ring, I'm tired of it, can we cut a deal? Then I promise I'll get out of your hair."

The deal was simple and at last Luke walked the stranger to the still-banging door and wished him a nice night while suggesting he seek occupancy at the inn. It wasn't until the door was battened down and Luke blew out the final lamp that he realized with a jolt, that he'd never once told the man his, or his wife's name. And with that sudden knowledge he dashed to his bed and pulled Alice close, listening to the quiet sound of a door somewhere in town banging wildly into the night.

CHAPTER 7

In the bright sunshine of the following day, Lucas Battles was recovered from his terrors of the evening prior, though he'd suffered nightmares about banging doors all the night long. Black John Hannah was in town, and Battles had been all too eager to whisper that less than welcome news into Sheriff Bob Beason's reluctant ear.

Now the lawman plowed through a sheaf of dodgers but finally sighed and had to admit that Black John's likeness was not among them. When Western men sat and shot the breeze, Beason had heard Hannah's name mentioned occasionally, but not as an outlaw, rather they argued about his place in the gunman hierarchy, usually agreeing that he was somewhere at the top of the list, above Wyatt Earp but below Longhaired Jim Courtright.

Beason scratched his head under his hat, a habit of his when thinking was called for. What the heck were Black John and his boys doing in a jerkwater town like Mustang Flat? They were way off their range, and wasn't it a strange coincidence that a stagecoach disappeared without trace just when they were in the vicinity? It was worth investigating, especially since Battles claimed Tucker and Scott had put up a reward for the return of their missing stage.

Beason rose from his desk and looked out the window.

It was the middle of the day, and the merciless sun pounded the dusty street like a sledgehammer. Across from his office Mrs. Mary Baldwin, pregnant again, and gray-haired Mrs. Penelope Lind stood talking under the awning of Luke Lawson's general store. Beason guessed they were gossiping about Bessie Blunt, a blond widow woman who was only as good as she had to be and seemed to entertain a steady clientele of gentlemen callers. To the west stood the Crystal Palace, the only saloon in town, half-a-dozen hipshot ponies and a few majestic mares and geldings tied to the hitching rail outside. A distance beyond the saloon lay what the townspeople called Little Sonora, a sprawling Mexican ghetto of wood frame and tarpaper shacks. Unlike the quietly dozing town itself, the village was noisy, alive with the sound of men, women, and children and dogs, and as always, the spicy aroma of cooking hung over the streets. Beason usually left the place strictly alone since, apart from the odd cutting, there was little serious crime.

According to Lucas Battles, Black John Hannah said he and his boys had come down from El Paso way. Beason turned from the window and, his curiosity aroused, made up his mind to take the old wagon road and scout to the north of town. If Hannah waylaid the Tucker and Scott stage, it could be in that area. It was a long shot, but worth the effort, and it would get him out of town for a spell . . . and the word was that the reward for the recovery of the stage was one-thousand dollars. Dreary Mustang Flat had a way of sucking the life out of a man, and he felt the four walls of his office closing in on him like a vise. Right then, the wagon circle on the Running-S didn't enter his thinking. For the time being at least, it was Sean O'Neil's problem, not his.

* * *

Sheriff Bob Beason followed the wagon road into the rolling, brush country north of Mustang Flat. Here and there flourished stands of gray oak, ash juniper, and creosote bush that could hide a stage from prying eyes. But only at a distance, not up close. Under a molten sun that scorched the color out of the sky and made Beason sweat, he reconnoitered a couple of likely places and found nothing except an empty pint whiskey bottle and the maggoty remains of a jackrabbit.

After an hour of fruitless searching, Beason drew rein and lit a cigar. Behind a haze of blue smoke, his face was like stone. He'd wasted his time on a wild goose chase and his hope to earn the Tucker and Scott reward had foundered on an empty wilderness of scrub and rock. Above him, the sky showed a few pale streaks of red, and a breeze explored the branches of the gray oak and juniper. He swung his horse around and then stopped. Listening.

What the heck was that?

There, he heard it again . . . a regular, metallic screech . . . fairly close . . . then silence again.

Beason's eyes swept the vast landscape around him and fixed on a brush-covered rise about a hundred yards to the east. The noise, whatever it was, seemed to come from that direction. The sound could be made by a wrecked stagecoach, a wheel turning in the breeze maybe. It was worth checking out. A cautious man, the sheriff slid his Winchester from the scabbard under his knee and laid it across the saddle horn. Only then did he knee his horse into motion.

Screech . . . screech . . . screech . . . loud and rhythmic, followed by silence.

The sound started up again, noisier now as Beason

approached the rise. His rifle at the ready, he rode around
the end of the ridge, a crumbling limestone rock face about
eight-foot tall and fifty yards wide, and then turned north
again into a flat, open, area strewn with bunchgrass, yellow
honey daisies, and pink sage. He drew rein, his eyes on the
badly decayed windmill that complained constantly as it
turned and screeched in the breeze.

Beyond the windmill, the ground sloped northward to
the burned-out ruin of a small cabin where black spars of
charred wood stuck up at all angles from the broken-rock
foundation. There seemed to be the remains of a barn and
a pig yard and two other buildings, probably a smokehouse
and a toolshed. Like the cabin, they'd been put to the
torch. To the sheriff's right there was a shallow, U-shaped
draw and then another, larger area of flat grass, much
scarred by the futile efforts of a plowshare that blunted
itself on bedrock and blighted a farmer's dreams.

Beason dismounted and scouted around the cabin.
Using the toe of his boot, he probed the ashes and uncovered scattered shell casings and a couple of blackened,
strap-iron arrowheads that had a story to tell. The Apache
or Comanche had attacked the farm and either they'd
killed everyone and then burned the place, or the settler
had won that round, but afraid and disheartened, had pulled
out, and the Indians had later torched the buildings. However it happened, there had been no happy-ever-aftering
for one starry-eyed pumpkin roller and his family. Beason
shook his head, kicked the dry ashes of the man's hopes
off his boots, and returned to his horse.

As the dreary day dragged to its close, the sky was
filmed with a thin layer of roseate cloud with no shading
or ripples, and the breeze had dropped, silencing the windmill's shrieks. Someone was watching him!

Beason had been bushwhacked enough that it was a

remembered experience, skin crawling, like walking naked into a portal hung thick with spiderwebs. He brought his Winchester to waist level and racked a round into the chamber. His head moved slowly, looking around at the surrounding landscape.

A giggle. Behind him.

The sheriff swung around, the rifle muzzle coming up fast, his finger on the trigger.

Darn it all! An Indian girl of about sixteen, ragged and underweight, stood staring at him, smiling. She wore a cloth shawl over a beaded buckskin dress and moccasins, and her hair was parted in the middle and hung loose without braids to her thin shoulders. Beason pegged her as Apache, probably, judging by her red, flannel shawl, Lipan. The gaze from her large, lustrous black eyes was direct and unwavering, but, by the standards of the time, she was too undernourished to be considered even remotely pretty.

Never one for small talk, Beason let out his pent-up breath and said, "Who the heck are you, and why are you here?"

An alarm bell ringing in his head, he waited for the girl's answer. It never came. She giggled again, turned, and ran into the brushy draw, disturbing a flock of quail that exploded into the sky like a scattergun blast.

Angry now, the sheriff heaved his vast bulk into the saddle and went after the fleeing girl. His horse breasting through brush at a canter, he saw the girl just ahead of him, but she dived into the entrance of a dome-shaped wickiup and vanished from sight.

Beason drew rein outside the untidy tree branch and brush structure and said, "Come out of there, girl. I'm an officer of the law and an important man in these parts, and I mean you no harm."

A few moments dragged past in silence and then the buckskin flap that closed the entrance twitched, opened, and a withered old man dressed in a white tunic and pants stepped outside. Like the girl, he was probably Lipan and had little reason to welcome an armed white man on a horse, and it showed in his face, wary, somewhat fearful, and stiff with resentment.

"Now see here," Beason said, donning his pomposity like a cloak, "I am an officer of the law, and I am here on a most serious investigation." He scowled. "Darn it all, I can't speak your heathen tongue, so you don't understand a word I'm saying, do you?"

"I understand," the old man, said, his voice like a creaking gate. "I have spoken with white men before."

"Good, then we're getting somewhere," the sheriff said. "Now listen up because I'm not a man who likes to repeat himself. I'm looking for a stagecoach, you know, big red people wagon pulled by horses, s-t-a-g-e c-o-a-c-h. Comprende?"

"I understand."

"Have you"—Beason laid his forefingers against his temples and then pointed them in the old timer's direction— "seen it?"

The man nodded.

"Where?"

"Near this place."

"Can you show me where it is?"

"My granddaughter can."

"Bring her out here."

"There is little to see. Ashes maybe."

"I'll be the judge of that. And as an officer of the law, I must warn you that both you and your granddaughter are now suspects in the disappearance of the Tucker and Scott stage and liable to prosecution."

The old man pointed skyward.

Beason looked up and then said, "Yes, the sky is red, and it will be dark soon, so bring the girl to me. Instanter!" The Lipan sighed and ducked into the wickiup. A moment later the girl appeared, and the sheriff said, "Show me where you found the stage."

"It is not far," the girl said.

"You speak English. What is your name?"

"My name is Ela."

"Well, Ela, did your grandfather tell you that you are both suspects in the stage's disappearance?"

"No."

"He should have. Now show me the way and watch your step. I'm an officer of the law, and I don't take any sass or backtalk."

"I do not understand," the girl said.

"Darn it, just lead me to the stage," Beason said, exasperated.

CHAPTER 8

The Lipan girl walked in front of Sheriff Bob Beason for thirty minutes, some of that time spent on stretches of the old wagon road. The darkening day lingered, as though reluctant to surrender to the night, and when Ela stopped and pointed ahead of her it was still light enough to see. Then the girl did something that Beason thought strange. Her face full of fright, she looked up at the purpling sky and quickly covered her head with her shawl.

"Heck, girl, it isn't going to rain," he said. "Probably hasn't rained here since Adam was a boy." He screwed up his eyes, scanned into distance and then said, "It's a buffalo wallow. Stupid girl, you led me to a wallow. Back in the day when there was still buffs, West Texas was covered with thousands of them."

The girl shook her head. "Fire," she said. "Fire from sky. Stupid white man know nothing." Then she gathered up her dress, fogged it out of there and didn't look back.

Beason watched the girl go and then decided the wallow, about fourteen feet wide, was curious enough to take a looksee. Buffalo wallows were rapidly vanishing from the West, and this could be among the last of them.

As the day shaded into a cobalt blue twilight, he urged his horse forward . . . and rode into a charnel house.

"My God, that ain't a sight for the eyes of a Christian man or for a heathen either," Bob Beason said aloud. He was shaken to the core, unable and unwilling to believe what his eyes were telling him.

Blackened, shattered bones, both human and animal, were strewn the length and breadth of the depression that was about three foot deep with a raised area in the center. A large area of bedrock was exposed, the limestone and dolomite smashed by some devastating impact. As his horrified gaze took in the scene, Beason suspected a howitzer shell had exploded there but immediately dismissed the thought. He rubbed his stubbled jaw, considering. It would take one heck of a shell to leave an impact crater that big, and who would drag a huge cannon all the way out here in the first place? A lightning strike, maybe? Beason dismounted. The day was waning fast, and he'd little time to solve the mystery.

As he'd done at the burned-out cabin, the sheriff used the toes of his boots as excavating tools. Apart from horse skulls and huge leg bones, there were several human ribcages and three skulls that he could see. Other bones from fragmented arms and legs, all blackened from fire, were scattered everywhere, and Beason dug out more pieces of skull, a couple with teeth intact, and decided that at least eight people had instantly died there and almost as many horses. Scraps of scorched wood and leather covered the area, and from just under the charred surface of the ground he uncovered a metal wheel hub and several iron tires. An oil side-lamp, almost intact, had been blown outside the crater.

As Bob Beason went, he wasn't one of the Frontier's smarter lawmen, but in the dim light he reached an inevitable conclusion . . . he'd found the Tucker and Scott stage. No mortal hand had wrought this destruction. Something, a falling star perhaps, had hurtled from the sky and struck the stage, shattering the vehicle and its passengers and horses to pieces in a fiery instant.

Flickering expressions came and went on Beason's face . . . horror . . . fear . . . and then, dawning in his eyes like a man who'd just been overcome by a great truth . . . fire and brimstone had been hurled from the sky, just as the holy man squatting on Sean O'Neil's land had prophesied. The wrath of the Lord had begun, and the Tucker and Scott stage was the first victim.

Was Mustang Flat next? And then the entire country? And then, to the ends of the earth, the whole world?

Darkness crowded out the day, and the first stars appeared, and when Beason rode back to the old Lipan man's wickiup a rising east wind danced the flames of his fire. He drew rein and said, "Got coffee on the bile, have ye?"

"You are welcome to have some," the Lipan said.

Beason swung out of the saddle. "I'm not much of a one for night riding," he said.

"The sun strengthens you by day and the moon restores you by night," the old man said. "It is your time to rest. The sun, the darkness, and the winds are all listening to what we now say."

"You're right, old timer, they're listening to me say it's time for these old bones to hit the hay," Beason said. He stripped his saddle, ground tied his horse on a patch of grama grass, and then returned to the fire.

The Lipan poured coffee into a tin cup and handed it to the sheriff. He turned his head, said something to the girl in the wickiup and she appeared holding a wooden bowl in her hands. The old man took the bowl and gave it to Beason. "Eat," he said.

Beason, not a man to scoff at food, identified roasted jackrabbit, dried agave cakes and crushed berries. He ate heartily, slept soundly and when he woke next morning, the Lipan were gone . . . and so was his horse.

CHAPTER 9

About the same time Sheriff Bob Beason settled in for his dinner with the old man and his granddaughter, Black John Hannah killed a man.

Later the good citizens of Mustang Flat agreed the shooting was justified, that Hannah was defending himself, but Lucas Battles said the slain man, a kid with a minor gun rep named Jack Doyle was as dead as a five-ace poker hand as soon as he stepped into the saloon, all horns and rattles and on the prod.

Black John and his boys had eaten a late supper at the Red Dust Inn and afterward decided to call it a day and retire to their rooms, except for Hannah, a chronic insomniac, who opted for a nightcap at the Crystal Palace. As the oil lamps cast a welcoming amber glow in the empty saloon, he sat at a table drinking Hennessy brandy, idly talking to Battles about the squatters on the O'Neil range. But the conversation stopped when Jack Doyle stepped inside, wearing his swaggering arrogance like a musketeer's cloak.

Black John had been up this road before, and it took him all of two seconds to peg the kid as a wannabe looking for trouble. The storm clouds were gathering, but he said nothing tense, waiting to see how the thing played out.

Doyle was twenty-one-years-old that fall, a man of medium height and build who obviously spent all his money on gun gear and not his wardrobe. Shabby to the point of raggedness, two things saved him from saddle tramp ordinariness. One was the nickel-plated, pearl-handled Colt he wore in a tooled holster at his waist, the other his finely made boots and chased silver, jingle-bob spurs. Lucas Battles, a perceptive man, reckoned the ranny wearing those boots and spurs wasn't the feller who'd bought them in the first place.

Doyle stepped to the bar and demanded, "Glass."

"Glass of what?" Battles said.

"Just the glass."

Battles shrugged and slammed a shot glass on the bar. "You hungry, young feller?" he said. "I got crackers and cheese. You like cheese?"

Doyle smirked, revealing prominent front teeth, took the glass and stepped to Hannah's table. He picked up the brandy, studied the label, smirked again, and filled his glass. He downed the drink and poured himself another.

Hannah turned his head toward Battles, his eyes never leaving Doyle. "How much does a shot of Hennessy cost, landlord?" he said.

"It's mighty hard to come by. I charge fifty cents a shot," Battles said.

Hannah nodded and then said, "Young feller, you owe me a dollar."

"You're pissing into the wind, Hannah," Doyle said. "I never pay for my own drinks."

"You know my name. What's yours?"

"You don't know it because I ain't put it out yet. It's Jack Doyle. Mean anything to you?"

Hannah's face wrinkled in thought. "Jack . . . Jack in the beanstalk . . . jack of all trades . . . crackerjack . . . doilies . . ." Hannah shook his head. "No, it doesn't mean a darned thing to me."

"No matter," Doyle said. "Soon everybody will know my name."

"How come?"

"Because folks will point me out as the man who killed Black John Hannah in fair fight. Gun-belted men will step wide around me, and the prettiest whores will flutter their eyelashes."

"You want I should get the sheriff, Mr. Hannah?" Battles said.

"No, that won't be necessary. Mr. Doyle is going to sit down and have a friendly drink and me and him will talk. Hey, here's a thing, Jesse is long dead, and they say Frank is selling men's shoes in Dallas, what do you think of that, Mr. Doyle? Ain't life strange sometimes?"

Doyle blinked, and his blue eyes hardened. "I don't give a darn about Frank James."

"Then what do you want to talk about, Jack? Women? Good-looking young buck like you, I bet you got stories to tell."

"You want to talk. Well, where I come from, only a yellow-belly tries to talk his way out of a shooting scrape."

"Where are you from, Jack? My guess is somewhere up in the Montana Territory."

"Darn you, Hannah, I followed you all the way from El Paso, a long hard trail and me eating nothing but beef jerky and drinking rank water, but you know what kept me going? I'll tell you what kept me going, the certain knowledge that you would make me famous."

"Advice," Hannah said. "Walk away from this." His face still, free of emotion. "You want no part of me. I'm hell on earth."

"I want all of you, mister," Doyle said, his hand lowering to his gun. "Now, on your feet and get your work in."

Battles said, "Leave it be, Jack. Be neighborly. Sit and have a drink with Mr. Hannah and me and we'll have us some laughs."

"You shut your trap." Doyle's wild stare moved to Hannah. "You won't stand, then I'll kill you where you darn well sit."

The kid's hand blurred as he went for his gun, but the shocking impact from a .41 caliber bullet fired from a Remington derringer put a brake on his draw. It was a hit to the gut, just under the navel, and Doyle was smart enough to know he was a dead man. But still game, his Colt leveled, and Hannah fired again. The derringer barked like an angry junkyard dog from under the table, and Black John's second shot slammed into Doyle an inch lower than the top button of his pants. The kid staggered, then screamed in pain and rage, and got off a shot. A miss. His bullet slammed into a Pabst beer sign on the opposite wall and sent it crashing to the floor. Backing up, with his waning strength, Doyle tried desperately to bring his Colt into play, his eyes fixed on Black John who was now on his feet.

"Catch!" Battles yelled.

He tossed a hammer-back Greener to Hannah, who grabbed the scattergun in mid-flight and fired from the hip. BLAM! BLAM!

Two rounds of buckshot slammed into Doyle and

dropped him. When Hannah stood over the young man, he was still alive. "Darn you, it wasn't a fair fight," he whispered, blood streaming from his mouth. "You pulled a sneaky gun."

Black John smiled. "Son, I had the drop on you the moment you walked into the saloon."

"Not . . . fair . . ."

"Life ain't fair, kid," Hannah said. "And gunfighting sure as heck ain't fair either. You kill a man any way you can."

"I should've shot you in the back."

"That's one way, and as good as any," Hannah said.

Doyle's eyes opened as though he'd just learned a great truth . . . and then all the life that was in him fled.

The saloon door opened, and two men stepped inside, Luke Lawson the mercantile owner and the cadaverous Clem Milk, the town's undertaker. Battles answered the question on their faces.

"The kid drew down on Mr. Hannah," he said.

Milk kneeled and inspected the body. "This gentleman is deceased," he said.

"We know that," Battles said. "Where is Beason?"

Lawson said, "He's not to home."

"Where is he?" Battles said again.

"I've no idea. His horse is gone."

"Well, I told you what happened," Battles said. "It was a fair fight."

Black John Hannah reached into his pocket, produced a five-dollar coin, and tossed it to Milk. "Bury him," he said.

Milk said, "I can do a right nice timber coffin and . . ."

"Mister, I don't give a darn what kind of coffin he gets," Hannah said. "Just plant him."

Battles looked at Lawson, locked eyes with the man and said, "Fair fight, Luke."

Lawson nodded. "Whatever you say, Lucas. Whatever you say."

CHAPTER 10

A man proud of his small feet, Sheriff Bob Beason's tight-fitting boots had punished him for hours and now in the gray dawn light every shuffling, wincing step was a mortal agony. He'd no idea how far he'd walked, his saddle on his shoulder, miles probably, but all he saw in front of him was the wagon road vanishing V-shaped into the distance. When the sun came up, the heat would grow intense, thirst would ravage him, and Beason suffered melancholy images of his white, bleached bones, grinning skull, and arched ribcage, lying at the side of the trail, objects of idle interest to any passing traveler. Pain spiking at tormented feet that swelled horribly in boots made on a narrow last, imagine then the sheriff's unbounded joy when he heard behind him the creak and clank of what could only be a wagon. He turned and beheld a sight he knew well, the yellow-painted conveyance of Solomon Cohen, the peddler.

Cohen drew rein on his nag, smiled, and said, "Out for a stroll, Sheriff?"

"Darn it, am I glad to see you," Beason groaned. "I don't think I could've walked another step." He dropped the saddle. "And this darn thing weighs a ton."

"I'm sorry to see you so distressed," the peddler said. "So what happened to you?"

"I was attacked by Apaches." Beason blinked. "They killed my horse."

"Sorry to hear that," Cohen said. He shook his head. "Funny, I never heard anything about Apaches playing hob around these parts."

"Well, they're out there," Beason said. "Take my word for it."

"Oh, I do, I do," Cohen said. "The customer is always right. I see you're limping, sheriff. What ails you?"

"Sol, my feet are killing me. Hey, do you have a salve for that?"

"Do I have a salve?"

"Yeah, Sol, a cream or something for aching feet."

"Well, you're in luck, Sheriff Beason. I have the very thing. I'll have you fixed up in no time."

"Bless you, Sol. You're true blue."

You know me, sheriff . . . anything I can do to help."

With a spryness that belied his sixty-odd years, Cohen jumped down from his seat, rooted around in the back of the wagon, and came up with a small ceramic pot.

"Is that a cure?" Beason said.

"Yes, it's just what the doctor ordered."

"Then slather it on me."

"Sheriff, you don't slather on this precious unguent. My dear sir, this elixir comes all the way from the mystic land of the pyramids, the very antique salve that soothed the sand-burned feet of the pharaoh . . ." The peddler paused and then said, "Amenhamatankah the Great. He swore by it and bought it by the gallon for his hundred wives." Cohen made a sweeping gesture and held the pot alongside his head. "And I have good news, sheriff. For today only" —he slapped, the jar—"I'm selling this fabulous nostrum at cost . . . just seventy-five cents, and it's worth three times that amount."

"Will it work?" Beason said.

"He asks me if it will work?" Cohen said. "Why, of course it will work. After Amenhamatankah put this stuff on his scorched feet he was so relieved he built a pyramid, maybe two or three."

"I'm willing to try anything," Beason said. "I'm in misery. Every step I take is killing me."

"Good, then sit yourself down and we'll get those boots off."

The sheriff sat and wrassled a boot, first heel and then toe, but the footwear steadfastly refused to budge. "Darn, it won't come off," he said.

"Let me try," the peddler said.

Grunting with effort, and as Beason shrieked, Cohen pulled, twisted, pulled again, but without success. Sweat beading his forehead, he said, "The trouble is your feet have swollen up, and the boot's as tight as the skin on a sausage."

"Heck, I know that. Am I not suffering the agonies of the damned here?"

"Desperate times need desperate measures, sheriff."

"What does that mean?"

"It means I have to cut them crucifiers off'n of you."

Beason was horrified. "I paid two months wages for these boots!"

"Then just as well that this is your lucky day," Cohen said. "I'll be right back."

Sol Cohen scrabbled around in the wagon, found a pair of boots, studied the size, and tossed them back. After three more tries he finally came up with a square-toed pair that seemed to fit the bill.

"Yes, just as I thought, these beauties are on sale today,"

Cohen said. "Just this morning I knocked ten dollars off the price. To you, sheriff, only twenty dollars the pair."

His face twisted in pain, Beason said, "They don't look like they was once thirty-dollar boots to me."

"Ah . . . but looks can be deceptive. I sold a similar pair to a puncher in San Antone who told me that walking in these here boots was like treading barefoot through a field of dewy bluebonnets. Now, he was a close friend of old John Chisholm and them, so who can doubt his word? But"—the peddler shrugged and spread his arms, the footwear dangling from one hand—"if you don't want them, then wear the pair you got." "The pair I got are killing me," Beason said, his face a pathetic portrait of pain.

"Then it's obvious to me that the boots must be removed instanter," the peddler said. "Sheriff Beason, it breaks my heart to see a man of your exalted status suffer so."

Beason thought about that and said, "All right, cut them off'n me. I can't stand the pain any longer."

Solomon Cohen reached into pocket and produced a Barlow folder. He held up the knife. "This beauty happens to be on sale." He read the expression on Beason's face and said, "Well, we'll keep that for another day."

"Cut, darn you, cut!" the sheriff yelled. "And mind how you go."

"Fear not," Cohen said. "When it comes to cutting boots off swollen feet, I'm as skillful as a Harvard-trained surgeon."

On the peddler's part, that was considerably stretching the truth.

Sheriff Bob Beason's agonized curses turned the air around him blue as Cohen's blade haggled at the tough leather of the man's left boot, sawing and cutting, nicking flesh here and there, drawing blood, as sweat ran off his face and his panting breath came hard and fast.

Finally, the peddler cut the boot to the ankle and yanked it free, drawing a yell of pain from Beason as blood rushed back to his foot like searing acid. "Darn butcher!" the sheriff roared, swatting at his tormentor. "Torturer!"

Solomon Cohen shrugged and said, "Now the other one."

"Oh, my God," Beason groaned.

"Let me have at that other boot, sheriff," the peddler said, frowning. "It's for your own good. Be brave."

The sun was up, the morning hot, and the mare in the traces tossed her head at flies. The sky was a uniform blue without a trace of cloud.

Beason lay back, extended his leg, and growled, "There it is, do your worst."

The right boot was tighter, the leg more bloated, the procedure more tortuous, and Beason caterwauled even louder, damning Cohen for a scoundrel and lowdown. But finally, applying lessons learned from his previous attempt, the peddler cut the boot free, this time leaving Beason's leg more or less intact.

"Solomon Cohen, be darned to ye for a villain," the sheriff said. "You've ruined my boots and cut me and them all to pieces."

"And fine boots they were," the peddler said, shaking his head. "What a pity. Now, off with your socks."

Beason was immediately suspicious. "Why?"

"We must apply the potion of the pharaohs to ease the pain in your feet."

"They still hurt like heck."

"Never fear, sheriff, soon you'll be walking in a field of bluebonnets, remember? Now, off with the socks."

To a chorus of Beason's mixed groans of relief and

pain, Cohen rubbed his elixir into the man's feet, and when he finished, the sheriff admitted that the swelling had gone down considerably, and they felt infinitely better.

"Of course, they do," the peddler said. "The pharaohs have never failed me."

"What was the name of that pharaoh feller again?" Beason said.

Cohen drew a blank and rubbed his greasy hands on a rag he'd taken from the wagon. He shook his head and blinked a few times. "It's bad luck to mention the great pharaoh's name more than twice a day. It angers his restless spirit, you understand. Ask me tomorrow. Now, that will be twenty dollars and seventy-five cents for today. Cutting off your boots and rubbing your feet are both free of charge."

"I haven't tried the new boots yet," Beason said, grudgingly counting sweaty banknotes into the peddler's hand.

"Wait until the foot swelling goes down further before you put them on, sheriff. You'll think you're walking on air, I promise."

"I'll try them when we reach Mustang Flat," Beason said.

"I'm not going to Mustang Flat."

"Then where?"

"I plan to make a round of the ranchers. The ladies love to see me."

"What about me?"

"Well, my first stop will be the Running-S, Sean O'Neil's place. You can borrow a horse there." Cohen smiled. "Sean's brother Johnny loves his cigars, so I always keep a stock on hand. At cost, of course, a courtesy to a regular customer."

"There's trouble on the O'Neil range," Beason said.

"What sort of trouble?"

"Big trouble. He'll tell you when you see him."

"Can you walk to the wagon on your poor feet, sheriff?"

"Yeah, I guess I can." Beason stood and picked up his socks and new boots. "Not very fancy, are they?"

"They're built for comfort, not looks," Cohen said. "How are the feet?"

"Fair to middlin'."

"Then don't wear your new boots until we reach the O'Neil place. In the meantime, wiggle your toes."

"I'll be sure to do that," Sheriff Beason said.

CHAPTER 11

By nature, Jess Hayes was a curious man. Work-shy and none too bright, he made his living scrounging in Mustang Flat or riding the grub line. But there never was a rancher who could get an honest day's work out of him, and he was not a popular man. When he smelled the fragrance of prime beef roasting, he figured it was an ideal place to scrounge a meal and maybe a dollar or two from the pilgrims and a safe spot to spread his blankets.

As events turned out, Hayes made a choice that would be the death of him.

The day was well gone, and the vast expanse of the sky ranged from pale pink to fiery red toward the horizon. The air was tinged with smoke from fires burning inside the circled wagons, and as he rode closer Hayes heard the melodious laugh of a woman. He grinned, his empty blue eyes narrowing as he tugged on his sparse goatee and pondered the possibility of a little slap and tickle with the wife or daughter of some slack-mouthed rube. He nodded and swallowed sudden saliva. Maybe, just maybe, he could make that happen.

Hayes drew rein and studied the circle. All seemed well. He saw people coming and going between the wagons, and their enclosed oxen shuffled and raised dust. The smell of roasting meat and the unmistakable tang of baking bread or biscuits was a tantalizing invitation to any passing stranger. He made up his mind and kneed his horse forward.

"Hello, the wagons!"

Within seconds two men stepped out of the circle and answered Hayes' call. Both carried rifles. "What do you want?" a bearded man yelled.

"Just a passing rider looking for supper and a place to lay his head," Hayes said.

"Go away, we have nothing for you here," the bearded man said.

"Now, that ain't sociable," Hayes said, suddenly angry.

"Be off with you!" the bearded man yelled, his hands moving on his Winchester.

"What's going on here?"

An older man in a red robe stepped from between the wagons. He had an air of command about him.

"Just a rider looking for some grub. Name's Jess Hayes, and I've come a fair piece today."

The three men huddled together in conversation and then the robed man said, "Do you know the world will soon be destroyed by the wrath of God?"

Hayes shook his head. "No, I didn't know that. And I'm right sorry to hear it."

"Well, you know it now," the robed man said.

"I'd still like to eat supper with you," Hayes said.

"You can find supper at any of the surrounding ranches," Micah said.

Hayes was smart enough to realize he was in the company of some kind of Bible pounders, and he played his trump card. "I know, but some invisible force drew me here. It was as though the Lord was calling me because He knew I needed help."

The three men consulted again and then the robed man said, "My disciples consider you an honest traveler, quite harmless, and they say it's our Christian duty to feed you. Dismount and lead your horse into the circle. You'll be safe with us."

Hayes smiled. "I'm much obliged, old timer."

"My name is Micah."

"Sure, it is, and a ten-dollar handle if ever I heard one," Hayes said.

Jess Hayes was made welcome and after a supper of beef and beans, he bedded down under a wagon. But he was a light sleeper, a legacy from his early years as a horse thief and sometime cattle rustler. He woke to pale moon-light, silent wagons, and the soft *chink . . . chink . . .* of coin that had roused him. Someone was counting money, and like a snake charmer's flute, it lured Hayes to full wake-fulness. When cash was being handled, Hayes wanted his share. He rolled out from under the wagon, sat upright, and looked around him. Most of the interior of the wagon circle was in shadow, and nothing moved. Even the usu-ally restless oxen lay still. Out in the grassland, coyotes yipped and a rising prairie wind slapped at the canvas covers of the wagons and tugged at Hayes' thin hair. Then from behind him the unmistakable chime of coins again, a whole cascade of coins falling into . . . what? A treasure chest? What in hades? Hayes turned his head and at the far side of the circle saw a red robe, an exclamation mark of color in the gloom. The man who called himself Micah had his back to him, and it was he who seemed to be counting money. This was worth investigating. Maybe, the thought slimed across Hayes' mind like a crawling snail, worth killing for. He got to his knees and picked up his gun belt. No, not the Colt, this had to be silent work. His sheathed Green River knife was a better option. Hayes drew the blade. At that point he'd considered murder but favored negotiation. Micah was counting money well after the midnight hour, and Jess Hayes, a man with criminal tendencies himself, felt assured him that the wagon master was up to no good.

Hayes had laid his boots aside with his gun belt, and now he rose to his feet and walked toward Micah in his sock feet, silent as a wraith, hardly daring to breathe. He was right behind the man when he whispered, "Can't sleep, huh?"

Micah jumped, slammed shut the lid of a box that sat on a pedestal in front of him and then swung around and said, "What in God's name are you doing here?"

"Woke up to the sound of money and came looking," Hayes said, grinning. "I surely love the sound of money."

"This gold is an offering to the Lord when he comes to destroy the earth and must not be touched."

Hayes' greed flared. "Let me see it."

"It is gold coin, but much more than that," Micah said. "It is farms, livestock, life savings, wedding rings and other jewelry all converted into gold for the Lord when he comes to visit his vengeance on the earth and destroy every living thing with fire and brimstone. Only those within the wagon circle will be saved. Hallelujah!"

"Yeah, hallelujah," Hayes said, his eyes glittering. "Now let me see inside that darned box."

"No. It will only be opened again when the Lord comes, and He will be here very soon."

Hayes looked around him as a black cloud passed across the face of the moon, its edges laced with silver light. Sleep lay heavily within the circle, and the wind whispered among the wagons, as though reluctant to disturb the peace. A man who usually counted his assets in nickels and dimes, Hayes was seduced by the allure of gold and suddenly driven half-mad by greed. He decided to gamble. The rubes were snoring, his horse was close, and only this frail old coot stood between him and a treasure that could keep a man in whiskey and whores for years. Jess Hayes had figured the odds and decided to make a play.

He raised his knife and shoved its keen edge against Micah's throat.

"Don't make a sound grandpa or I'll cut your throat," he whispered. "Open the chest."

"The box is heavy. You can't carry it away from here."

"Let me worry about that." The knife edge pressed closer. "Now open it, darn you."

"This will be your doom," Micah said.

"The heck it will. Now open it."

The man used both hands to open the box that brimmed with large gold coins.

"Double eagles, by God!" Hayes said. He dug into the coins and let them trickle through his fingers. "There's a king's ransom here. Help me load it onto my horse."

"There is only one king, the lord God," Micah said. "And he will not be mocked."

It was then, as the holy man, suddenly as sinewy and muscular as a python, twisted away from him that Hayes realized he'd made a major mistake. Micah parried the younger man's knife arm and at the same time slid a stiletto blade between his ribs. Hayes gasped in pain, staggered, and his eyes grew as large and round as the double eagles in the treasure box.

"How . . . how?" Jess Hayes stammered.

"Like this," Micah said, stabbing a second time.

Hayes shrieked and slowly dropped to his knees, grabbing onto the older man's red robes as he fell. Micah bent over and whispered into Hayes' ear, his voice suddenly hard and harsh, "My mamma didn't raise a pretty boy, but she didn't raise a dumb one either." The stiletto went in again, this time to the hilt just under Hayes' Adam's apple. Cold steel in his throat, the man couldn't shriek again. All he could do was die.

After he stepped away and let Hayes fall, Micah wiped his blade on Hayes' shirt and replaced the knife in the leather lined pocket of his scarlet robe. He then threw back his head and yelled at the top of his voice, "Hallelujah!"

The oxen stirred, wagons swayed, and people came running.

"An avenging angel of the Lord was here," Micah called out, his arms open wide, his face turned to the star-splashed sky. "He saved us from destruction."

A tall man with a broken nose and a black beard spread across his chest, spoke for the crowding others when he said, "What has happened this night, chosen one?"

"The man we trusted with our hospitality turned devil," Micah said.

"Oh, my God," a woman wailed, and a ripple of horrified cries rose from the sixty-eight men, women, and sleepy children gathered in the darkness.

"The devil tried to steal the treasure of the Lord and was struck down by an angel wielding a mighty sword," Micah said. "Oh, it was a wondrous sight to see."

"Tell us, prophet," a woman called out. "Oh, tell us."

"The angel was dressed in silver armor and wore a tall white plume on his helmet," Micah said. "Hallelujah!"

"Did he have wings?" a man yelled.

"No wings. He just appeared, punished the wrongdoer

and then was gone. He neither looked at me nor spoke, but through the slits of his helmet, his eyes burned like emerald fire."

"Chosen one, is the Lord's offering safe?" the black-bearded man said.

"Yes, it's safe and sound. The devil didn't get a chance to lay profane hands on the gold."

"Then we are blessed," an older woman with a white shawl over her head said.

"Yes, we are blessed, twice blessed, because we now know that the Lord sets store by our sacrifice and saved his gold from evil," Micah said. "Hallelujah!"

People crowded closer to look at the crumpled body of the dead man.

"See, where the sword of the Lord struck him," a man said. "Look at the blood."

"That is evil blood, and it will scald like acid," said another.

"He is already burning in purgatory," a woman said. "God will surely damn him."

"Good people, return to your beds and pray for our salvation when the Lord comes in all his righteous anger," Micah said. "Tomorrow we'll bury the evil one away from our sanctified wagons so that no part of him remains above the ground. Let all memory of him be banished from our thoughts. The Lord worked a great wonder tonight and we should all be thankful."

"Hallelujah!" said voices in the crowd.

An hour later, the wagon circle was again silent but for the whispering wind. Jess Hayes lay still in opalescent moonlight, a dead man making no sound.

CHAPTER 12

About the same time the ill-fated Jess Hayes entered the wagon circle for a free meal, Sheriff Bob Beason drove up to the O'Neil ranch house, cussing out Solomon Cohen for a snake-oil salesman and low down.

Johnny O'Neil happened to be out front, enjoying an evening cigar, when the pair arrived. "What are you all riled up about, Sheriff?" he said.

"Riled up? I'm more than riled up. Sol Cohen sold me a pair of boots that are killing my feet. Look at the darn things, Mr. O'Neil. They fits where they hits and that's about it."

"Sheriff, I told you they have to be broken in," Cohen said patiently, the voice of reason. "Walk on them for a while, and you'll be comfy as a bug in a deep pile rug."

"Scoundrel!" Beason yelled. "You told me these were thirty-dollar boots."

"Twenty-dollar boots. They were on sale, remember?"

"I can't say I'm partial to boots myself," Johnny said. "But I think Sol is right. They'll be fine once you break them in. Nice-looking boots, by the way."

"Mr. O'Neil, I always listen to the advice of a man of your stature, you being a world champion pugilist and all, but in this case you're wrong, wrong, wrong. I've been swindled, by God. Just look at Sol Cohen. Isn't that the face of a guilty man? I want a refund."

"And then you'll have no boots at all," the peddler said.

"But I'll have happy feet and twenty dollars back in my empty pocket."

The cabin door opened, and Sean O'Neil stepped outside. "Howdy, Sheriff Beason," he said. "It's always a great pleasure to see your smiling face at the Running-S."

"The pleasure is all yours O'Neil," the lawman said, surly.

"Why are you here?" Sean said. "I hardly think Sol Cohen brought you here on a social visit."

Beason didn't have time to answer as Maria Perez burst out of the door and ran to the wagon. "Mr. Cohen, what do you have for me?"

"The little peddler smiled and said, "For you, young lady, everything your little heart desires. I've got lace, ribbons, hair bows, calico cloth, gloves, shoes, kerchiefs, straw hats and perfumes from Paris, pins, needles and thread, pens, paper and ink, and laudanum that will cure all female afflictions and on sale just for today, white linen collars and cuffs that will add new life to any worn-out dress." The peddler paused dramatically and then said, "And a limited supply of silver rings, bracelets and necklaces from the mysterious land of Cathay, all at cost."

Maria clapped her hands, jumped up and down and said, "Show me, Mr. Cohen. I want to see everything."

Johnny O'Neil grinned and said, "You'll spend all your money on Sol's trinkets."

"And he's a robber," Beason yelled.

But neither Maria nor Solomon Cohen listened, both exploring the peddler's wagon and its exciting cornucopia of wares.

Sean asked his question again. "Sheriff, why are you here, horseless."

"It's a long story. And as you can tell, I need to borry a hoss."

"Then come inside and tell me what's happened to you."

"I need a drink."

"That can be arranged," Sean said.

"The baby's sleeping, so we need to be quiet," Sean said, as he poured Sheriff Bob Beason a whiskey.

"I'll be quiet," Beason said, whispering. "I hate babies, nasty, smelly, little, short-tailed roosters." He picked up his drink, downed it in one gulp and pushed his glass toward Sean who filled it again. "I had the bright idea of going after the missing Tucker and Scott stage, to cash in on the reward, like."

Sean smiled. "Did you find it?"

"Yeah, I found it, or what's left of it."

Surprised, Sean said, "You're a scout, Beason, a reg'lar Dan'l Boone."

"No, I'm not. And old Lipan man and his granddaughter led me to it."

"Was it broken up? Where were the passengers?"

"I'm coming to that," Beason said, frowning. "Don't interrupt my story, O'Neil. You're dipping your quill into my ink."

"Sorry, sheriff. Go right ahead."

"Well, the Lipan girl took me to a place where she said the stage was, and she was right. But there was nothing left of it but charred wood and metal and the bones of horses and people. The ground around the ruin of the coach was scorched, as though by an almighty fire. It was a terrible place."

"What . . . what happened?" Sean said. He helped himself to a drink and again refilled Beason's glass.

"You ain't gonna believe this," Beason said. "I can scarce believe it myself, and I was there."

"Lay it on me," Sean said.

"The Lipan girl said something fell from the sky and hit the stage. Exploded it, I guess, and the folks inside with it."

Sean sat back in his chair. "Beason, she told you a big windy. Stuff doesn't just fall from the sky and firebomb a stage."

"O'Neil, the girl threw her shawl over her head when she got near the place, as though she feared she'd be next to get hit. I've been lawman a long time and I can tell when someone is lying. The Lipan girl wasn't lying."

"Then what was it that hit the stage, Beason?" Sean said.

"How the heck should I know?" the sheriff said. "Maybe one of them shooting stars we see all the time in Texas hit ground just as the Tucker and Scott stage was passing."

"It's a mystery all right. Could've Apaches done it? You say you had a brush with them."

"Apaches might tear people apart, but they don't do that to horses. The entire six-horse team was wiped out, bones lying everywhere. It was an awful sight. And I didn't have a brush with the Apaches. I made that up."

"Why?"

"I didn't want Sol Cohen spreading the word that Sheriff Beason's hoss was stole by an old Lipan man and his granddaughter."

"I won't say a word," Sean said, stifling a grin.

"Now, about that horse . . ."

"It's almost dark. You can stay the night, you know."

"No, I want to get back to Mustang Flat. God knows what mischief them Mexicans have gotten into since I've been gone."

A squeal of delight from outside made Sean smile. "Maria's found something she likes, spending the money I underpay her for housekeeping around here."

Beason got to his feet. "The wagons are still parked on your range, huh?" he said.

"Yeah, they're still there."

"You got to do something about that, O'Neil."

"So do you, sheriff."

"I'll look into it." Beason scratched his stubbled chin. "When the time comes and then goes for the end of the world, my guess is they'll hitch up and go back to Kansas."

"I hope that's the case," Sean said. "I don't want a shooting war with a bunch of pumpkin rollers and their women and children."

Beason nodded and sighed. "As an officer of the law, neither do I. I got to be going. What hoss?"

"Take your pick. There's a nice little gray mare in the last stall on the left that will take you where you want to go."

"I don't like grays," Beason said, making a face. "They smell bad."

"Then choose another one. Don't look a gift horse in the mouth, sheriff. Anybody ever tell you that?"

"No, nobody ever told me that," Beason said.

"Well, sir, I just told you now," Sean said.

Chapter 13

If he had even a single customer, Lucas Battles would stay open, so it came as no surprise to Sheriff Bob Beason when he rode into Mustang Flat under a midnight moon that oil lamps still burned in the Crystal Palace saloon. And that was all for the better because Battles, a talkative man, would bring him up to date on what had happened around town in his absence.

Beason dismounted, looped his reins to the hitching rail and stepped inside, his feet thudding on the timber floor as he ambled in boots that were too big for him.

Lucas Battles stood behind the bar, talking to a pair of tall, wide-shouldered gents that were alike as two peas in a pod. Both had lean faces, the skin lying tight to heavy cheekbones, thick black eyebrows and coal-black eyes that seemed flat and dead. Both were unshaven and their skin had an ashen pallor that spoke of many years without sun.

Yuma penitentiary, Beason guessed as he stepped to the bar, and by the look of them, recently released.

Battles beamed at the sheriff, as he habitually did to all regular customers, and said, "Bob, where have you been? There was a heck of an excitement, and you missed it all."

"I was out on an official duty," Beason said, his eyes on

the strangers. "Whiskey," he said, placing his Winchester on the bar, and then, "What excitement?"

"Black John Hannah killed a man."

"When?"

"Why, last night, right here in the Crystal Palace!"

Beason sampled his whiskey, then, "How did the scrape go down?"

"A kid trying to build a gun rep braced Black John and then got shot for his trouble." He saw the concern in the lawman's face and added quickly, "It was a fair fight."

"Who was the kid?"

"The name he put out was Jack Doyle. I summed him up and decided he didn't come to much."

"But he drew down on Black John?" Beason said. "That took sand."

"And there you have the truth of it, sheriff. The kid drew down on Black John and Mr. Hannah put two quick bullets into him, nice as you please."

"The city will bury the kid, I guess."

"No, Black John paid Clem Milk to plant him. He's a generous gent, is Mr. Hannah, especially to them he's plugged, it seems."

"Another drink, Lucas," Beason said. His eyes lifted to the two drifters at the bar. The light from the oil lamps above their heads gleamed amber in the whiskey glasses in front of them, the levels unchanging, apparently nursed by men down to their last dollar. "I haven't had the pleasure."

The pair looked surprised, then one of them said, "I'm Lon Gallagher. This here is my twin brother Ben." Lon's pallid, hard-boned face revealed a glimpse of malevolence, as though he resented the intrusion.

"Where are you boys from?" Beason said, prepared to be sociable and official at the same time.

"Originally from up Kansas way," Lon said. "But we've been drifting."

"Looking for work," Ben said. He was tall and thin, his wide shoulders much stooped. His black eyes were unfriendly, a hint of the man's natural temperament.

"Name's Sheriff Bob Beason. What kind of work?"

"Anything that comes along," Ben Gallagher said.

"Maybe you should speak to some of the local ranchers. The fall gather is coming up."

Lon said, "Maybe. But we ain't drovers."

"Then what are you?"

The twins looked at each other and then Lon said, "We're just common laboring men."

Battles grinned. "Not much call for that in Mustang Flat. The Mexicans do all the digging around here."

"You boys both wear guns and as far as I saw when I rode up, the horses outside ain't mustangs. Top dollar mounts for laboring men?" Beason said before downing another shot of whiskey.

"We saved our money and bought them cheap," Ben said.

"And maybe you hire out them pistols of yours now and again, huh?" Beason said.

"No, we don't, and enough with the questions," Lon said. "I told you, we're honest travelers looking for work and that's all we are."

"Laborers on horseback. And I'm the law so you boys will answer as many questions as I feel like asking," Beason said, the whiskey in his blood making him courageous.

"That ain't so unusual. What's a drover but a laborer on a horse?" Lon said.

"He has a point, sheriff," Battles said.

"I guess so," Beason said. "But it all sounds a tad suspicious to me. If you boys plan to spend time in Mustang Flat, keep in touch. Drop by my office every day and say howdy."

"Sheriff, you're suspicious of everybody," Battles said. "Even my maiden aunt."

"Lucas, you don't have a maiden aunt."

"I know, but if I had one, you'd be suspicious of her."

"Sheriff, you're a questioning man, and I got one for you," Lon said.

"Ask away," Beason said. "I'll have an answer. I always do."

"All right, then where can me and my brother bed down tonight?"

"The Red Dust Inn is your best bet. That's where John Hannah and his boys are holed up. They seem comfy enough when Black John ain't shooting folks."

A flicker of . . . something . . . showed in Lon's carbon eyes, lasted for a moment, and then was gone. "We're working men," he said. "We can't afford fancy hotels."

Battles said, "Then your second-best bet is the livery stable right there on the edge of town. John charges seventy-five cents a night for man and horse, and he has coffee in the morning for an extry nickel."

"That's more our style," Lon said. He downed what was left of his drink, turned to his brother, and said, "You ready, Ben?"

"I'm ready," Ben said. He looked at Beason. "I can't say meeting you was a real pleasure, sheriff."

"It seldom is," Beason said. "Now you boys keep in touch like I told you, you heah?"

"Go to hell," Ben Gallagher said.

Beason watched the brothers leave, men in shabby ditto

suits, derby hats, and lace-up ankle boots who walked with little grace, like farmers crossing a fresh-plowed field.

"Do them two look like trouble to you, Lucas?" the sheriff said.

"I don't know. Maybe. They haven't yet met up with Black John Hannah and his boys. That could be a problem."

"I reckon they'll pull in their horns where they're around Black John," Beason said.

"I sure hope so," Battles said. "I don't want my place shot up."

"And neither do I," Beason said. "Darn it all, Lucas, law enforcement is getting complicated in these parts. Why is Black John hanging around? What's the attraction? And them Gallagher brothers are in town for a reason, and the chances are they're up to no good. I got a nose for stuff like that, and I don't like what I smell. Mark my words, storm clouds are gathering over Mustang Flat."

"Seems like," Battles said.

CHAPTER 14

Sean O'Neil's recently hired hand, a tall, lank man named Jasper Reese, reined in his running horse, dismounted outside the ranch house, and rapped on the door. When Sean answered, the puncher said, "Boss, there's a grave dug on our southern range."

"A what?" Sean said.

"A grave, boss, six feet long and I don't know how deep."

"Is there a marker?"

"No marker. Just a grave and it looks fresh."

Sean turned his head. "Did you hear that, Johnny?"

"Yeah, I heard it. Jasper, you sure it's a grave?"

Reese, who had the face of a dyspeptic preacher, was a man of a singularly melancholy nature, but surprisingly he played the banjo, and his vocal version of *Sweet Angie's Bluetick Hound* was always well-received.

"Sure, I'm sure, boss," he said. "I've seen plenty of graves afore in my time."

"Sean, I bet this has something to do with the squatters on our range," Johnny said.

"I tend to agree with you." Sean said. "Now they're burying their dead on my land, darn them." He thought for a moment and then said, "Jasper, ride into town and get Sheriff Beason. He's useless as teats on a boar hog, but I want him here when I warn those squatters to use an undertaker."

Jasper Reese, as superstitious as any cowboy, said, "Burying a man on grazing land is gotta be bad luck, boss."

"I reckon it is. Now go fetch Beason, and we'll get this thing settled."

As he watched the hand ride away, Sean said to his brother, "Johnny, I'm heading for the south range to see the grave for myself. Look after things while I'm gone."

"I'd rather go with you. I do appreciate Billy and Maria, but a squalling baby sometimes gives me a headache," Johnny said. "She says little Billy is teething, and he sure reckons to let the whole state of Texas know about it."

"It's a three-hour ride," Sean said. "Too long for a man with a bad leg."

"We can take the buckboard," Johnny said.

Sean was about to object but then Billy erupted in an ear-splitting bawling, wailing tantrum that threatened to blow the roof off the ranch house, and he said hastily, "I'll get the buckboard."

The sun hadn't reached its highest level in the sky when Sheriff Bob Beason in company with Jasper Reese stepped into John Baxter's livery and found the Gallagher brothers sitting on a bench outside drinking coffee. Beason was quite pleased with himself since he'd suddenly just now hatched a plan that would keep the twins away from Black John Hannah and his boys. At least for a while. He didn't really expect trouble, since saddle tramps like the

Gallaghers were beneath the notice of a big-time badman like John Hannah, but he didn't want to be fooled either.

"Mornin', boys," he said. "How would you like to make a dollar?"

"Each?" Ben said.

"Of course," Beason said. "Cash on the barrel head."

"Is it gun work?" Lon said. "Like we told you, we don't do gun work."

"Not for a dollar, we don't," Ben said. His hair stood straight up, like the bristles of a shaving brush.

"No gun work," Beason said, smiling his sincerity. "You'll be assisting me on my official duties."

"What kind of duties? We don't arrest folks either," Ben said, his morning surliness on show.

"No, nothing like that. You'll help me solve a mystery," Beason said.

"A mystery?" Ben echoed. "What mystery?"

Beason beamed like a schoolmaster regarding a particularly bright student. "Good question," he said, "And here are a couple of clues: Why is there a grave where there should be no grave, and who lies within?"

"Where is this grave, a churchyard?" Ben said. "We don't do no churchyards."

"No, sir, it's out there on the wide prairie, on the O'Neil range to be precise. And here," he took Reese by the elbow and pushed him forward, "is the man who will lead us there."

"Right pleased to make you gents' acquaintance," the puncher said.

The twins ignored that, and Ben said, "Cattle range, you say."

"Yes, my boss Sean O'Neil's ranch. He runs Herefords out there. Now we're having some trouble with a nesting wagon train, but my guess is them pilgrims will move on pretty soon when their water runs out."

A more perceptive man than Bob Beason would've noted the sudden exchange of glances between the Gallagher brothers and wondered at it, but the incident went unnoticed and unremarked.

For all of five seconds, Ben stared at the lawman with his black, bird-of-prey eyes, and then said, "We'll solve your mystery, sheriff. Give me and Lon a few minutes to saddle up."

"Crackerjack!" Beason said. "I'll pay you when we return to Mustang Flat."

Jasper Reese took Beason aside and said, his face troubled, "Sheriff, them rannies jumped on your two dollars pretty darned quick as soon as you mentioned the grave was on my boss's range. That was kinda strange, wasn't it?"

Beason shook his head. "No, it wasn't strange. I figure they thought the job was in town, painting fences or digging ditches or something, but when I mentioned a ride out onto the range, they jumped on it. It was the prospect of grass, fresh air, and sunlight that made those boys change their minds. Depend on it."

"I still think it was a mighty quick turnaround," Reese said.

Beason smiled. "Cowboy, you sound like an old maiden aunt who hears a rustle in every bush. I have a law enforcement officer's instinct for these things, and those Gallagher boys are straight shooters . . . at least for today."

Reese stopped talking. It dawned on him at that moment that Sheriff Beason was an idiot.

CHAPTER 15

"It's a grave all right," Sheriff Bob Beason said. "The question is whose?"

"It's short and narrow," Sean O'Neil said. "It could be a woman."

"Could be . . ." the lawman said, head bowed, his face thoughtful. Then, looking up, "O'Neil, these two are the Gallagher twins, Lon and Ben. I deputized them just for today."

Sean gave the two a perfunctory nod, that neither of the men returned the gesture.

"Why do you need deputies, Beason?" he said.

"Just being careful, O'Neil. I'm sure this grave is connected to them folks in the wagons. Was this a natural death or is there cold-blooded murder involved?" Then to Johnny, "What do you think, Mr. O'Neil?"

"I'll leave the thinking to you, sheriff."

"No doubt a wise choice. I am well experienced in these matters."

Sean's gaze tracked a Harrier hawk's progress across the afternoon sky, a sharp-edged silhouette that looked as though it had been cut from black paper with a razor. He turned his attention to Beason again. "We have no way of knowing who or what it is. It could be a dead dog."

"Yes, we have," the sheriff said. "O'Neil, I see shovels in your buckboard, we'll dig up the . . . whatever it is . . . and take a look-see. It's time for my deputies to earn their wages."

"You want us to dig up a dead man?" Lon said, staring at Beason with an air of bitter distaste.

"Yes, you and Ben. Go get your shovels."

"You sure you want to do this, sheriff?" Sean said. "Whoever or whatever is down there could've been dead for a long time."

"Not so, O'Neil," Beason said. "Look at the dirt. That grave was dug not long ago. He, she, or it will be as fresh as a daisy."

"Boss . . ." Jasper Reese, his voice wary, as though he was afraid to be overheard, said to Sean, "the sheriff brung his borried roan back. Maybe I should take him home to the stable."

Sean, aware of all the cowboy superstitions, smiled and said, "Sure Jasper, take the horse back to the ranch. See that you give him a scoop of oats."

Reese, a puncher with his pants on fire, grabbed the roan's lead rope, mounted his own pony, and galloped away as though the hounds were after him. He didn't look back.

"What's the trouble with him?" Beason said.

"I guess he doesn't like to dig up bodies," Johnny O'Neil said.

"It's a chore sure enough," the sheriff said. "But no matter how unpleasant, the work of law enforcement has to be done. Lon, Ben, get to digging."

At first Sean figured the brothers would refuse, but

when Lon whispered something urgent into Ben's ear, the man listened and then nodded and grabbed a shovel.

The grave was shallow, the covering earth loose and the corpse was not the daisy Beason had promised.

"I can see him well enough, you don't need to yank him out of there," Beason said. He spat. "God, he smells like he fell off a manure wagon."

"He's a corpse, sheriff," Sean said, trying hard to breathe. "What the heck did you expect?"

The body's face was dry-ash gray, the glazed, unseeing eyes open and putrefaction had already started its work.

"Right, cover him up again," Beason said. "I've seen all I needed to see."

"Cover him up? Sheriff this is my range, I'm not about to turn it into a graveyard. Pull him out of there and get Clem to plant him properly or toss him for the coyotes, but you can't leave him here."

Beason huffed, "Well, he stinks and I've seen all I needed to see."

"And what do you see?" Sean said.

"I see a chicken thief and all-round nuisance by the name of Jess Hayes," the sheriff said. "He didn't amount to much, but what the heck was he doing way out here?"

"Getting himself murdered," Sean said. "He has a bad wound to his throat."

"Saw that," Beason said. "And another further down." He looked at Sean. "Apaches maybe?"

"Sheriff," Sean said, his irritation obvious, "Apaches don't bury dead white men, only live ones."

Beason nodded. "Then the suspects are obvious, them plow wranglers with the wagons punched Hayes' ticket and buried him to get rid of the evidence."

"Why?" Sean said.

"Why? I don't know why," Beason said.

"Maybe he stole one of their chickens, huh?"

"O'Neil, murder makes this official investigation a serious matter and I'd appreciate it if you'd render it the seriousness it deserves."

"All right, so where do you go from here, sheriff?" Sean said.

"From here? Why, to the wagon circle, of course. They have some questions to answer."

"Beason, the last time you tried that they near blew your head off," Sean said, gesturing to the sheriff's holed hat.

"This time it's an official murder inquiry, and I'm bringing down on them the full majesty of the law. My deputies will ride at my side. Is that not so, boys?"

"Whatever you say, sheriff," Lon Gallagher said, smiling slightly.

Sean didn't like or trust either brother. In their ditto suits and plug hats he figured they looked more like big-city gangsters than Western men. Both had contemptuous eyes, but they never looked at you directly, their glance was always sidelong, and it gave them the appearance of venomous serpents. Beason wouldn't recognize them as such, but Sean had enough experience of such men to peg the Gallagher twins as professional thugs who would lend a hand to any criminal enterprise that came their way.

Then Sean asked himself a question: What were men like those doing in a backwater like Mustang Flat? He had no answer, and that troubled him.

"O'Neil, you want to ride along in the buckboard?" Beason said.

"No, I had enough trouble the last time," Sean said.

"Probably just as well," Beason said. "Murder investigations are best left to professionals."

"Get that corpse off of my range, sheriff, or Johnny and I will be dumping him on your doorstep." Sean shot

Beason a meaningful glance and the portly sheriff threw his hands up in despair. "These pumpkin rollers are making law enforcement more complicated by the minute."

As he watched sheriff Bob Beason, bookended by the Gallaghers, ride away, the putrefied corpse wrapped in a canvas tarp and tied to Ben's horse, Johnny O'Neil said, "What do you think, Sean?"

"About what?"

"Beason's idea that the people in the wagons murdered . . . what's his name?"

"Jess Hayes."

"Yeah, murdered him and then buried him on our range?"

"I don't know, but I guess it's possible."

"Well, we'll soon know the answer. Sheriff Beason will get to the bottom of this mystery."

The two brothers exchanged glances, and then both laughed. In fact, Sean was so amused he was still smiling when he climbed on the buckboard and he and Johnny headed for the Running-S.

CHAPTER 16

"I will soon get to the bottom of this mystery," Sheriff Bob Beason said. "But you boys stay close. Them pilgrims with the wagons are mighty notional."

"Sure thing, sheriff," Lon Gallagher said. He turned to his twin and grinned, a grin that again went unnoticed by Beason.

Just how notional were the pilgrims was quickly revealed when ten riflemen stepped out from between the wagons and lined up facing the sheriff. They didn't look friendly.

Beason drew rein and said, "Now see here, put those rifles away. I'm here on official business." He let that sink in and then added, "I'm talking murder here, cold, black-hearted murder."

The reply, if a well-aimed .44-40 rifle bullet can rightly be called a reply, blew Beason's hat off his head. An inch or two lower and the two-hundred grain lead bullet, moving at twelve hundred feet per second, could've bored a tunnel though the sheriff's skull quite effectively. Beason probably didn't know the ballistics of the cartridge, but he was aware, from firsthand knowledge, what a large caliber bullet did to a man's head.

For a moment the sheriff sat his mount stunned. He now had two bullet holes in his hat, four if he counted the exits, and this kind of reception at the wagon circle was wearing mighty thin.

Beason's anger flared hotter than the overhead sun. His face crimson, he yelled, "Be darned to you, you've shot at an officer of the law, and this is your second offense. I could lock you all up in Huntsville and throw away the key. Now, give me the road and allow me passage through the wagons."

"You wish to speak to Micah, God's prophet?" a man at the end of the line called out.

"That's the very feller," Beason hollered. "Get him out here so my official homicide investigation into the murder of the nuisance Jess Hayes can commence."

"There was no murder here," one of the riflemen said. "We are peaceful people."

"I'll be the judge of that. Now go get whatshisname. I'm not a patient man."

CHAPTER 17

"Get him out here so my official homicide investigation can commence . . ." Micah mimicked the self-important wheedling of the sheriff. He was irritated beyond belief. The stupid hick sheriff was back, interrupting his ritual bath no less. He knew why he was here. The grave of Jess Hayes could not have remained a secret for long.

Within the canvas tent reserved exclusively for the prophet, three beautiful yet emaciated young women worked tirelessly, heating pails of fresh water over a fire, filling the washtub, and perfuming the steaming bath with salts scented strongly by frankincense and copal resin. Micah dropped his red robes and handed them off to one of the women who quickly spirited them away for cleaning, and within moments returned with a basket laden with fresh robes and towels for drying. Micah stepped into the tub and leaning back, smiled as he felt the heat of the bath ease his many aches and pains.

The prophet of God relished in more than the warm relief of the tub. He enjoyed soaking clean while the filthy young women continued to serve at his feet, since he knew it had been weeks since they were allowed to bathe.

Yet they served him without contempt despite being repeatedly exposed to his naked form, and the thought made him smile.

If he lifted his right hand, the women scurried to bring fresh warm water—certainly they wouldn't let the prophet catch a chill. There was a time shortly after they'd left Kansas when he'd bathed in pure milk instead of water, having read that the Egyptian pharaohs had done the same, but as they had only one thin cow left in the camp who produced little milk he'd been forced to compromise. Now, the pilgrims agreed to take turns going without to sacrifice their paltry milk ration to be used for the prophet's sacred bath. The young children protested against this as their stomachs clenched with hunger, but the prophet was chosen by God, and children must honor their parents. A fact Micah was eager to drive home with his leather strap.

She'll be a beef stew soon, he thought about the cow.

"See here . . ." He struggled so with the names of these women . . . Something with an L . . . Laura? Linda? No, Liza.

"Liza, put down your labors for a moment and rest so I may teach you." He watched as the girl set her basket of men's clothing, topped by a scarlet robe, on the ground and approached him. "Kneel!" Micah violently lurched forward, sluicing water over the tub edge, soaking the girl's brown linen skirt until it clung to her long legs. "Always kneel before the prophet when he addresses you."

Cowering, the girl swiftly kneeled in supplication, long dark ringlets tumbling in question marks over her forehead. "Yes, prophet." She spoke just above a whisper. "I will remember in the future."

Distantly aware of the other women in the tent, he dismissed them, "The rest of you may go. Now!" The wiry blonde fled the tent in relief, impatient to return to her infant son, but Emma, the tall redheaded woman he kept warm with at night only pulled back, eager to watch the show.

Micah placed his blue-veined hand with its thick, yellowed fingernails beneath the woman called Liza's chin and lifted her gaze to meet his.

"You are heavy with child," he said.

"Yes, prophet. My time is near."

"Then for you and your unborn child's sake, you'll do as I say, woman, and talk to the sheriff. I'll tell you what you must say to him. Do you understand?"

"I think so, anointed one."

"Good, this is what you will tell Beason. Are you ready?"

"Yes, prophet."

"Know that Beason has arrived here, an ungodly unbeliever who means us harm."

"Yes, prophet, I know," Liza said. "He and two others."

"Beason wishes to question me about the vengeance handed out by an angel of God on the thief who called himself Jess Hayes and tried to steal the treasure of the Lord."

Fear widened the girl's brown eyes, but she said nothing.

"You were there, weren't you Liza?" Micah said. "You saw what happened."

"No, Prophet, I was asleep in the wagon when the angel came," Liza said, shaking her head. She seemed confused.

"No, that is not what you will tell the thrice-cursed Beason."

Liza was shocked. "But . . . but what do I tell him, prophet?"

"Listen to me, girl," Micah said, steam from his bath rising around him. He looked skinny, shriveled. "When a falsehood is told in the cause of righteousness, it is transformed. It becomes a lie no longer but a monumental truth. Do you understand?"

"I think so," Liza said.

"Good, then here's what you will tell Beason: You were kneeling outside your wagon, saying your evening prayers, when the lustful Jess Hayes set upon you, seeking his way with you. Ere you were undone, you fell to your knees and beseeched the Lord to help, and He, in his sacred anger, sent an angel with a mighty sword to save you, one of his chosen. Hallelujah!"

Liza, just sixteen years old and already married to a man twenty years her senior, was exhausted from the hard life in the wagon circle and carrying her child, and her normally bright mind was muddled. Her confusion was evident. "But, prophet, that didn't happen," she said. "The man was trying to steal the treasure we will gift to God after the great destruction and the angel saved you from him. I heard you say that."

"Yes, I said that, but it was not what you will tell Beason," Micah said. "The less said about the treasure the better. If word gets around that we have gold coin here, it will attract bandits like steel filings to a magnet. Do you understand?"

"Yes, I believe so," Liza said.

"Remember, Hayes had his wicked way with you and filled you with despair. You must say that to Beason. Touch his cold heart."

"I will try," Liza said. "I'm a good girl."

Micah reached out a hand, coiled his spindly fingers into a fistful of the girl's hair and twisted until she cried out in pain. "You stupid bitch, you will tell the sheriff exactly what I told you to tell him, and if he asks further, you will say that we swiftly removed the corpse of Hayes from our land, fearing its evil. You will tell him all these things because they are the truth before the eyes of God," Micah released his hold on the girl's hair but shoved her head away from him with such force that she stumbled and almost fell. "Of course, you will do as I say, Liza, because you are such a devout girl. But if you don't, I promise you I will cast you out of the circle and you will burn with the unbelievers."

Micah shoved his face forward, so he was nose to nose with Liza. "Do you understand?"

Tears staining her cheeks, the girl said, "I understand."

"Good, now help me get dressed, we don't want to keep the lawman waiting." Micah stepped from the tub naked, letting the bathwater drip off his gray skin as Liza and the redhead quickly moved to dry and dress him in his scarlet robe of office.

Emma drew closer to Liza, her green eyes hard and mean. She whispered thinly into her ear, "Liza Hart, I saw you upset the prophet. What did you say that troubled him so?"

"Nothing. I said nothing to him," Liza said.

"You're a liar," the redhead said. "You little witch, you will not escape the terrible fire, not now."

Sobbing, Liza buried her face in the skirt of her dress and ran.

When Micah stepped from within the shade of his tent, he saw that the sun had finished its morning display of red and pink, and the sky was mottled blue and white. The prophet watched the progress of a vulture flock swirling like a black tornado above the camp. "Hallelujah," Micah muttered, "Hallelujah."

CHAPTER 18

"Ah, Sheriff Beason, to what do we owe the pleasure of your visit to our humble circle?" Micah approached, cinching his heavy robe about his waist, flocked on all sides by much larger men armed with rifles and dark scowls. The prophet looked over the sheriff and Lon and Ben Gallagher, then stopped dead in his tracks and shoved a hand into the air, four stiff fingers extended.

"Four days until the coming of the Lord and the terrible night of the hail of fire and brimstone!" he yelled. "Four short days, I tell you. God just spoke to me as I knelt in prayer and announced when the Day of Judgement will arrive. Hallelujah!"

As the pilgrims with the wagon train cheered and yelled Hallelujah, Micah's voice rose above the clamor. "Four days!" And then, louder, "Let loose the oxen! We no longer need them."

A team of boys drove the huge animals out the wagons onto the grazing land, to the cheers of the people who now crowded outside the circle.

Then . . .

Sean O'Neil and perhaps half the population of

Mustang Flat would've picked up on the significance of what happened a moment later, but as always Sheriff Bob Beason was oblivious, an error on his part that would later cost many lives. Micah's eyes fixed on the Gallagher twins and now the men's gazes formed a triangle that locked together for an instant. It was there, then gone, a fleeting moment in time. What was its significance? Whatever it was, Beason chose to ignore it, in fact he steamrollered over the proceedings with his bellow.

Beason harrumphed, "First of all, you deranged old coot, you owe me a new hat. Second, I am mighty tired of dragging myself out here to deal with you rotten scoundrels over one darn thing or another. Now as an officer of the law I am here to inform you that everyone in this camp is a suspect in the murder of one Mr. Jess Hayes. I am well within my rights to drag all of ye, men, women, children, and horses into Mustang Flat to be held until such a time as the murderer comes forward with a full and truthful confession. I might just add charges for shooting a lawman and ruining his hat, if you ain't all too lowdown to admit who done it."

Micah held out his hand to calm the tension as his human shields shouldered their rifles to fire.

"We recognize no law here outside of the righteous testaments of the Lord, and your threats mean nothing to such pure pilgrims as ourselves. Whoever shot your hat was simply protecting our peaceful wagon circle and the chosen people within. However, I can tell you exactly what became of Mr. Hayes to set your mind at ease. Liza, will you come forward?"

The young woman stepped from the gathered crowd with head bowed and cheeks flushed, her damp hair leaving a gray shadow on the shoulders of her dirty white blouse. Her elbows and arms were bloomed with purple and yellow bruises and traces of blood, and her movement came stiffly.

Beason glared at the girl. She looked to be no older than sixteen and had a distinctive beauty despite being painfully thin. Her belly swelled into a round shape, and the sheriff wondered if it was a baby or the bloat of extreme hunger.

"Liza, tell this . . . gentleman . . . of your most horrifying yet blessed encounter, glory be to God." Micah said.

"Glory be to God!" the gathered crowd of pilgrims chorused.

Beason rolled his eyes in response.

The girl spoke so softly that Beason strained onto tiptoes in his too-big boots to lean forward and listen, ever conscious of the armed men behind her.

"I, well, you see the man . . . the bad man, he came upon me praying and . . ."

"When was this?" Beason barked, making her jump in fright.

She glanced around frantically, her eyes settling on Micah.

"Friday last, it was, dear," he replied.

"Ye—yes, Friday last, your honor."

"I'm not a judge, girl. Call me sheriff. Tell the truth now, painful as it may be," Beason snapped.

"Oh. Your sheriff, it were Friday last that I were lost in prayers to bring blessings upon the prophet when the bad man came upon me. He . . . he hollered real lustful words I cannot repeat, your sheriff, and meant to . . ."

She choked back a sob, "He meant to violate me and then steal the treasures we've collected to settle our debts with God the Almighty."

"It ain't 'your sheriff,' it's just, oh heck never mind, then what?"

Liza drew a deep breath, her eyes downcast as she toed

circles in the dusty ground with her worn-out boot. "Then as he reached for me, a mighty angel descended from the heavens, and our glorious prophet heard the call and ran to my aid. The bad man tried to hold me but the angel, who wore real purty armor and had eyes what glowed, used a mighty silver blade to strike the man dead."

"Hallelujah!" The crowd cried in jubilation.

"The prophet caught me as I collapsed, I were so a'feared, your sheriff, that my baby would be harmed, but I were saved! Then the angel spoke and said to bury the man far away so as his demon blood wouldn't taint our soil and burn our souls away. I . . . I don't know what came after that, your sheriff, the other good Christian women here helped me lay to rest."

Micah nodded and patted Liza on the back. It was not lost even to a poor excuse of a lawman like Beason that the girl shrank at his touch.

"After that, we . . . well, my husband and the others, removed the evil bad man and buried him in the dirt so he could finish his voyage into hell. That is all that happened, Mr. Beason, told true from start to end."

The Prophet Micah then spoke in booming bass tones, hushing the whispering crowd.

"Now you'll remove yourself from our presence less the lord see fit to strike you down next. Hallelujah!" His eyes were polished flint and held sheer malice. Lon and Ben shared a side-eyed glance as Beason turned red as a beet with indignation.

"All right, see here, you deranged lunatic, I don't believe one word any of you darn fools have said. I expect you to head into that divine treasure of yours and find me a double eagle to replace my hat. The fellow you murdered was a thief and a drunk, but he was no raper, unlike some men." He glanced pointedly at the young girl's pregnant belly.

"You may have us outnumbered here today, but don't think I will be eternally defeated by some grubby old man in a dress and his roving band of fools!" Beason bellowed.

The crowd gasped in shock and began whispering fervently, and somewhere in the gathered throng gun hammers cocked.

The twins tightened their grips on their guns, surveying the pilgrims with cold, hard eyes.

Micah sighed but remained eerily calm.

"Fine, I will take from God's owed penance to replace your hat. Come, Jethro, take out a double eagle for this insufferable man. He shall repay it in Hell."

Jethro, a mountain of a man with filth caked into every weathered crack of his skin, slipped into a canvas tent behind the crowd.

The Gallagher brothers intently watched the top of his head as it wove through the camp, and Lon nudged Ben with the toe of his boot and grinned. He leaned over to his brother and whispered quietly, "Sheriff will repay that double eagle in lead, soon enough." The two men chuckled as Beason sat oblivious to the terrible mess he'd fallen into.

"If it will remove your presence from our camp so we may enjoy our final days upon this earth in peace, then leave now. We will await your return within the four days left to us."

Frustrated, angry, Beason said, "You people don't know who you're dealing with, but you'll soon find out to your cost." Then, "Lon, get my hat."

Lon looked at his brother, defiance stiffening his face, but Ben merely nodded. Lon swung out of the saddle and retrieved Beason's hat. As he handed it to him, he said, "What now, Sheriff?"

"Back to Mustang Flat," Beason answered. "I have to study on this situation. It is apparent that these pilgrims have no respect for the supreme authority of the law, and I'll need to find more superior reinforcements than you pair."

"Where are you gonna get these superior reinforcements?" Lon said.

"Heck if I know," Beason said.

CHAPTER 19

The same time Beason and the Gallagher brothers were making their way back to Mustang Flat, Sol Cohen was making a deal. "I assure you, Mr. Holton, that these boots will someday bring you a fortune in resale. In fact, I've got the certificate of authenticity to accompany them, free of charge just for you." The peddler held up the cut, bloody boots of Bob Beason for one of Black John Hannah's boys, Tommy Holton, to examine. Holton was a fast gun with a slow mind, and as he'd stepped outside the Red Dust Inn the peddler had correctly read him as an easy sale. Holton had already bought tobacco and a button, but now he was admiring, according to Sol Cohen, the very boots Sam Bass had once suffered being cut off his bleeding feet, after his battle with Texas Rangers in Round Rock, Texas. Holton took a long drag off his cigarette and studied a spell, "I heard they took him in 'fore he died, so he didn't die in a shootout wearing them boots, mister."

Sol was quick and replied, "Yes, yes, they had to cut them off you see, notice the hurried manner of the cuts? The poor man was swelling up and bloody, so they worked fast. Today only as a special offer for an esteemed gentleman like yourself, these display pieces are selling for . . ." Sol poked about in his cart as if searching for a price. "Oh! Splendid! For the low price of just thirty dollars."

Holton balked, "Thirty dollars for some cut up, blood-soaked boots? Have you lost your mind, peddler?"

Cohen held his hands up in a display of innocence, "Okay, okay, since you're a true-blue young man, you are, aren't you? Yes, of course. I'll sell you these museum-quality boots for a discount of just twenty dollars and throw in another pouch of tobacco, as well. Remember, once you hit a major city you can sell these for display at a price of maybe hundreds of dollars!"

Tommy Holton had no idea what a museum even was, but he liked the sound of hundreds in cash to resell something he bought for twenty. After Black John and the gang had settled their treasure-finding battle with the pumpkin rollers, they planned to head back to El Paso. "Hey, peddler, does El Paso have a mausoleum?"

Sol blinked in confusion but then caught on, "I'm sure they do, son, in fact they keep mummies of the great Egyptian pharaohs on display to please the tourists. Sam Bass's boots would surely hold a place of honor alongside other historical legends."

Holton smiled, "And I'd get my name up there, too, right, for being the one who found the boots?"

Sol knew he had him hooked now, "Why of course, in fact I imagine they may name a whole wing after you!" He spread his arms wide as if showing a marquee. "The Tommy Holton Wing of Western Antiquities," he declared.

Holton tossed his cigarette butt to the ground, "All right then, let's do it. Twenty dollars and extree tobacco as you promised. Don't forget my certificate of . . . auth . . . aut . . ."

"Authenticity!" Sol finished for him. "Yeah, that."

Sol whipped out a paper that he'd handwritten to say:

This certificate authenticates these boots
to have been cut off the corpse of known
outlaw and notorious gang leader Sam Bass,
murdered by the most noble Texas Rangers
on July 21, year of our lord 1878,
in Round Rock, Texas.

"That's that. Now, about those mystical Egyptian pharaohs, I have something else a hardworking fella like yourself may be interested to try . . ."

CHAPTER 20

"Rider coming in," Johnny O'Neil said. "I hear him," his brother Sean said.

The day was fading, the evening sky blushing pink, and the lamplit cabin was fragrant with the hearty stew that Maria had simmering on the stove. Patches, Johnny's recently adopted calico kitten, full of milk, lay on a cupboard shelf and blinked like an owl. As the sound of hoofbeats came nearer, Sean rose from his chair and stood by the door, close to his hanging gun belt.

Outside the rider drew rein and after the passage of a few moments rapped on the door. Sean opened to a young, grinning puncher with a huge bunch of wildflowers in his hands.

"Howdy, Mr. O'Neil, my name is Larry Green and I brung these"—and then as though he'd been coached on what to say—"for Miss Maria Perez compliments of my employer Mr. Dick Peterson and he says to wish you all a pleasant evenin'."

"Come inside," Sean said. "Can I get you a cup of coffee?"

"Thank you, no, sir. Ah . . . the flowers come with a

handwritten note and I'm to wait for an answer from Miss Perez. That's what Mr. Peterson says, beggin' your pardon, sir."

The woman was in her bedroom, a frilly, pink place that Sean avoided like the plague, and he called out, "Maria, you have a gentleman caller."

"But I'm not the gentleman, ma'am," Larry Green said, blushing slightly. "I'm calling on behalf of the gentleman."

"Now here's a mystery," Maria said as she stepped out of her door. "Are all those flowers for me?"

"Yes ma'am. Picked fresh today by Mr. Dick Peterson's own hand. It took him the best part of an hour."

Maria took the flowers, smiled, and said, "How thoughtful of him."

"And I also have a note from Mr. Peterson that he wrote all by himself," Larry said. He took a cream-colored envelope from his pocket and passed it to Maria. "I'm to wait for an answer, ma'am."

"This is exciting," Johnny O'Neil said. "Who knew Dick Peterson was such a man of mystery?"

A slight frown gathering between her eyebrows, Maria opened the envelope and read the note:

WILL YOU MARRY ME?
Dick Peterson, Esq

"Well, what does it say?" Johnny said, enjoying this.

"Mr. Peterson wants to marry me," Maria said.

"Bully!" Johnny said, clapping his hands. "I knew it was love at first sight." He winked at Maria, and she glared in return.

"Well, this is quite an entanglement, isn't it?" Sean said.

Maria said nothing. She stepped into her room where

she kept her pen and ink and at the bottom of Peterson's note she wrote:

A man should have the nerve to come and ask me.
Maria Perez, spinster

She folded the note, pushed it back into the envelope and said, "You may give this to Mr. Peterson."

Larry Green took the envelope and said, "I hope you wrote down good news, ma'am. My boss is in a terrible state. The cook told me he's as nervous as a frog in a frying pan, and he says he's never seen him like that afore."

"Just . . . give him the note," Maria said.

"Yes, ma'am," the young puncher said.

He touched his hat to Maria, nodded at Sean and Johnny, and left.

After Maria returned to her room, Johnny said, "Sean, what just happened?"

"I don't know," Sean said. "Dick Peterson must've wrote something mighty powerful."

"A love poem maybe?"

"Could be, but I never pegged Peterson as a poet. He's a good cattleman though."

"Sounds like Maria is crying in her room," Johnny said.

Sean shook his head. "Women cry for all kinds of reasons."

"It's a mystery," Johnny said.

"A mystery no man has solved yet."

"Should I talk to her?" Johnny said.

"No, let her be. But if you plan to make her your bride, I suggest you solve this trouble by asking her instanter."

Johnny sighed. "I love her, Sean. I'd give the world for her. But is it right to saddle a beautiful young woman with an old, busted man like me? Maybe she'd be better off with Peterson who could give her far more than I ever can. She and Billy deserve so much more than me. That's where the problem lies."

Sean shook his head. He'd hashed out the same conversation many a time since Maria entered their lives, and no matter what sage advice he offered his brother, it was ignored.

Johnny picked up the calico kitten and held her in front of his face. "What problems do you have, Patches, huh?"

"What does she say?"

"She says nary a one."

"Lucky cat," Sean said.

CHAPTER 21

The autumn afternoon had settled in warm and still when Johnny O'Neil knocked on Maria Perez's door. The girl had wept for most of the day and served them a mostly silent lunch with red, puffy eyes before slipping back into her room. "Maria, it's Johnny, can I come in?"

Silence, and then, "Why, Johnny? I'm not in a state for visitors." Johnny sighed and rested his scarred forehead against the door. "I know, and I think that may be mostly my fault. Please?" The door swung open suddenly, and Johnny nearly fell into the room. "You'll need to be quiet. I've just managed to get Billy to sleep by rubbing brandy on his gums. My poor sweet boy. Dr. Grant said I could give him this." She held up a small glass bottle labeled DR SETH ARNOLD'S INFANTILE REGULATOR that held a dark brown liquid. "But I'm holding off because I don't trust it much."

Johnny nodded, "You're a good mother, Maria, that's a natural fact. Do what your gut tells you."

Pacified some by the compliment, Maria stepped back and let Johnny enter her room. In the corner, a frilled bassinet stood with a sleeping Billy within, and beside it was her small, wooden bed and a dressing table covered in potions and notions. Frilly pink fabrics and white lace seemed to be everywhere, and the battered old pugilist stuck out like a fox in a henhouse. Maria gestured to the dressing table chair, and Johnny sat while she perched on the edge of her own bed. The only sound was the quiet coos and gurgles Billy made in his sleep. "I . . . Well, I wanted to tell you something because I feel like maybe I haven't done right by you at all," Johnny began, eyes downcast. Maria sat on the edge of her bed, clinging to an embroidered handkerchief so tightly her knuckles turned white. Johnny fiddled with the buttons of his shirt and then continued. "See, I love you, in fact from the moment I first saw you I loved you."

Maria laughed. "Johnny, the moment you first saw me I was throwing rocks at you and threatening to kill you and your brother once I got a gun."

Johnny grinned. "Exactly, that's why I fell for you. And every day since, I've fallen harder, and of course I love little Billy just as much. The trouble is"—he sighed and shifted his weight, measuring his words—"the trouble is that you're about as perfect a gal as could ever exist. And me . . . I'm just a battered old pug who ain't much to look at, with a bum leg, who can barely ride a horse and is trying to play at being a rancher when really . . . well, Sean is the one who knows what he's doing. I'm just along for the ride. So, when a fella like Peterson comes a calling, I don't feel right keeping you from the life he could give you. He's rich, handsome, younger than me by quite a bit, and would let you live like the very royalty you are. Do you understand what I'm saying?"

Maria stood, her chocolate eyes blazing as color flushed her cheeks. She tossed the handkerchief to the floor. "Yes, I understand exactly what you're saying Mr. Johnny O'Neil. You're saying that you are a giant *pendejo,* a fool, a fool and a coward!" Her voice was steadily rising, and Johnny sat dumbstruck as she jabbed her tiny finger in his face as though she was ready to punch him. "You are a stupid, stupid man, Irish!" she raged, placing her hands on her head, grasping her hair as though suddenly besieged by a fearsome headache. Billy awoke and began caterwauling loud enough to wake the dead. Maria breathed deeply and regained her composure though tears now flowed freely from her reddened eyes. She scooped up the baby and soothed him on her shoulder, but he was not easily consoled. "Get out." She spoke firmly with her back turned to Johnny, yet her voice cracked with emotion. Billy peeped over her shoulder at the big man with interest before resuming his crying.

Johnny groaned and, grunting his frustration, stood from the too-small chair and left the woman he loved, quietly latching the door behind him. He made his way to the kitchen and retrieved the bottle of Old Crow, taking it to the porch without a glass. He gulped deeply straight from the bottle before taking a cheroot from his case and lighting it with shaking hands. The prairie was serene outside of the muffled cries of the baby and Maria's soothing singing. Not for the first time Johnny wondered if he was making a terrible, irreparable mistake.

CHAPTER 22

"So, we're agreed that it's a go for tomorrow morning just after sunup?" Black John Hannah said.

"They'll scatter, boss," Con Ransom said. "Them rubes have never come up against professional guns before."

"Scatter?" Hannah said. "Adam, will they see us come at them and cut and run?"

"Maybe," Curtis said. "Unless the crazy man who leads them decides to put up some kind of fight."

"Bill?" Hannah said.

Bill Stern, his slightly slanted reptilian green eyes reflecting the grin on his lips, said, "We drop a few on the way in and they'll break. Guaranteed."

Black John and his boys sat around the table in his cramped hotel room, a bottle of whiskey and glasses on the table reflecting the yellow light of the overhanging oil lamp. The air was hot and tight and smelled of man sweat and dust.

"Then here's how we'll play it," Hannah said. "We ride up to the wagons, nice as you please, tell them we want to join the pilgrims and once we're among them cut loose and drop as many as we can in the first volleys."

"They won't stand," Curtis said. As was his habit when

he was thinking, he held his iron rosary in his gun hand. "Boss, you and the others grab the treasure box and let me take care of their leader."

Hannah smiled. "Why him, Adam?"

"Because he's a false prophet, an enemy of Christendom and therefore an abomination. He must suffer the penalty of death."

Joe Hall guffawed. "You can take the boy outta the seminary but once a chalice chaser . . ."

Curtis' anger flared. "Joe, that ain't funny."

"Heck, I was only making a joke," Hall said. "Shoot the holy joe if you want. I don't care." Joe Hall spoke with a slight lisp, the result of having suffered a gunshot wound to the side of the head. His copper-colored hair bore a trench of scar tissue on the right side and he kept it close cropped, believing it made him look scary. He was right.

"Enough," Black John said. "I won't have quarreling among ourselves. Joe, apologize to Adam for your remark." A pause, then, "Do it now!"

"Sorry for my remark," Hall said. In fact, Hall wasn't sorry for anything he'd done in his violent life, the chalice chaser comment included, but he wished to keep the peace, and Adam Curtis was a dangerous and mighty sudden man. There was always that.

For his part, Curtis didn't push it. "Apology accepted," he said. "I'm a bit on edge tonight."

"It's the heat," Black John said. "This darn town is as hot as a Deadwood whore's sheets."

That last broke the tension and men laughed.

"Well, it's settled, tomorrow is the day," Black John said.

"The day we all get rich," Stern said.

"Darn right," Con Ransom said. "Darn rubes, I'll walk on top of their dead to get to the treasure box."

"I guess we all will," Hannah said. He stood, a big man making his presence felt in a small room. "What do you say we head for the Crystal Palace and have Lucas Battles burn us some steaks?"

"Sounds good to me," Leo Meyers said. "And fry up some taters to go with them."

"You love your grub, Leo, don't you?" Black John said.

"Sure do. One of the good things about hell is you can burn a steak anytime you want one." "I wonder how the coffee is?" Ransom said.

"Black as mortal sin and boiling hot, I imagine," Curtis said.

"Served by naked ladies," Stern said.

"And all of them . . . lewd," Curtis said.

Black John Hannah grinned. "Hold on boys, you make me want to get to Hades way before my time."

"John, I'm sure it will wait for you," Curtis said.

The laughter that followed was interrupted by a hesitant, timid tap on the door.

"Get that, Hank," Black John Hannah said to Hank Ward, who'd been quietly sipping his whiskey as was his nature. "Probably the proprietor demanding his room rents."

It wasn't the manager at the door, but Sheriff Bob Beason, flanked by the Gallagher twins. Beason looked determined, the twins uneasy. All three were armed.

"A friendly visit, I hope, sheriff," Black John Hannah said.

"Official business, I'm afraid," Beason said. "May we come in?"

"It's going to be crowded in here," Hannah said. "Who are those boys with you?"

"Deputies."

"Well, tell your deputies to stay in the hallway."

"You heard the man," Beason said. "Remain in the hallway. I'll be out soon."

Lon and Ben Gallagher didn't argue the point. They stepped back and leaned against the far wall, their faces expressionless.

Beason stepped into the room and Hannah closed the door behind him. Frontier hotel rooms were small and cramped and eight large men made for a crowd in the confined space.

Black John picked up the whiskey bottle. "Drink?" he said.

"Don't mind if I do," Beason said. "I need something to cut the dust."

When the sheriff had his drink in hand, Hannah said, "What can I do for you?"

Beason downed his whiskey, thumped the glass on the table, and said, "Shall I come to the point about what I want? Cut to the chase, as they say?"

"Please do," Black John said, aware of Bill Stern's amused grin. "Speak your piece, don't dance all over the floor with it."

"In short, Mr. Hannah, I need a posse," Beason said.

"A posse?" Black John said. "What kind of posse?"

"The kind that will help me get rid of a nest of murderous vipers currently encamped on the rancher Sean O'Neil's range."

Before any of his surprised boys could say a word, Hannah said, "You mean the pilgrims in the wagon train that everybody in town is talking about?"

"The very same. They say the world will end in a hail

of fire and brimstone in four days." Beason consulted his watch and said, "Now almost three days. This is a very serious matter, Mr. Hannah, because I hold all of them responsible for the cold-blooded murder of the nuisance Jess Hayes."

"And what do you want us to do about it?" Black John said.

"Ride in my posse and help me arrest the man responsible for Hayes' death." Beason suddenly swelled up and looked pompous. "This has become a personal matter since the vagabonds have tried to assassinate me. My hat has been twice shot off my head." The sheriff removed his hat and waggled two fingers through the bullet holes. "Darn murderous low-downs."

As Tommy Holton choked, stifling a laugh, Black John Hannah thought over Beason's offer. Could the star-strutting buffoon's posse work to his advantage? He would have the law on his side when he attacked the wagons and that might make a difference. Slight maybe, but anything that gave the pilgrims pause was worth considering. Beason could be disposed of later and his mouth permanently shut.

Finally, Hannah said, "Sheriff, let me talk this over with my friends. We plan to walk across to the Crystal Palace to eat a steak. I'll give you my decision then."

"I plan to make my arrest, or arrests, tomorrow," Beason said. "And I must warn you that there could be danger. Mr. Hannah, I'll be frank with you, I need men with sand, I say sand, sir, and I think you and your men fit the bill."

"You can depend on us, sheriff," Bill Stern said.

"As the day is long," Con Ransom said.

"Those are the words I need to hear," Beason said.

"We'll let you know, sheriff," Black John said. "Meet

us in the saloon, an hour or so from now. Say just before midnight."

"I'll be there, and my hopes will be high," Beason said. He smiled. "Mr. Hannah, it's men like you, and my humble self, that make our Republic great."

"Darn right it is," Hank Ward said, suppressing yet another grin.

CHAPTER 23

Little Sonora was vibrant with noise. Children yelling at play, chickens clucking, and lively music coming from all directions gave the shabby tarpaper shacks and leaning buildings the ambience of a large city. The enticing aroma of tamales, chili con carne, and menudo filled the dusty streets, but Joe Hall wasn't in search of supper. He made his way from the Crystal Palace to the small cantina that stood behind it, where the Mexican men gathered to drink tequila and share exaggerated stories of their work-day adventures in hope of provoking laughter or sympathy. Small, battered gambling tables dotted the room and a few men tried their hand at poker, a game that sometimes re-sulted in the weekend cuttings Sheriff Bob Beason let pass with little investigation.

Joe Hall was here because the saloon offered cheap whores, and with his blood up about the posse, he wanted to release some of his pent-up energy. He bellied up to the sagging bar where a short, hard-eyed man was busy pol-ishing glasses. "Cervesa, por favor," Hall said, the only Spanish he knew. When the bartender handed over a frothy beer, Hall sipped it slowly and surveyed his options.

Only two women graced the saloon, both looking bored and dressed in frilly red and black dresses with knee-high black stockings. A beautiful dark-haired girl with bite mark scars on her shoulders sat with her feet up, reading a book beside a beat-up old piano. She glanced at Hall when she felt him staring at her and offered a weak smile. The white man had a face only a mother could love, and the prominent scar running down the side of his head didn't help. Hall looked mean and menacing, but whores would do business with anyone if it meant putting food on the table.

The girl was a beauty, Hall thought. Her obsidian eyes sparkled in the lamplight, and a lush cascade of black hair flowed loose down to her mid-back. Hall picked up his beer and approached her, getting straight to the point. "Habla ingles, yeah? How much, love?" he asked, his lisp prominent.

The girl studied him then set down her book and placed her feet on the floor. "Si, of course I understand English. Three dollars for everything, if that's what you want. But no kissy-kissy and cuddling you white men always want. Service only and then you go away. Shoo. Get some tequila and unwind. Comprende?"

Joe Hall grinned. "Comprende."

The girl stood and took his hand to lead him to the back room, but Hall stopped her. "No, outside, I like it standing up."

The girl frowned. "You can stand up in here, it's just a small room with a bed."

Hall tugged her toward the exit. "I know, but that's boring, come on and we'll take care of business in the alley. I'll throw in an extry two dollars if you let me have it my way."

Although she felt ill at ease for a notion she couldn't quite justify, the lure of extra money won out in the end, and the whore allowed Hall to guide her outside. Pedro, the bartender, watched the pair exit and he, too, felt a niggling sensation of danger deep in his gut. Setting down the glasses, he reached beneath the bar where he kept both a Winchester rifle and a long knife for reassurance. Who could understand the notional nature of white men? But still . . . something felt off. Pedro poured another round of tequila and beer for the gathered men at his bar and then decided to follow.

In the dank, dark alleyway behind the Crystal Palace, Joe Hall finished his transaction with the beautiful young senora and grinned. Tears filled the girl's eyes, and her nose was bloodied from being smashed hard into the wall of the cantina. She hastily adjusted her dress, the five dollars tucked into her bosom, and made to head back into the warm glow of the building.

"Just a minute," Joe Hall said, his eyes gleeful with malice. "I've got something extry for you since you did such a good job." The girl turned to face him and that was all he needed. Fast as a rattlesnake he pulled a long knife from his boot and slit her throat, the fine, sharp blade cutting through her cinnamon flesh like silk. As blood poured from the wound, she collapsed to the dirt, eyes wide with terror and confusion. Hall bent down and covered his fingers with the hot blood before bringing them to his mouth and licking them clean. "Delicious," he said, as peaceful and delighted as a man tasting his fond mama's peach pie. He retrieved the five dollars from her corpse and when he stood, two rounds from a Winchester rifle exploded through his back, stopping his heart in an instant. A scurry of footsteps filled the alley and then all went silent, the blood of both Joe Hall and the pretty señorita mingled into a single stream that trickled slowly down the dusty alley and into the light.

CHAPTER 24

As Sean O'Neil turned down the oil lamps at the Running-S, over in Mustang Flat steaks were eaten and decisions made in the Crystal Palace saloon.

As Black John Hannah said, "Riding with the sheriff and his deputies can't hurt and might even help."

"Sure, let them ride along," Bill Stern said. "Once we pick up the treasure, we can get rid of them right quick. I'm looking forward to putting a bullet into the pompous ass of a lawman."

"Here he comes, treat him right," Hannah said. "We need him, at least for a while."

Bob Beason bellied to the bar, ordered a whiskey, and then said, "Well, Mr. Hannah, have you come to a decision?"

"Yeah," Black John said, "we'll be your posse for a day."

Beason grinned and thumped his fist on the table. "Crackerjack! We'll clear out that nest of rogues. I'll show them who's boss around here."

"What about that rancher, what's his name?" Hannah said.

"You mean Sean O'Neil?"

"Might he throw in with us?"

Beason shook his head. "O'Neil punches cows and that's all he does. His brother Johnny was a prizefighter, but a leg injury has slowed him down and besides, he's not much good with a gun. No, we can't expect help from the O'Neils."

"Too bad," Black John said. "But no matter. Tomorrow morning we'll put on a show that will never be forgotten in this neck of the woods."

"There's one thing I need to mention," Beason said. He looked tired, bags pouched under his eyes, and his skin had the gray tinge you see on a man who is sick or near exhaustion. For all his big belly, Beason was robust, so it was a lack of sleep that showed on him. "There's talk of treasure stashed in those wagons. Have you heard that?"

Black John didn't miss a beat. "No, sheriff, that's news to me," he said.

"Personally, I think it's all idle talk," Beason said. "But if there is a treasure, we must make sure the pilgrims don't try to run off with it."

"Don't worry, sheriff," Bill Stern said. "If we see that happen, we'll stop the thieves dead in their tracks."

"And then return the money to the proper authorities, of course," Black John said. "You being the proper authority of course, sheriff."

"I knew I could count on you boys," Beason said. "It's a pleasure to work with professionals. Now I think I'll turn in, busy day tomorrow. For all I know, maybe even a historic day that will be long remembered in West Texas."

"It will be historic, all right," Black John said. "You can count on it."

Beason's tired brain couldn't wrassle with the implications of that remark, and he tossed it out of his head like dirty dishwater. "Well, until tomorrow then. I'll meet you boys outside the Red Dust Inn at first light."

"We'll be there, sheriff," Black John said. "We wouldn't miss it for the world."

CHAPTER 25

"Sheriff! Hey sheriff! Come quick!" a young Mexican man accosted Bob Beason as he stepped out of the Crystal Palace, aggravating the tired man to no end.

"Oh heck no, I've got no time for the shenanigans of Mexicans tonight. What is it, another cutting? A stolen chicken? The law is busy, young man, busy with important law business. I'm sure whatever it is will wait until tomorrow." The sheriff scowled and tried to waddle away, the siren song of his bed calling loudly, but the young man grabbed his arm.

"Unhand me you—"

The man interrupted. "It's a white man! There's a white man dead in the alley and a dead whore with him."

Beason sighed and scrubbed his face with his hand. "Which white man?"

The young man cast him a sly glance. "How should I know? You all look alike."

Beason glared at the man. "Show me."

Sheriff Bob Beason stood with the undertaker Clem Milk, who had an instinct for showing up whenever bodies were found, and observed the scene. An inarguably beautiful señorita with a broken nose and slit throat lay beneath the crumpled form of a copper haired white man with two giant gunshot wounds to his back. The pair lay entwined together like a pile of garbage in the dark alley, their bodies cooled and pale. The dead girl stared skyward with an expression of sheer terror forever frozen on her face, and the man lay face down in the dirt, a bloodied knife still clutched in his hand.

Beason sighed. "I recognize that ugly head with the scar. He's one of Black John Hannah's men." The sheriff toed the corpse with his boot, and the body rolled enough to expose the dead man's face. "Yep. Hall, I think, Joe Hall. Guess he decided to murder this girl and someone caught him in the act. I don't suppose we'll ever figure out whodunit, but he would have been hanged for murdering the whore anyway, so justice was done."

Clem moved his lantern around and pointed, "Sheriff, there's footprints going to and from the cantina, look."

Beason puffed up his chest, "I saw them, Milk. I am a highly trained representative of the law, and I miss nothing!"

Clem shared a look with the Mexican who'd fetched the sheriff, and both struggled to hide their grins. "Of course, Mr. Beason, that's why I came straight to find you. Why, I thought, 'If anyone will solve this murder, it'll be the highly trained sheriff.'" The man's voice was dripping with sarcasm, but Beason either didn't notice or didn't care.

"Yes, you did the right thing, son. What is your name? For the official record like." Beason whipped out a notebook and stub of pencil.

"Mateo Vasquez, but my amigos call me Matty."

The sheriff jotted it down. "And you saw nothing at all?"

"No, I thought I heard the gunshots, but we hear them all the time. I didn't pay much attention. I was walking home bringing food from my Tia's house to my Madre, she's been ill, you know—"

Beason rudely interrupted. "Just the facts, you mustn't waste the law's time. I have no need for stories. Give me the details of this crime instanter."

Matty frowned. "Sure, sheriff. Anyway, I was walking past and saw blood coming out of the alley, see down there." He pointed to the entrance of the alleyway where a thin stream of blood had run and eventually pooled. "So, I came to see if someone was hurt and . . . well, they were hurt bad, so I ran to find you."

"It seems to me that justice was served, although I suppose the girl may have attacked Hall first and it was self-defense. Matthew, did she have a weapon when you found her. Come now, tell me the truth, it will set you free," Beason said.

The young man flushed with anger but kept his voice steady, "Mateo, my name is Mateo. And no, I didn't touch a thing. You think all Mexicans are criminals, sheriff?"

Beason harrumphed. "Of course not, but I must examine all the facts before I settle a case. I suppose I'll go speak to the patrons in the cantina. Milk, take the bodies away. I'll notify Black John Hannah. He ain't going to like it."

The undertaker set upon his work as the sheriff waddled off to the cantina. Most of the Mexicans spoke English, but all present, including the bartender, who'd hidden his Winchester rifle under his mattress, insisted they saw and heard nothing. As far as Beason was concerned there was nothing left to investigate. A dead Little Sonora whore and a dead gang member were the least of his concerns.

CHAPTER 26

Micah, despite his earlier exertions with the woman sharing his narrow cot, was unable to sleep. The moment of truth was fast approaching, and everything must go as planned. The Gallagher twins had his fullest confidence. City-bred thugs and not particularly intelligent, they would do as they were told, and they'd no qualms about killing. Man, woman, or child, it made no difference to Lon and Ben. Later, after the heist was made, he'd gun them if he could, pay them off if he couldn't. But even that reassurance did little to ease his racing mind.

The woman beside him stirred. "Chosen One, why are you still awake?" she said, her voice drowsy from sleep. "Do you want me again?"

"No, not now. I was at prayer," Micah said.

"Then I will pray with you."

"No, go back to sleep," Micah said. "I'll wake you later."

"Then I'll await your command," the woman said.

She turned on her side and was soon slumbering again.

Micah lay still, reluctant to rouse the woman a second time. He suddenly felt a need, a burning desire to visit the scene of the crime, if it was truly a crime to fleece a bunch of dimwitted sodbusters, and go through the plan again in his mind. His scheme, spawned a long time ago in Kansas, had gone way too far to risk any last-minute blunders.

Micah sat up in the tangled sheets and reached for his nightgown. The woman didn't stir. He pulled the garment over his head and then his skinny legs, and this time the woman whimpered in her sleep. He patted the woman's naked hip as he would an agitated puppy and said, "Shh . . . shh . . ."

The woman whimpered again and then her breathing became soft and regular as she slept.

Micah grinned. What was her name? Ah yes, Emma. It seemed Emma had been dreaming about her skinny, bald husband again.

Still smiling, he made his way out of his tent without disturbing the woman further, and stood stock still in the darkness, his eyes scanning the compound. Saddle horses, people, everything was in its place as it should be. There was no sound and nothing moved. After a tense couple of minutes, on silent feet Micah crossed to the far side of the circle to the treasure chest. The wagons behind it must be moved apart to allow free passage out of the circle once the money was transferred to sacks for transportation. Gunplay was unlikely, but he figured the Gallaghers could handle it, but more likely the getaway would be clean. The rubes would believe that the treasure had to be moved to protect it from evil forces during the great destruction and the whole business would go as planned. But Micah still felt uneasy. Why? Then it dawned on him. The hicks themselves might be the problem. What if they objected to God's treasure being removed from the security of the circle? A solution presented itself. He and the Gallaghers could shoot their way out. Micah dismissed that immediately. They'd face a score of rifles wielded by angry farmers, odds too great for three men to buck. There had to be another way.

And then a revelation . . .

He'd have another vision. That very morning.

Micah smiled in the moonless gloom. God would warn him that evil was at work, and godless men planned to steal the treasure. "Chosen One, my sacred offering is at risk and must be moved to a place of safety."

Micah did a little jig of delight. That was the answer.

The Gallaghers he'd pass off as trusted converts recommended by the Lord to help move the offering to a place of safekeeping, to be returned when the skies reddened and flaming clouds began to rain fire and brimstone.

Yes, it was perfect, and no gunplay involved. The slack-mouthed hayseeds would swallow his tale hook, line, and sinker.

Now in a much better frame of mind, Micah made his way back to his tent. It was time to wake Ella or Emma or whatever the heck her name was . . .

Jim Petite huddled near his wagon and the fire he'd built for himself and his beloved wife Emma, who was nowhere to be found. With a rag, he tried his best to scrub the dried mud off the knees of his trousers without much luck. Then he set back to frying up the salt pork, cooking Emma's share in the hopes that she'd return soon enough. He knew that she was chosen by Micah for private prayer sessions and sometimes would share supper in his tent, and though it filled Jim with jealousy, he knew he must cast aside those feelings to become closer with God. The rain showed little sign of slowing, and all around the camp pilgrims were doing their best to make dry places to sit and share a cup of coffee and a meal. Rolling thunder echoed across the prairie, and bright bolts of lightning spread in the distant darkness like dead trees coated in silver. Jim shivered and pulled his poncho closer to stave off the cold. He'd had many misgivings about following their prophet, yet signs from God always appeared in his moments of weakness and renewed his faith.

The mood of the camp seemed sullen tonight, and as he gazed around the circle, he saw few smiles being shared. He hoped they were doing the right thing. God forgive him, but he was afraid of the end times and if the thin prophet in his red robes wasn't truly the chosen one . . . what would happen to them all then? Exhausted, damp, and lonely, Jim finally ate Emma's share and crawled into the leaky wagon in hope of a dreamless sleep until the bright, welcoming sun would rise again.

CHAPTER 27

A theater audience would've given Micah's perform-
ance a standing ovation.

Under a gray sky, as people prepared breakfast within
the wagon circle, low fires burning their dwindling supply
of wood, he stepped into the middle of the throng, let out
a terrible, anguished cry, and suddenly dropped to his
knees. The pilgrims stopped what they were doing, leaving
salt pork to sputter in frypans, and crowded around their
leader, their shocked faces concerned.

Micah raised his arms, threw his head back, and stared
skyward. For a few moments, he appeared to listen intently, and then he called out, "I hear you, Lord! And I am
sorely afeared." Again, the man appeared to listen as
around him people kneeled and prayed, and a few women
sobbed. "Yes, Lord, it shall be done!" Micah yelled. "The
evil ones will not lay blasphemous hands on our offering.
Thank you, oh Lord, for your help and guidance."

If there were a few skeptics among the pilgrims, their
misgivings vanished when nature intervened . . . a happening so timely and bizarre that historians later said must
have made Micah rejoice.

The sky above the wagon circle had been gray all morning, now it turned black as a fast-moving thunderstorm rolled off the Gulf of Mexico and the clouds exploded with a tremendous bang over the wagon circle. A flash of lighting forked across the heavens like the signature of a demented god and shimmered on rain falling in sheets, cascading like steel needles. The hissing campfires trailed smoke as their flames were battered into oblivion. Then as quickly as it appeared it was gone. The storm grumbled eastward, and the sky began to clear.

Hallelujah!

Men and women fell to their knees on the muddy ground, their hands clasped in prayer, and Micah rose to his feet and walked among them.

"Good people, all ye chosen, be of good faith because we are not alone," he said. "God told me that he has appointed two men, stalwarts who are faithful to our cause. They will join us and point the way to where the Lord's treasure must be concealed until we return it to ourselves as the first fiery bolts begin to fall."

More cries of Hallelujah and Micah was triumphant. He strolled among the faithful, his hand moving from bowed head to bowed head, and grinned inwardly. Thank'ee West Texas weather . . . your thunderstorms come right when they're most needed.

CHAPTER 28

"We didn't need this rain," Sheriff Bob Beason grumbled. "I didn't even bring my slicker."

Riding beside him, Black John Hannah glanced at the torn sky and said, "It'll pass. Keep your mind on what's ahead."

"You think they'll let us just ride in there?" Beason said.

"Having second thoughts, sheriff?" Hannah said.

"I don't think we can waltz into the wagon circle, is all I'm saying."

"Then we'll shoot our way in," Black John said. His horse had no liking for thunder and fought the bit. "There's nine—well, with Hall dead there's eight of us, plus you and those twins. Ten men is plenty and we have eleven, that gives us a spare."

"Eleven men and we're facing a score of riflemen. And two of us are a tad dubious."

Bill Stern laughed out loud. "Heck, sheriff, a bunch of rubes armed with squirrel guns ain't riflemen."

"One of them was marksman enough to knock my hat off my head twice," Beason said.

"But not good enough to blow your brains out twice," Black John said, smiling. His smile faded and he said, "Two of us are dubious? I trust my boys, how about your deputies?"

"If it comes to shooting, I don't know."

"Don't know what?"

"If we get into a scrape, I don't know if they'll gun-fight."

"You picked a fine time to tell us," Black John said, scowling his irritation.

"What do you think?" Beason said.

"I think the rubes might use them as target practice. If they're shooting at them, they're not shooting at us."

"If it comes to it, they'll shoot at all of us."

"Shooting ain't hitting," Stern said. "Me and the others hit." He shook his head and spat. "Darned plow wranglers, what do they know? I've shot enough of them to know they're useless."

"I reckon we'll find out pretty darn quick how much they know," Black John said.

Stern made a face and his eyes searched for Hannah's in the gloom. "Not you, too, boss?" he said.

Black John's teeth gleamed. "Bill, never underestimate a wolf until you've skun him. Let's brace those pilgrims before we do any bragging."

"Suits me, boss," Stern said. "Heck, I do enjoy gunning rubes."

The remainder of the ride was made in silence that Black John didn't break until the wagon circle came in sight. "There it is, boys," he said. "We go in smiling and a-grinning like we're visiting kinfolk. Let me do the talking."

"And me," Beason said. "I'm the law, remember?"

"We're not about to forget that, sheriff," Bill Stern said. "The very sight of you will make them quake in their boots."

Beason looked for the tease in Stern's face, saw none and said, "We're almost in rifle range."

"Figgered that," Black John said. "Nobody's shooting yet. Maybe we put the crawl on them already."

But a moment later a shot that blew Beason's hat off his head gave the lie to that statement.

"Darnit," the sheriff said. "Who keeps doing that?"

"Somebody who can't decide if he wants to kill you or not, Beason," Stern said. "You better hope he doesn't make up his mind any time soon."

A few moments later Black John Hannah drew rein, a raised hand halting the others. The Gallagher boys were holding back, a few yards behind the rest.

"Hello, the wagons," Hannah yelled.

A man's voice answered. "What do you want?"

"I'll tell it straight out," Black John said.

"Then tell it."

"We've seen the light," Hannah said. "We want to join you and escape the fires of hell to come."

A few seconds pause, and then a man from within the circle, his voice edged with anger, roared, "You're too late! Go away!"

"Let's talk about that," Hannah said.

Then Micah's voice, "Go away and don't show your faces around these wagons again. You're not wanted here."

"Open a space. Give us the road," Hannah said.

"No."

Black John Hannah was a successful outlaw and former peace officer, and he did not lack smarts. Yet he was about to make a crucial mistake that would cost him dearly. The only reason for his action that comes to mind is that storming the wagon circle and stealing the treasure had become an obsession. He forgot, or paid no heed, to the warning first given in the War Between the States that underestimating an enemy's intelligence, strength, and aggression makes you vulnerable. When it comes to violence, expect anything from anyone and it could be almighty sudden.

"All right, let's take 'em, boys!" Black John yelled.

"Nooo . . ." Beason cried out, the horrified wail of a man in mental agony. His voice was drowned out by a thunderclap that shook the ground, and Black John's men paid him no heed.

Beason took no part in the charge . . . that turned out to be a pitiful farce.

Firing their revolvers at the run, Black John and his men made for a five-foot gap in the wagon circle, the result of a barricade of empty barrels and packing crates that were earlier pushed over by the exiting oxen, and never rebuilt. But the space was heavily defended, as Black John quickly learned.

He and his boys ran into the devastating fire of at least a dozen riflemen, a wall of lead that Hannah and his boys hurtled into at the gallop.

Bill Stern was the first to be hit, wounds to his right leg and upper chest. Game to the end, a superb shootist, Stern drew rein and fought back, a Colt in each hand. He killed a man at the gap, wounded another, and then went down under a hail of bullets, his slim body shredded, blood everywhere.

Black John saw a disaster in the making and yelled, "Back! Back!"

But it was too late for Con Ransom, who sat slumped in the saddle, shot to pieces, his dead, blue eyes open, staring into eternity.

Bullets zipping past them, Black John and Adam Curtis retreated out of rifle range. Tommy Holton and Hank Ward were slow to retreat, and Ward had his horse shot from underneath him and was crushed by the beast before a well-aimed shot to the head ended his suffering. Holton was shot in the shoulder but made it to where John and Curtis stood, howling in pain and clutching the bloody wound. Elliot Flint took a shot to his thigh and in his panic fled past his compatriots into the prairie. There was no sign of the Gallagher twins, but Sheriff Bob Beason, his face ashen, sat his horse at a safe distance. Leo Myers lay bloody and ashen at the edge of the circle, still alive but just barely and not for much longer. Hannah drew rein in front of him, his eyes flinty and accusing. "Beason, you yellow-bellied coward," he said. "You and your deputies could've made the difference."

Beason's anger flared. "I wouldn't have made the difference! Darn your eyes, Hannah, nobody could've made a difference. A group of men with pistols don't attack a wagon circle defended by at least a score of riflemen. Not if they're in their right mind, they don't. Black John, you're an arrogant man who thought the very sight of you would put the crawl on a passel of scared rubes. Well, it didn't work out that way, did it?"

"This thing ain't over, Beason, not by a long shot," Hannah said.

"Leave them be. In a few days they'll be gone."

"They killed four of my boys and have maimed two. I can't forget that. And I won't forget you either."

Black John swung his horse away and Beason watched him leave. Now it dawned on him why the man joined his posse so eagerly . . . he knew of the treasure and aimed to take it . . . until the pumpkin-rollers ruined his plans.

The morning sun glinted on the nickel-plated star pinned to Beason's shirt. It had two words engraved on it, CITY SHERIFF. Once those words meant something to him, something noble, but that was a long time ago. In the intervening years he'd countless times dragged the badge through the dirt, and the words and what they stood for had lost all meaning. Perhaps there was still time to make amends.

Beason swung out of the saddle, retrieved his shot-up hat, and then, to look less aggressive, led his mount toward the circle. He walked in a profound silence, quieter by far than a cobwebbed tomb. Only the air spoke to him, the acrid tang of gunsmoke reminding him that overly proud men had died there.

A man stepped through the gap in the wagons and yelled, "That's far enough."

"I come in peace," Beason said. *I come in peace . . .* what a stupid thing to say, he thought. Given the circumstances, could he come any other way?

"State your intentions," the man at the gap said.

"There are four men dead on the ground here," Beason said. "And a dead horse," he added for good measure.

"And two more within the wagon circle and a woman who won't last until midnight."

"I can send a doctor," Beason said.

"Too late for doctors. Mrs. Emma Petite has a belly wound. She can't live."

"I'm Sheriff Bob Beason."

"We know who you are. I could shoot you down where you stand."

The sheriff ignored that and said, "I'll send out Clem Milk the undertaker from Mustang Flat for your dead. They can be buried in a proper cemetery."

The rifleman turned his head, talking to someone, then he faced Beason again and said, "That will be much appreciated. Why would you do that for people you hate?"

"I don't hate you. But a man was murdered and one of your people did it. I still have a job to do."

"An avenging angel of the lord killed the man. He was not slain by mortal hand."

"You know, Sean O'Neil was right about you people, and I was wrong," Beason said. "He told me to leave you the heck alone and you'd eventually go away."

"A wise man, sheriff. You should have listened." Micah stepped out of the wagon circle. "We'll be gone from here in a little over forty-eight hours, and by the forty-ninth hour, we will be in paradise while your bones are turning to ashes. Hallelujah!"

Beason realized that this conversation could go around and around until his head spun. He cut it short. "I'll send the undertaker."

"Tell him we now have three dead," Micah said. "Emma Petite, a holy and devout woman, passed away a few minutes ago."

"Sorry to hear that," Beason said.

"You're sorry, we're all sorry, and mostly because you brought those gunmen down on us," Micah said.

"That wasn't supposed to happen. I came here to talk."

"I believe you," Micah said. "If I didn't, you'd be dead by now. Go away, and never come back. The day of destruction is nigh."

Micah turned on his heel and stepped through the gap.

The rifleman motioned with his Winchester. "Go now."

Sheriff Bob Beason mounted and headed for Mustang Flat. On his way he checked the bodies of Con Ransom and Bill Stern, Stern's face, though bloody, was at peace. Ransom was the opposite. Gut shot, his features were contorted in pain, his gray lips drawn back from his teeth in a snarl, damning death for the terrible fate that had befallen him.

CHAPTER 29

"Boss, big doings at the wagons," the excited puncher said. He sat his horse under a gold-colored sky strewn with islands of small purple clouds.

"What kind of doings?" Sean O'Neil said.

"Looks like there's been a fight. I seen Clem Milk there, boxing bodies."

"Did you see Sheriff Beason?"

"No. He ain't there. Just Milk and two of his helpers. But I counted five coffins in his wagon, and two more in the works."

"All right, I'll come take a look see," Sean said. He turned to his ranch foreman, a man named Joe Dean and said, "Joe, call it a day. We'll finish this stretch of fence to-morrow."

The man nodded. "Sure thing, boss."

"And tell Maria and Johnny I'll be home in time for supper."

When the wagon circle came in sight, Clem Milk and his helpers were still there and Sean O'Neil rode up to the little scarecrow of an undertaker, dismounted, and said, "What happened?"

"The way I heard it, the sheriff led a posse against the pilgrims, planning to make an arrest, and got all shot up."

"Is Beason alive?" Sean said.

"Yes, he is, complaining that he got his hat blowed off his head for the third time."

"Who are the dead?"

"Two men and a woman from the wagons, and four gunmen who work for Black John Hannah."

"What's Hannah's claim to fame?" Sean said.

"I don't know all of it, but the moccasin talk is that he's an outlaw of some kind out of El Paso and other places, and mighty sudden with Colt's gun. He already killed a man in Mustang Flat."

"Anybody I know?"

"I doubt it. A youngster on the make by the name of Jack Doyle. Seems he was trying to build a gun rep and drew down on Black John. Poor kid, I buried him the next morning. Mr. Hannah paid to have him laid to rest decent."

"Big of him," Sean said.

Milk shrugged. "It's fast-on-the-draw men like Black John that help keep me in business." He turned to one of his assistants. "Looks like we're all loaded up, Sam."

"Yeah, we're ready to go, Mr. Milk."

The undertaker looked past Sean, held something in sight for a moment and then said, "Uh-oh, now what do these fellers want?"

The pair dismounted at a distance, a move that rang an alarm bell in Sean's mind. Drawing a gun can be unhandy on a horse and he'd made the acquaintance of those gents earlier, the Gallagher twins, men in big city suits with a thuggish attitude acquired on the mean streets. Both were heeled, wearing a belt gun, and neither showed the slightest sign of being neighborly.

Lon Gallagher stopped, looked over Milk and his assistants, dismissed them, and said to Sean, "What the heck are you doing here? O'Neil, isn't it?"

"Yeah, it's O'Neil, and this is my range," Sean said. "That's what the heck I'm doing here."

"You're a funny man, cowboy," Ben said. "I don't like funny men, and I don't like cowboys."

"And I don't like strangers on my land," Sean said. "And I don't like the look of you or your brother. You boys are too close, crowding me, and I won't be crowded. To sum up, get mounted and flap your chaps off my ranch."

"You're playing with fire, waddie," Ben said.

"And I'd guess you are, too. Did you hook up with the fire and brimstone crowd in the wagons?"

"That's none of your business," Ben said.

"You're on my range, so I'm making it my business," Sean said.

In a small, timid voice, Clem Milk said, "Sam, clear a space in the wagon."

Ben said, "I'm giving you one chance, O'Neil. Mount up and get out of here. I won't give you another."

"Answer me," Sean said. "Did you throw in with the folks with the wagons? And if you did, explain why."

Ben sighed and said, "Lon, this boy just won't learn. Why don't you read to him from the book?" Lon smiled and said, "All right, cowboy, here's chapter and verse . . . if you don't ride on out of here now, I'll drop you right where you stand. Do you compre?"

"Gallagher, don't haul iron on me," Sean said. "I don't want to kill you."

Ben laughed. "Confident, ain't he?"

"Don't even try it, boys," Sean said. "My draw was made in the devil's lair."

"And cute with it, too," Ben said, grinning.

"He's a big talker," Lon said. "I've met his kind before."

"Don't push me," Sean said. "I don't want trouble."

"You mean gun trouble?" Ben said. "Is that why your knees are knocking?"

"Let it go and get off my range," Sean said.

"I'm not letting go," Lon said. He grinned. "You want Texas fast, O'Neil? All right then, I'll give you fast."

His hand dropped to his gun. Sean O'Neil put two bullets into Lon before he cleared leather. At a range of just ten feet both rounds smashed through the man's breastbone and instantly destroyed his heart and blew apart a lung. Lon died with his eyes wide open, without ever knowing what hit him.

Ben, yellow to the core, shrieked, an animal cry of anguish and terror. "I'm out of it!" He clambered into the saddle, ignored Sean's yell of "Halt!" and galloped for the wagon circle.

His blood up, Sean slid his Winchester from its saddle scabbard and levered a round into the chamber. He drew a bead on Ben's back, his finger on the trigger, but after a moment lowered the rifle.

His face as white as his name, Clem Milk said. "You let him go."

Sean watched Ben Gallagher ride into the circle through a gap in the wagons and said, "He was running for his life and his back was to me."

"You don't shoot a man in the back?" Milk said.

"Not as a general rule," Sean said.

He looked down at Lon's face, ugly and twisted in death.

Milk again, as timid as ever, said, "Why did he do it?"

"Because he was a city thug who considered a gun just another tool, like a sap or a club or a shiv. He'd no right getting into a Texas drawfight. I tried to warn him that he was way overmatched."

"Room for one more, Mr. Milk," the man called Sam said. "We're gonna need a bigger cemetery."

"Load him up," Clem Milk said, adding, "Mr. O'Neil, what do I tell Sheriff Beason?"

"Tell him what you saw, Clem. And let him know I want to see him," Sean said.

He looked at the wagon circle. It seemed that Ben Gallagher had been welcomed with open arms. What in God's name was going on in there?

CHAPTER 30

"What the heck is going on with those pilgrims?" Johnny O'Neil said.

"I wish I knew," Sean said. "I reckon they'll all be gone in a few days after the fire and brimstone doesn't arrive, so I guess we may never know."

"I'd bet the farm that it's something to do with the treasure they're supposed to have," Johnny said. "Some folks could be interested in that, including Black John Hannah and those Gallagher twins you met today."

"There's only half a pair of twins left," Sean said.

"I know," Johnny said. "Sean, I'm sorry you had to shoot one of them today. What was his name?"

"Lon. He gave me no choice. But I'm not about to dwell on it."

"Don't let it eat on you," Johnny said. "No amount of regrets will bring him back."

Sean said, "I won't boast on it, but I don't regret it, Johnny. I killed Lon Gallagher in a fair fight. It was either him or me."

Johnny's smile was hesitant, and he opened his mouth to speak, then shut it again.

"Ask it, brother," Sean said.

"It's a Texas question."

"I can answer most of those. Speak."

"Was he fast?"

"No. But he was game."

"And murderous."

"That was my impression."

"Oh, dear," Maria Perez said, staring out the window into the waning day.

Sean followed her gaze and in pretend surprise said, "Why, it's Dick Peterson. Now what is he doing here? Has he come a-calling?"

Maria flew into a panic. "Here, Sean, hold the baby. She shoved little Billy into his arms and fled into her bedroom.

In a panic that equaled Maria's, Sean said, "Johnny, take him. I know nothing about holding babes."

"He'll be all right," Johnny said, grinning.

"He's squirming like a frightened piglet. I can't get ahold of him, and he knows it."

Johnny rose and took the baby. "You've a lot to learn about little ones, brother."

"Let me do it at a safe distance, huh? Suppose he throws up all over me?"

"Then you wipe it off with a cloth."

"Oh my God, that sounds dreadful," Sean said.

He rose and answered the door to Dick Peterson's rap. "Howdy, Dick. Come in," he said. "Here to visit?"

For a moment, Peterson seemed confused. Then he managed, "I've come to see Miss Maria."

"She's in her bedroom, but I'm sure she'll be right out. Take a chair, Dick. Coffee?"

"If it's all the same to you, Sean, I could use a drink."

Sean smiled. "I'm sure you could."

He poured a bourbon as the big rancher took little Billy's hand and made coo-cooing noises that chilled Sean's blood. Mercifully it soon stopped, and Peterson regained his chair. After a gulp of whiskey, he said, "I heard you killed a man today, Sean."

"You heard right."

"That was after a big fight at the wagons."

Sean nodded. "You heard that right, too."

"How did it all come up?"

Using as few words as possible, Sean told about Bob Beason's posse and how his planned arrest of the killer of Jess Hayes had ended in disaster with seven people dead. "Eight if you include Lon Gallagher," he said.

"I keep hearing the name Black John Hannah," Peterson said. "He killed a man in Mustang Flat, and you say he and his boys rode in Beason's posse?"

"They sure did. Hannah lost four of his gun hands in the scrape."

"Did this man Lon Gallagher ride with Hannah?"

"Not as far as I know. Gallagher was a member of the posse, so Beason probably deputized him and his brother."

"It seems Gallagher drew down on you for no good reason," Peterson said.

"He had a reason all right. He didn't want me anywhere near the wagons."

"And his brother is now with them."

"Seems like."

Peterson shook his head. "Very strange." His eyes were fixed on Maria's bedroom door.

"I think the treasure is involved," Johnny said.

"I was told about the treasure," Peterson said. "You think there's any truth in it?"

"Who knows?" Johnny said. "Those pilgrims are a mighty odd bunch. They might make up all kind of stories."

"Best you stay away from them. They'll move on soon."

"That is my intention," Sean said. "There's been enough blood spilled already."

Maria's bedroom door opened a crack, and then halted, as though she was having second thoughts about making her entrance. Then it opened wider, and she stepped into the room to smiles of approval from the men present. The girl wore a pink, floral print dress with a ruffled neck and puffed sleeves, recently purchased at cost from Solomon Cohen. Sol assured Maria the dress was so fashionable that old Queen Vic had approved it for her own ladies in waiting. True or not, it certainly made a big impression on the menfolk, especially Dick Peterson and Johnny O'Neil.

In considerable haste, Peterson swallowed the last of his whiskey, rose, and ushered Maria into his chair. "I've come in person to ask you a question," he said.

"Ask, and I'll do my best to answer it," Maria said, her cheeks pink.

"I wrote it down," the big rancher said.

"Then it must be a big question," Maria said.

"It is. Oh yes, it is."

Peterson pulled a folded paper from his shirt pocket and handed it to Maria. She opened the paper and read:

WILL YOU MARRY ME?

Peterson handed the girl a stub of pencil and said, "Write down your answer."

Maria paused, her face clouded with racing thoughts,

and her body wavered as if pained, then laid the paper on the table and wrote:

I CANT. I AM SORRY.

"Yee-hah!" Peterson yelled, presumptively. "She's gonna—" The rancher's handsome face fell, and he slumped in the chair. "Oh. I see," he said, pouring a double bourbon and swallowing it with haste. Sean glanced at Johnny, who kept his eyes downcast and sat still as a statue, a muscle twitching in his jaw. Peterson extended his hands and Maria took them and rose from the chair. The rancher held her at arm's length and looked deep into her chocolate eyes, now glittering with tears. Quietly he asked, "May I ask why, Maria?" The girl took a deep, quivering breath and glanced at the O'Neil brothers, saying nothing.

"Johnny," Sean said finally, "come outside, I want to talk to you, and bring the baby. Show him the sky. He likes that."

"Why?" Johnny said. Then he saw Maria and Peterson still clasping hands and added quickly, "Oh, yes, I understand."

He stepped outside with Sean, and Billy looked up at the sky, red rose petals of cloud strewn across an indigo backdrop, holding fast to its promise of tomorrow's sun.

"What do you want to talk to me about?" Johnny said, smiling, taking delight in the baby's delight.

"I want you to head into Mustang Flat for supplies tomorrow," Sean said. "I'll be tied up all day . . ."

"With fencing. I can't help you with that since barbed wire and me ain't on friendly terms, but I'll sure bring home the groceries."

"I thought you might, since you eat most of them,"

Sean said. "I'll give you a list in the morning. Billy sure likes that sky, huh?"

"Yes, he does, and he loves watching cows."

"We'll make a rancher out of him yet."

"I don't think so. Maria says she wants her son to go to college."

"Then he'll be a gentleman rancher. Plenty of those around, even belted earls, I'm told."

Johnny smiled. "During my boxing days in Boston I once knew a belted earl, an English gent called the Earl of Strathmore, and a fine man he was, too. He could gamble for days at an end without sleep, drink any man under the table, and he boasted that he'd bedded ten thousand whores on five continents."

"I guess he died of exhaustion, huh?"

"Listen to Billy. He's making baby talk to the sky. Ain't that darlin'? Now where was I?"

"I asked you what happened to the Earl of Strathmore."

"Oh, yeah. Well, it was a tragic case. The earl gambled away his fortune and fell into penury. I tried to help him, but he was too proud to accept charity. Then came a frosty, wintry morning in Boston town when he stumbled out of a poorhouse into the path of a speeding coach and four and was killed instantly. Now here's the irony of the thing, Sean. The coach belonged to a rich railroad and mining magnate, another Englishman by the name of Sir Marmaduke Tweng, and he and the earl had once been close friends. Sir Marmaduke was distraught and buried the earl on his own property and erected an eight-foot gravestone that still stands. Funny thing, all Tweng wrote on it was, 'The Earl of Strathmore. Sporting Gent.'"

"A story that would bring a tear to a glass eye," Sean said.

"Wouldn't it though," Johnny said. "Ah well, let's go

back inside. The sky is fading, and little Billy here is getting fussy."

"Another excellent supper, Maria," Johnny O'Neil said. He dabbed his mouth with his napkin and then said, "Are you feeling all right. You look peaked?"

"I'm fine." Maria said. She quickly cleared the plates and then said, "Well, I suppose I do feel as though I need to lie down awhile. Excuse me." And with that, she disappeared into her room where little Billy was sleeping soundly.

"When do you think is a fine time for a wedding?" Johnny said.

Sean smiled. "You're asking a man who has never been married."

"Maybe someday." A sly twinkle in his eye, Johnny said, "Maybe a woman like Maria."

Sean didn't hesitate. "If she can cook like Maria, why not?"

"Why not indeed," Johnny said, patting his distended stomach.

Johnny said, "What do you think, Sean?"

"I think you're a darned fool if you don't march in there and ask her to marry you. You'll lose her for good Johnny. You almost did."

Johnny scrubbed his face with his hands. "You're right. I'm an idiot. I'll set it right, Sean."

The young rancher stood and squeezed his brother's shoulder. "I know you will," he said and then retreated to his quilts, exhausted from the day.

CHAPTER 31

That evening while Maria Perez broke Dick Peterson's heart, a flustered Dr. Grant had two patients with gunshot wounds carried into his surgery. Luke Lawson and the Scottish rancher Sandy McPhee had been recruited by Bob Beason to transport the wounded men from the wagon circle on the prairie and into Mustang Flat on a wagon, Luke at the reins as Sandy did his best to stem the bleeding with little success.

Seeing the condition of his patients, the doctor shook his head. "These men have lost a lot of blood. I don't have high hopes for their survival."

Tommy Holton groaned in pain, his face ashen and spattered with his own blood. "Help me, Doc, it hurts real bad, make it stop, God please make it stop . . ."

Dr. Grant drew up morphine in a syringe and administered it to Holton, "I can only give you a little, son. I have to put you under anesthesia and try to get the bullet out. I suggest you make your peace with God now. The bullet didn't go straight through, and it may have nicked your heart or lung. Do you understand what I'm telling you?"

As the morphine surged through Holton, he felt a rush of euphoria mingle with the pain, and he muttered an unintelligible response. Dr. Grant shook his head and moved to take a look at Elliot Flint. The dark-haired man had been unconscious since he'd fallen off his horse on the range. The bullet had pierced his thigh but come clean out the other side and missed hitting bone.

"He can wait," Grant said, "Sandy, I need you to help me with the anesthesia. It's ether and you must be careful to listen to my instructions. Luke, you stay with this fellow and keep pressure on his wound. Hopefully he doesn't wake up."

The two men shared a glance and grimaced. Neither had signed up to get involved with surgical proceedings but they felt obligated to stay. "You need a nurse, doc," said McPhee.

"Chop, chop, we must begin" was the doctor's only reply.

He showed Sandy McPhee how to hold the ether mask and control the droplets, and once Holton was out began the task of retrieving the bullet. Using long forceps, he dug into the wound and the squelching sounds made Sandy blanch pale beneath his red hair. "Don't you dare faint on me, McPhee, or I'll have your hide."

Finally, Doctor Grant located the bullet and with a cry of victory pulled it free and dropped it into a metal pan with a loud clunk. "It didn't break up, thank God. No major organs dinged, either. He was lucky, but I doubt he will ever be able to use the arm properly again."

"Perhaps that is for the best given his trade," he added. After rinsing the wound clean, the doctor sprinkled sulfa within and made swift work of stitching it closed. "If he can avoid infection, I dare say he'll live. Sandy, take away the mask and let him wake." Grant moved away and rinsed his bloody hands in a pail of water before moving onto Elliot, who was beginning to stir. Luke Lawson was green around the gills and eager to return to the far less bloody life of his mercantile.

The door to the surgery opened with a bang and a plump, red-faced women rushed inside, huffing for breath. "I'm here, Doctor Grant, I came as quick as I could. Oh, how awful it is, so many dead!"

Luke and Sandy immediately made for the door, eager to flee. "Mrs. Pierson you're just in time to help me with this chap here. But check on the other one first. He's just come off the ether. Boys you can leave now, I'm sure these gentlemen will owe you a great debt."

It was not lost on the men that Grant, snide as ever, didn't thank them directly. They left without a word, and though they closed the surgery door behind them, it swung open and began banging in the wind of the thunderstorm outside.

CHAPTER 32

"Damn it, Adam, this ain't over," Black John Hannah said. "The killing ain't over. Somehow, somewhere, I'll make a slaughter of those pilgrims."

"There's only two of us, John," Adam Curtis said. "Con, Leo, Hank, and Bill are lying cold and dead in Milk's back parlor and they ain't coming back. Tommy and Elliot aren't coming back for a long time, either, even if the doc gets the lead out of them."

"You turning yellow on me, Adam?"

"Nope. I can't say as I am, but a team of wild horses couldn't make me brace that wagon circle a second time."

"We need a plan or a darned infernal machine," Black John said. "And that's not a plea to God . . . it's a cry for help to the devil himself."

"John, you tread in dangerous waters," Curtis said. He produced his rosary and wound its iron beads around his fist. "Satan is a trickster. He'll play you for his own amusement."

"And do I care?" Hannah's voice was loud in the small, shadowy hotel room. "I want to win, not lose like we did. My boys were shot down like mad dogs. If the powers of Purgatory can make me a winner, then so be it."

"Satan won't make you a winner. He'll use you for his own evil purposes and then destroy you in the end."

Hannah smiled. "I'll take my chances."

A rising wind sighed around the eaves of the Red Dust Inn and somewhere a door banged and banged again.

"Boss, I don't like this," Curtis said. He held the iron beads in his fingers. "There's a danger you may summon powers you can't control."

"Spoken like a true preacher. Adam, we're headed for hell anyway, so why not take advantage of it?"

"But we must strive for heaven, John. Why does that door keep banging?"

Hannah reached out and grabbed both of Curtis's hands and squeezed with his powerful fingers. The iron beads dug into the other man's flesh and grated on bone. Curtis twisted his face in pain, his mouth hanging open, his breath coming in short, eloquent gasps.

"Adam, are you with me or agin' me?" Black John asked, his face taking on a look of demonic glee. "Are you willing to use the powers of darkness to get what we want?"

Curtis gasped. "That door . . . banging . . . banging . . ."

Black John squeezed harder, stronger, and it seemed that Curtis's hands crunched under the onslaught.

"For me or agin' me?" Hannah said over and over like a chant.

"I'm for you, John," Curtis said. Then, his eyes wild, "Listen. Now every door in the building is banging open and shut." He rose to his feet and yelled, "Somebody shut those blasted doors."

SLAM! SLAM! SLAM!

The doors, wherever they were, finally closed with deafening finality, like portals to Hades.

"Did I booger you, Adam?" Black John said, smiling,

sitting back in his chair. "I was only funnin' about all that devil stuff."

Curtis flexed his stiff, pained gun hand, and his rosary fell to the floor. "John there are some things you don't jest about, things outside of our knowledge that are better left alone."

"You mean the devil?"

"I mean don't dabble in matters you know nothing about."

"And you do?"

"Yes, I do. I once saw Satan's work at first hand."

"When you were a papist priest?"

"When I was studying to be a priest."

"Then tell me about it. Here, have a whiskey." Black John poured the drink that Curtis picked up with his left hand. "Now go ahead, Adam, scare old scratch right out of me."

"You sure you want to hear this?"

"I got nothing else to do."

"All right, then I'll tell it as I remember. It was a while ago."

"Let's hear it."

"The seminary of St. Joseph was a small one in Philadelphia, ivy covered gray sandstone walls and arched windows, and not very important," Curtis said. "I was seventeen when I was accepted as a seminarian, and from then on my life was centered on prayer and study."

"Sounds exciting," Hannah said.

"It was a quiet life and nothing ever disturbed its tranquility, but that all changed on my nineteenth birthday."

"So, what happened, birthday boy?" Black John said. "Did they bake you a cake?"

"No, but it was a day I'll never forget. On that day an old priest, he must have been well over eighty, arrived at

St. Joseph's at midnight in a closed carriage with a couple of Jesuits. I was told the priest's name was Father Thomas O'Rourke and that he was dying of cancer. The Jesuits wanted him to spend his remaining time in peace and serenity. I was one of two seminarians appointed to take care of him. What I didn't know then, and what I wasn't told, was that Father O'Rourke was possessed by a demon, an evil entity named Legion that had made him stark, raving mad."

Black John grinned. "Like me?"

"John, God will not be mocked."

"A slight smile played on Hannah's lips. "Sorry, go on with your story. I'm listening."

"Most of the time Father O'Rourke sat in a chair by a window and seldom spoke. But when he did, he rolled around on his cot and screamed the most profane gibberish you ever heard. I tolerated that because the man was clearly mad, only his eyes disturbed me, depending on the time of day they changed color from brown to green and back again. When they were green it was a sign Legion was visiting and the Jesuits warned me that on those occasions, I was to tie the old man to his bed so that he couldn't harm himself. And he stank, a smell I can't describe, rotting flesh is the closest I can come to it, but much, much worse. Every time it happened that smell made me sick to my stomach and Father O'Rourke would laugh and raise his head, trying to breathe on me. His breath was hideous, repulsive, indescribable."

"I would've put a bullet into the sidewinder," Black John said.

Curtis ignored that and said, "Then came Christmas Eve 1876, and I sat by him because he was clearly dying. He'd refused the Last Rights and Legion roared and threatened to tear apart the young priest trying to administer them. The priest took fright and left in a hurry, and I was left with a dying madman on my hands."

"Unlucky you, huh, pardner?" Black John said.

"It got worse."

"I figured it would."

"Legion didn't want Father O'Rourke to die. He, it, whatever, kept lifting him from the bed, shaking him, growling like a wild animal. I threw myself on top of the priest and held him on his cot. And then, thank God, Father O'Rourke let out a great sigh and died. I saw his face then. Before he died it was a mask of hate, lust, envy, greed, and anger, but in an instant it changed into that of the kindly old priest he had once been. Then every door in the seminary opened and shut, sounding like cannon fire on that quiet Christmas Eve. Bang! Bang! Bang! Legion announcing his departure. I heard priests and seminarians alike cry out in fear followed by voices raised in words of prayer."

Black John Hannah downed a whiskey, gulped, and said, "It was the wind."

"No, it was Legion."

"I mean the doors banging here in the Red Dust Inn. It was only the wind. Listen, it's picking up out there."

Adam Curtis smiled. "Maybe. Or maybe Legion paid us a visit."

"Heck, back there at the seminary you were lucky you escaped with your life."

"But I didn't escape unscathed. Legion left his carte de visite," Curtis said.

He unbuttoned his shirt, yanked it open, and revealed five deep scarred furrows that ran from the bottom of his throat to his waist. "Darn, man, those are claw marks," Black John said. "It's like you had a run-in with a cougar."

Curtis pulled his shirt closed. "Not a cougar, John, something infinitely more terrible . . . a demon."

Hannah shook his head, his face ashen. "Adam, all that I said about the devil and stuff don't go. Tell God I didn't mean a word of it."

"Tell him in your prayers tonight," Curtis said.

"Adam, I have to say this, you're a real strange feller," Black John said. "Why didn't you become a priest?"

"I don't really know." Curtis's fingers strayed to his dreadful scars. "Maybe these. But one day, I just packed my bag and left St. Joseph's forever. Then came the day I bought a revolver, discovered I was pretty good with it, and decided to take the long-rider's trail."

"Then you met me."

"Then I met you and decided to be your personal chaplain."

"You sure put the fear of God into me tonight."

"Fear God, and your enemies will fear you, John."

"All right, we'll talk again in the morning and come up with a plan for relieving them pilgrims of their treasure."

"I'll study on it," Curtis said.

There were seven guests in the Red Dust Inn that night, and in the morning five of them complained to the management that constantly banging doors kept them awake all night. Neither Black John Hannah nor Adam Curtis were among the complainers.

CHAPTER 33

Breakfast was late at the Running-S thanks to Maria scorching the scrambled eggs and burning the biscuits the first time around.

Sean and Johnny didn't complain. The woman's state of mind was understandable, and anyway, her second attempt at breakfast was tolerable.

"I'm so sorry about the biscuits," Maria said as she lifted well-scraped plates from the table. "I don't know what I was thinking."

"Matters of the heart," Johnny said, smiling. "That's what you were thinking."

"Perhaps it was," Maria said.

Sean said, "Don't listen to Johnny's teasing, Maria. Everything will be just fine. Dick Peterson is a good man, and I'm sure in the end you'll both find true love and be very happy." He directed a pointed look at Johnny who suddenly became very interested in lighting his cheroot.

A tap-tap on the door, and Sean called out, "Come in, Joe."

Joe Dean, hat in hand, stepped into the cabin and said, "We're all, ready, boss."

"Did we find those extra fence posts?" Sean asked his foreman.

"Yes, sir, they were at the back of the barn under a tarp."

Sean rose to his feet, put on his hat, and buckled into his gun belt. "My horse saddled?"

"Yes, sir."

"Good then, I'll be leaving. Johnny let Maria look at the supplies list and see if there's anything else she needs." He stepped out the door. "See you both this evening. "

It was gone noon when Johnny O'Neil drove the buckboard down Mustang Flat's dusty main drag. There was no one on the street, no one venturing outdoors when the sun was at its highest in the faded blue sky. As Johnny reined in his two Morgans a dust devil spun past his rig and then collapsed to a puff that fell silently onto the street. A door banged open and shut somewhere in the Red Dust Inn and banged again.

Johnny applied the brake, climbed down from his seat, and then stepped onto the shady porch that ran the full length of Luke Lawson's mercantile. His front was decorated with tin signs advertising tobacco, shoes, cigars, soda pop, and a dozen other items, and the windows were crammed with notions and cheap jewelry, high-heeled ankle boots, ribboned straw boaters that were then in fashion and other dainties to entice passing womenfolk.

When Johnny stepped inside the double door he paused for a few moments, enjoying the mercantile's distinctive aroma, a mix of ripe cheese, pickles, kerosene, feed, hanging haunches of bacon in white sacks, leather, and the ever-present tang of cigar and pipe smoke.

"Good afternoon to you, Mr. O'Neil," Luke Lawson

said, beaming from behind a counter almost completely covered by merchandise, stacks of denim pants, candy jars, tobacco displays, all of them crowded out by a huge cash register, a coffee mill, and brown wrapping paper on a cast iron roller with a ball of string attached. "It's been a while."

"Howdy, Mr. Lawson," Johnny said. He held up a sheet of paper. "I guess you can tell it's been a spell by the length of this list."

"Ah, let me fill that right away," Lawson said. "In the meantime, browse around if you want, I've got lots of items on sale just for today."

"Don't mind if I do," Johnny said.

The mercantile was laid out exactly like hundreds of others scattered across the frontier, long counters, rounded glass display cases, side walls lined with shelves, drawers, and bins while other items like buggy whips, horse harnesses, lantern, pails, and coiled ropes hung from the ceilings. Shelves carried meat and peaches in cans, dried beans, household items, soap, patent medicines, spices, crockery and dishes and boxes of rifle, shotgun, and pistol ammunition in solemn boxes. A pot-bellied stove bookended by two chairs and an upturned barrel with a checkerboard on top always completed the furnishings.

When Johnny's list was filled and Lawson's two half-grown sons had begun carrying the supplies to the buckboard, the mercantile owner said, "See anything you like, Mr. O'Neil?"

"Yes, this," Johnny said. He laid a woman's hair comb on the counter.

"Ah, for the lady in your life?" Lawson asked.

Johnny smiled. "Yes, but keep it quiet for a spell, Luke."

"You made an excellent choice, Mr. O'Neil, as I would

expect from a man of your stature. What you have here is a bridal hair comb all the way from Paris, France. The pearls are the genuine article as is the opal centerpiece, and the comb itself is made of silver. Mr. O'Neil, one look at this comb and any bride's heart will beat faster."

"How much?" Johnny said, fearing the answer.

"For today and today only, just five dollars, and it comes in its own box."

Johnny was stunned. "Five dollars. That's almost a week's wages for some of our punchers back at the Running-S."

Lawson slowly shook his head. "Mr. O'Neil, this exquisite piece is a gentleman's gift to a lady. It's not a gewgaw a cowboy gives to his prairie flower."

Johnny pondered for all of ten seconds and then said, "All right, I'll take it. Box it up."

"Will I add it to your bill?"

"No, I'll pay for the comb myself." Johnny reached into a pocket and put a five-dollar half eagle on the counter.

Lawson beamed. "My congratulations to the lucky lady."

"I'll tell her that."

"Please do. And here's the bill for the supplies. Tell Sean he can pay me the next time he's in town."

"Next week probably. He told me he needs fence posts and barbed wire."

But Sean O'Neil was destined to be in Mustang Flat much sooner than that . . . after his brother killed a man.

CHAPTER 34

The buckboard creaked and swayed as Johnny O'Neil, a big man, climbed into the driver's seat. He gathered up the reins and then stopped, his unbelieving gaze trying to comprehend what was happening in the street just twenty yards in front of him.

A man, tall, heavy, black haired, with pouched, porcine eyes and a beard down to his navel, wielded a thick leather belt, whaling on a short, plump girl, very young, who shrieked every time a cracking blow landed on her already bruised back, shoulders, and face.

Sight . . . then sound.

"You darned treacherous whore, I'll beat the devil out of you," the man roared.

The girl pleaded, "No, husband! Don't hit me again!"

It was a plea that went unheeded. The girl had now fallen to her knees. The belt, wielded with tremendous strength, the blows driven by a white-hot anger, thudded on to the girl's head and shoulders, and now the boot went in, savage kicks to his victim's legs and body.

"We could all die in flames because of you," the man yelled, still hammering at his much younger wife, now in his blinding rage, with closed fists. "You are Satan's spawn. I'll cripple you so bad you'll never run away again."

The girl's shrieks had choked away to whimpers. She wrapped her arms around her husband's booted legs and whispered, "Mercy . . . mercy . . ."

But her assailant had no mercy. He kicked her away, and his flailing fists continued her terrible beating. The girl's face was now a scarlet mask of blood.

"Stop, you'll kill her!" Luke Lawson yelled. And then to Johnny who was about to climb off the buckboard. "No, Mr. O'Neil!" He turned to one of his wide-eyed sons, "Dan, go get Sheriff Beason."

The boy nodded and ran.

But Johnny had no confidence in Beason. The girl could be beaten to death before he got there. And now he watched her throw back her head and take a glimpse at the flawless blue sky. A final glimpse. Like a person about to be executed.

Johnny clambered out of the wagon and stepped into the street.

"You!" he yelled. "Let that girl be."

The bearded man, holding the girl by a handful of hair, said, "Go away, this is none of your concern."

"I'm making it my concern," Johnny said.

The girl turned her face to him and he thought he saw a gleam of hope in her eyes.

"She's my wife, and that means I can do anything to her I please," the bearded man said.

"Not when I'm around," Johnny said. "A man beating a woman, wife or not, is something I won't tolerate."

"Mister, get away from here while you can still walk."

Johnny thought the man's piggish eyes with their pouches and chin that disappeared into his beard made his face look weak. But shaggy black eyebrows and an unruly shock of black hair, graying at the temples, added strength, like Samson before he met Delilah. His shoulders were an ax handle wide and dangling from long, muscular arms, his hands, curved to make a fist, looked like iron meat hooks.

"Help me, mister," the girl whispered, words that earned her a vicious back slap across the face that stunned her into silence.

This man would be a handful, Johnny decided, but to save the girl's life he had to act, especially since there was no Bob Beason in sight to ride to the rescue. He walked toward the bearded man, painfully conscious of his dragging right leg that had robbed him of his once superb footwork. The man just stood there, a sneer on his face as Johnny came closer. Then WHAM! a tremendous straight right to the bearded man's chin dropped him like a puppet whose strings had just been cut.

The man lay there for several seconds and then, like Lazarus rising from the dead, sprang to his feet, his dukes up and ready.

Johnny was appalled.

He'd given this man his best shot, and he'd come back for more, fast on his feet, hammering at Johnny with lefts and rights that stung. And then came a beautiful right jab from the bearded man that rocked him to his foundations and to his surprise Johnny saw the dusty street rush up to meet him. The bearded man then came in with the boot, a kick to Johnny's ribs that hurt like the devil and winded him. He rolled, got to his feet, and his opponent's wicked right uppercut flattened him again. His back in the dirt, an alarm sounded in Johnny O'Neil's head. The bearded man had either picked up the rudiments of boxing somewhere or he was a natural pugilist. And he was big, very big, with a granite jaw. It dawned on Johnny then that he could lose this fight. Slowed by his stiff leg, he got to his feet, absorbed a flurry of punches that rang his head like a bell, and then he slowed the bearded man with a right hook to the body that winded him, forcing him to disengage and backpedal. Johnny followed, crowding the man, landing more punches to the belly and ribs that took their toll. The bearded man was tiring, Johnny could see and sense it. And the man began to drop his guard every time he tried to land a punch. Johnny took another left jab to the chin that slowed him for a few moments, and then the bearded man dropped his guard again as he telegraphed a left hook. This was the moment of truth for Johnny. He had to end this fight without taking more punishment. He blocked the left, countered with a right cross that stopped the bearded man in his tracks. This was the moment of truth. Johnny's straight right had failed him before, but now he threw it again with all the punching power he could muster. POW! His fist landed on the bearded man's chin with tremendous impact, staggered him, and then the man stopped, dropping his arms as little tweeting birds flew around his head. He stared at Johnny with the incredulous look of a man who'd never lost a fight before, and then his swollen eyes shut, and he fell in a heap to the ground and didn't move.

"He's done. It's over."

Sheriff Bob Beason stepped in front of Johnny and pushed him back. "Let him be, champ. He's had enough."

"And so have I," Johnny said. "Luke, how is he?"

Luke Lawson had tried to revive the fallen man but now he rose to his feet and said, "Someone get Doc Grant. I think this man may be dead."

A scream, and the girl threw herself on her husband's

sprawled form. "Husband, talk to me. Say something," she shrieked.

"He's only been knocked out," Beason said to the girl. "He'll be on his feet in a little while."

But the girl made no reply, hugging her husband's body, her body racked by great, shuddering sobs.

When Dr. Grant arrived, he gently moved the girl aside and examined the bearded man. After a while his troubled young face looked up at Beason, and he said, "He's dead, sheriff."

"How come?" Beason said.

"He's been beaten to death," Dr. Grant said.

To Johnny, none of the blows the bearded man landed hurt as badly as that simple statement. *He's been beaten to death.* He felt sick to his stomach. He'd killed a man, a complete stranger that up until today he'd harbored no animosity toward. It was a senseless killing, carried out by himself, a man in the wrong place at the wrong time.

Dr. Grant spoke to the girl. "Young lady, I want you to come to my surgery where I can treat your cuts and bruises that are numerous and severe, I might add. What's your name?"

"Liza . . ." the girl sniffled. "Liza Hart." She looked at the dead man. "He's my husband."

Grant said, "Mr. O'Neil, did you have a hand in this female's injuries?"

Johnny was too stunned to be angry. "Of course not. The girl's husband went at her with the leather strap you see on the street there. I took it from him and that's when the fight began."

"A fight to the death it seems."

"That may have been his intention. It wasn't mine."

"Dr. Grant, that's enough questions from you," Beason

said. "I'm in charge here." He turned to Johnny. "Mr. O'Neil, it's with a heavy heart that I arrest you for the murder of . . . of . . . what's his name."

"My husband's name is . . . was . . . Medard after St. Medard of Picardy. His former name was Tom, but Micah gave him that name because Saint Medard, who often comes to visit the prophet, saw Tom reading the Holy Bible and remarked on his piety."

"You're from the wagons, young lady?" Beason said, scowling. "Speak up now, I want the truth."

"Yes, I'm from the wagons, and I stole a horse and ran away. Tom . . . Medard . . . followed me."

"And he beat you?"

"Yes."

"With a leather strap."

"Yes."

"Did you think he might kill you?"

"He wanted to take me back to face the prophet's justice."

"Would the prophet—God I feel like an ass calling the old coot that—have killed you?"

"I don't know. Maybe."

"Hmm . . . very interesting, very interesting indeed," Beason said.

Luke Lawson, who had no liking for the sheriff said, "And here's something else that's interesting. The dead man struck the first blow and started the fight. I was on my porch and saw it with my own eyes."

"I'm confused, was he dead or alive when he struck the first blow?"

"Beason, you darned fool, of course he was alive," Lawson said.

"All this will be noted down in evidence," Beason said.

"Darn it, Beason, there's no crime here," Lawson said. "It's a clear-cut case of self-defense. Mr. O'Neil was attacked and fought back."

"Once I interview witnesses and consider the evidence, I'll be the judge of that," the sheriff said.

"I'm the only witness," Lawson said. "There's was no one on the street except me, the dead man, his wife, and Mr. O'Neil."

"I see two unsaddled horses," Beason said.

"Horses can't talk," Lawson said.

"But it suggests Mrs. Hart and her husband left the wagon circle in a hurry," the sheriff said.

"Of course, it does, you numbskull. She made a run for it, and he followed," Lawson said, growing angrier.

"Be careful what you say, Mr. Lawson," Beason warned, frowning. "Verbal abuse of a peace officer is a serious offense."

Lawson gave up. He said to Johnny, "My eldest can handle a team and I'll have him deliver your supplies to the Running-S. He'll tell Sean what happened here."

"I'm obliged," Johnny said.

"Beason said, "And I'm taking you into custody, Mr. O'Neil, while I solve this mystery."

Lawson badly wanted to say, "There is no mystery, you fool!" But he kept his mouth shut. More talk would get him nowhere. To Johnny he said, "You know you have a friend in me."

"I know," Johnny said. He shook hands with Lawson and said, "And I appreciate it."

"That's your cell, but I'll leave the door open, Mr. O'Neil," Sheriff Bob Beason said. "I will not put a man of your boxing fame behind bars."

"That's true blue of you," Johnny said.

"Now, I'll pour us both a whiskey and get the checkerboard out. While we play, you can tell me about your fight with . . . whatshisname . . ."

He handed Johnny a whiskey and laid out the checkerboard. "Now tell me again, how did it come up?"

CHAPTER 35

"Why did Lon draw down on the rancher?" Micah said.

"The man's name is O'Neil, and he was pushing it," Ben Gallagher said. "He came up with one of them Texas fast draws and put two bullets into my brother before he'd even cleared his pistol."

"Darn it, now there's only two of us to move the gold out of here. Where's that drunken brute Tom, what did I name him? Medard?"

"He ran off after his little wife, haven't seen him since. We can manage, prophet."

"For God's sake call me Charlie when we're alone. My name is Charlie Wade, not that idiotic Prophet Micah handle I gave the rubes."

"I know," Gallagher said. "I recollect it was plain Charlie Wade back in Kansas when you first hired me and Lon."

"Cost me five hundred dollars to bribe that hick town marshal to let the pair of you go. If I'd known Lon was going to get himself gunned, I could've saved myself two hundred and fifty dollars."

"Charlie, that marshal had nothing on us."

"You and your brother were caught red-handed stealing a two-hundred-dollar stud horse, for pity's sake. That rancher feller, what was his name? Yeah, Kirkland, that was it. He was aiming to lynch the pair of you."

"We found the horse wandering in the street and claimed him," Ben said.

"Some townsfolk had a differing opinion on that. Well, it's all water under the bridge. We've got more important things to talk about," Charlie Wade said. "And first and foremost is we make the heist tomorrow night just after sundown."

Ben Gallagher smiled. "Just before it starts raining fire, huh, Charlie?"

The two men stood outside the wagon circle under a blue afternoon sky, the vast prairie rolling away in all directions to the far horizons where the heat hazes danced.

"Call me Prophet Micah when we're within the wagon circle. I don't want any last-minute slip-ups. I already told them about Lon, how the barbarians cut him down, an affront to God himself."

"What about the two who left earlier?" Ben said. "Is that going to cause problems?"

"No, that's simple. We say Tom Hart's wife decided she didn't want to be saved and he went after her," Micah said. "He'll bring her back here for my justice, and I'll see that she's never able to steal a horse again. She'll suffer the ultimate penalty for her whoredom and treachery."

"I look forward to watching that," Ben said.

"Yeah, I suppose you would. Let's get back into the wagon circle, and, Ben, talk to nobody, just stay to yourself. You've been sent by God to help these people, so remember that."

"I won't forget . . . Prophet . . . and my lips are sealed."

"We got tomorrow to make good," Charlie said. "The day after that we'll be rich men."

Ben smiled. "Good whiskey and the fanciest whores . . . I can hardly wait."

"Just be patient for another day," Charlie said, "and you'll get what's coming to you."

It's unlikely that Ben Gallagher, a not very intelligent man, heard the implied threat in that statement.

CHAPTER 36

"And that's all I can tell you, Mr. O'Neil," young Tim Lawson, a twelve-year-old towhead, said.

"And where is Johnny now?" Sean said.

"In Sheriff Beason's lockup, all sad an' stuff."

"Darn that man," Sean said. Bitter words. "Tim, I'll change the team and we'll use the buckboard to get us to town."

"Mr. O'Neil are you worried about what the sheriff might do to the champ?" Tim said, concern on his freckled face. Fighting Johnny O'Neil, the bare-knuckle brawler, was a hero to the kids of Mustang Flat.

"No, I'm more worried about what the champ might do to the sheriff," Sean said.

"Sean, why don't you take a couple of the hands with you?" Maria said.

"No, I don't want a show of force. If I scare the snot out of Beason, God knows what he'll do. The man's a chucklehead."

"Sean, I'm worried," Maria said.

"That makes two of us," Sean said. "Hopefully I'll be back with Johnny by sundown."

"I'll say a novena for you," Maria said.

Sean managed a smile. "Might help, can't hurt." He put on his hat, checked the loads in his Colt, then buckled on his gun belt. "Maria, I'm leaving you with a lot of supplies to put away."

"I can manage," the woman said.

"You always can, and I don't know how you do it." Then, "Right, Tim, let's get the fresh team harnessed. We're burning daylight."

"O'Neil, as you can see, I've given your brother all the comforts a man of his reputation and standing deserves," Sheriff Bob Beason said.

"A prison cell doesn't comfort a man," Sean said.

"A cell with the door open and that's how it will remain."

"Beason, I just spoke with Luke Lawson, and he says it's a clear-cut case of self-defense. The man . . ."

"Tom Hart."

"Threw the first punch."

"But there are complications," the sheriff said. "First of all, he was from the wagon circle on your range."

"What's that to do with it?" Sean said.

"I don't want to get those folks all riled up. They may take it into their heads to mount a revenge attack on Mustang Flat, and then where would we be?"

"Those people think they'll all be in heaven in another day or so. I doubt that they'll raid Mustang Flat," Sean said.

"And then there's the other matter," Beason said.

"What other matter?"

Beason stared into space for long moments, then said, "The matter of it not being a gunfight."

Johnny looked puzzled, and Sean said, "Beason, what the heck are you talking about?"

"Listen up, O'Neil, you too, champ." He talked directly to Johnny. "If you'd gunned Tom Hart and Luke Lawson said he drew down on you first I'd be the first to say self-defense. But a fistfight . . . I mean Lawson says Hart threw the first punch, but what kind of punch? A good-natured tap to the chest, a first blow that missed, or even a wallop that hit the champ's chin but did no harm?" Beason held up a silencing hand. "No, O'Neil, let me finish. You can see that none of those examples justify killing a man with one blow. That's why the matter calls for a thorough investigation."

"Darn it, Beason, he put me on my back twice. He had a punch like an anvil," Johnny said. "He hit me so hard I didn't feel the pain until now."

"Hmm . . . very interesting," Beason said, looking wise. "And certainly, I'll take all that into consideration in the course of my deliberations."

Sean's voice was measured, quiet. "Beason, if you and some idiot circuit judge railroad Johnny into a murder charge, I'll shoot him and you. That's not a promise or a threat, it's a natural fact."

"O'Neil, sassing a lawman does nothing for your brother's case," Beason said.

"There is no case, you darned fool. The rube hit Johnny and Johnny hit him back. That's it. There's nothing else. Case closed."

"You say," Beason said.

Sean shook his head. "Why am I wasting my time talking to you, Beason? All you're doing is giving me a headache."

"My job is to enforce the law, O'Neil," the sheriff said. "It is not to enforce justice."

"And you're doing a poor job of both," Sean said. He sighed. "I'll take Johnny home. You know where to find him."

Beason shook his head. "If Mr. O'Neil's case is decided in his favor, you can take him home. For now, he must remain in my jail. I'm sorry, but that's the law."

"Johnny, I'm talking to a brick wall," Sean said. "What do you think?"

"Let Beason do his duty as he sees it," Johnny said. "I'll stay here until he makes up his mind."

"And the champ will have every comfort befitting his status," Beason said. "His cell door will never be locked, he can play checkers, and I'll see that his meals are brought here from the Red Dust Inn, all at the town's expense, mind you." He sat back in his chair. "There, can I say any fairer than that?"

Sean didn't have to answer the question because Dr. Grant stepped into the office, Liza Hart in tow. "Sheriff, this young lady has something to tell you." He looked at Johnny. "Mr. O'Neil, this girl was beaten to within an inch of her life, and she's pregnant. I'm glad you stepped in when you did."

"An opinion that is duly noted, doctor," Beason said. "My God, but that child is badly bruised. What's her name again?"

"Liza Hart. And I think she'd be dead if it wasn't for Mr. O'Neil. Her brute of a husband could've killed her and the unborn baby."

"Another opinion that I've filed away. I have a mind like a steel trap." He beckoned to the girl. "Come closer, child. I know you face the full majesty of the law, but I won't harm you." He reached into his drawer and brought out a small, paper bag. "Here, have a pear drop. A child will never be afraid sucking on a pear drop." Beason waited until Liza popped the candy in her mouth and then said, "You have information to impart. Is it about Mr. O'Neil?"

"No," the girl said. "It's about the prophet Micah."

"Darn that man," Beason said. "It seems that name is all I hear. Who the heck calls himself prophet Micah, and what does it mean?"

Dr. Grant said, "Sheriff, Micah is a name of a prophet in the Bible, Old Testament, it means 'Who is like God?' I'm guessing it is the fellow's idea of a funny joke."

"He sure tricked those rubes in the wagon circle into believing that he's a prophet," Beason said.

"Well, I suppose it doesn't take much to encourage the already pious to believe. Many prophets have succeeded before him," Dr. Grant said. "It seems your man is following in their footsteps."

"That scoundrel," Beason said. "Now Liza, what can you tell me about this so called prophet?"

"It concerns the man who called himself Jess Hayes," the girl said.

She hesitated and Beason said, "Go on, girl. Tell us what you heard or saw. The law is listening."

"Well, remember when you visited the wagons and I told you about how Hayes tried to attack me and then an angel came down from Heaven and killed him?" The girl's upper lip was damp, and her voice was slow and hesitant, as though she considered her every word before she spoke.

Dawning recognition sparked in Beason's eyes. "That was you girl? Tell me true now. I knew that was a big windy. What really happened?" demanded Beason.

"I was standing outside my wagon, saying my prayers. Can I sit? I don't feel well."

"Here, little lady, sit here," Sean said, rising from one of the two chairs in front of Beason's desk.

"But then you'll have to stand," the girl said.

Sean smiled as he ushered her into the chair. "I'm used to standing around."

"Especially when other folks are working," Johnny said.

Everyone smiled at that, including Sean and the normally grave Dr. Grant.

Beason said, "Now tell me, girl, then what happened?"

"Jess Hayes and the prophet spoke for a few moments . . ."

"Speak up. I can hardly hear you."

Louder, Liza said, "The two spoke and suddenly Micah had a knife in his hand, and he stabbed Hayes twice. He didn't know I saw him."

"And did the prophet kill him?" Beason asked.

"Of course, he killed him," Sean said. "Beason, you dug up Hayes' body, remember."

"O'Neil, please don't interrupt the legal discourse of the law," Beason said. "Now, young lady, what happened next? Be concise, be alert, just tell me what I need to know."

"Later on Micah told me to lie, to tell the others that an avenging angel came down from heaven and killed Hayes with a mighty sword. He told me to say that Hayes was raping me when the angel struck."

"That's what you told me when I approached the wagons," Beason said. "You said an angel saved your honor."

"Yes, I did. It was all lies, and I didn't want to do it. But Micah had my husband beat the lies into me, all of them."

"Lying to the law is a very serious and punishable offense," Beason said.

"I think Liza has suffered enough, Sheriff," Dr. Grant said. "Don't you?"

"Perhaps, doctor. Bob Beason is always willing to temper justice with mercy."

"There is one thing more, sheriff," the girl said. "The prophet told us that since evil had entered the wagon circle, God had spoken to him in a great vision. The Lord told him the money chest, our sacred offering, must be moved to a safe place and only returned when the first fires began to rain from the sky."

"In other words, he plans to skedaddle with the treasure," Sean said.

"Seems like," Johnny agreed. "What do you think, Beason?"

"It all adds up. Yes, now I study on it, Micah, heck, I hate that name, is a fox in the chicken coop."

"So, what are you going to do about it?" Sean said.

"What can I do about it? I can't arrest him. Every time I've tried, I've walked into a wall of lead. Those rubes worship him, and they can shoot."

"After he grabs the treasure, which way will he go?" Sean said. "My guess is that he'll head for the Rio Bravo and cross into Old Mexico."

"Yeah, it's only a hop, skip, and jump to Chihuahua," Beason said. "I'd never find him there."

Dr. Grant said, "I want Liza to sleep in my surgery tonight where I can keep an eye on her. She took a vicious beating and is very weak. Is that all right with you, sheriff?"

Beason waved a hand. "Sure, doc, that's fine." Then a thought dawned on him. "Here, what do I do with her when she's well again?"

Grant shook his head. "That's your department, sheriff, not mine."

Beason sighed and said, "Mr. O'Neil you can go home with your brother. It seems it might get crowded around here." When Johnny rose to his feet, he said, "Keep in touch, mind. This thing ain't over until it's over."

CHAPTER 37

Sean O'Neil's buckboard still stood outside the sheriff's office when Black John Hannah ran out of cigars and crossed the street to the mercantile to buy a box of Cubans.

"Big commotion on the street earlier, woke me from my siesta," he said to Luke Lawson. "What was going on?"

"Fist fight. Johnny O'Neil got into it with another man, a pugilist by the look of him, and it was shaping up to be a real Pecos Promenade until Johnny hit the man too hard and killed him."

"I've heard that name," Black John said. "O'Neil is a former prizefighter, and now he and his brother have a cattle spread west of here."

"You heard the right of it. They run Herefords and seem to be prospering. I've got a new shipment of Cubans in the back, browse around while I get them."

"Yeah, I'll do that," Black John said.

When Lawson left to get the cigars, he cast a disinterested eye over the place. One mercantile was much like any other. Except . . . Glittering red light caught his eyes, twinkling in the beams of sun that shone on the display case like spun gold. A signet ring sat propped up inside a blue velvet box, the ruby colored gem gleaming brightly from its perch between the tooled silver crosses that made up the band. Black John was enthralled, though normally a man not keen on baubles and dandies. The ring emanated evil. He wanted it.

Luke Lawson appeared from the back door with two boxes of cigars in his hand, "Here we go, Mr. Hannah, nice and fresh for you." Black John was still fascinated by the ring and merely murmured an acknowledgment. Intrigued, Lawson set down the cigars and walked over to the jewelry display.

"See something you like?" he asked cheerfully, hoping for another sale. Black John looked up and saw that the shimmering red light was concentrated on Lawsons' temple and casting rivulets down his cheek, creating the appearance of a bloody gunshot wound.

"Yes, this ring. I'm not much of a jewelry man, but it is . . . interesting, isn't it?"

"Oh!" Lawson exclaimed, always excited to be given an excuse to tell a tale. "It was brought in just last night, real late, around midnight. I was closing shop when the strangest fella came in, maybe you know him since he seemed like a guy who'd . . . well, know you." Lawson nervously cleared his throat.

"He was wearing a cloak over his hat, and it's the darnedest thing, but I don't remember what his face looked like. Real tall, all in black. Anyhow, he came in and asked if I could send a wire for him, so I did. Then he wanted to know if I'd let him trade in that there ring for a box of Cubans and a pint of rum. Seemed like a deal to me, sure enough."

Black John jumped as the door to the mercantile banged hard in the wind. Lawson almost laughed at him but quickly thought better of it. "Don't know where that wind came from, was like this last night, too," he said.

"You know where the man went, the man in black I mean?" Hannah asked.

Lawson shook his head, "No idea."

"Well, do you remember what the telegram was about?"

"Oh, sure, it was simple, I wrote it down. Hang on," Lawson ducked away beneath the counter and then produced a piece of paper:

COME STOP MUSTANG FLAT STOP
GOLD FOR YOU STOP FAVOR PAID STOP

"That was all of it. Sent to a fella named Dallas Hamer. His name ring a bell . . . ?" Lawson dwindled off when he saw Black John's face. The man looked like he'd seen a ghost. The two men stared at each other for a long moment, then, "Luke, you sure? The name was Dallas Hamer?"

"Of course, I'm sure. Why, who's he?"

"No one we want to show up here, that's for darned sure," John said.

"Should I tell . . ."

"No! Don't tell anyone. Let me handle it if he shows up. Now, about this ring, let me try it on."

CHAPTER 38

While Black John cut a deal to purchase the ruby ring, Johnny O'Neil was settling in at home, relieved to be sprung from Beason's jail.

"I saw this among the supplies," Maria Perez said, handing Johnny O'Neil a thin, rectangular box. "I didn't open it. I thought it might be something you bought for yourself."

"No, it's something I bought for you," Johnny said. "Open it."

"Oh, it's beautiful," Maria said, staring into the opened box.

"It's a bridal comb, all the way from Paris, France," Johnny said. "I thought you might wear it on your wedding day."

"Oh, but Johnny, I have no wedding day," she said softly.

"Well," Johnny dropped onto one knee though his leg was stiff and pained. "Maria Perez, I have loved you since the moment I laid eyes on you. You deserve better than me so it's taken me some time to build up the courage . . . Maria, will you marry me, and allow me to raise Billy as my own son?"

Maria squealed her excitement and launched onto Johnny where he held her in a firm embrace. Tears were flowing from Maria, and Johnny felt like his heart would burst from fullness.

"Of course, I'll be your wife, you know that is all I have ever wanted. I thought you might never ask me."

"I'm a fool, Maria, I'm sorry if I made your heart hurt. Please forgive me?"

Maria stood on her tiptoes and cradled Johnny's face, showering him with kisses. "Of course I forgive you, you silly, stubborn man."

"Try it, Maria, the comb," Sean said. "Let's see how it looks."

"No, Sean, that could be unlucky," Maria said. "Johnny bought the comb for my bridal day—our wedding day— and that's when I'll wear it."

"Quite right, Maria," Johnny said.

"Brother, I didn't think you were such an expert on weddings," Sean said.

"I'm not, but I've been to a few back in Boston," Johnny said.

"And now you'll attend as the groom for a bride who will love you until eternity," Maria said.

"That I will, and I plan to dance with you the whole night through!"

"Johnny, you've got a bad leg," Sean said.

"So? If I stumble, I'll just make it part of the dance."

Sean laughed. "Johnny, you've got an answer for everything."

"And what Irishman hasn't?"

The sunset was spectacular that evening, spirals of gold and red on a cobalt blue backdrop. As they sat on the front porch, the faces of Sean and Johnny, weathered from wind and sun, caught the light, turning them into burnished men of bronze.

After a while Sean said, "If memory serves me right, day after tomorrow is when God will rain fire and brimstone on the earth and save the folks in the wagon circle."

"Judging by the sky, He's already warming up," Johnny said.

"You boogered?" Sean said, smiling.

"Nope. But what if they're right and we're wrong?"

"I reckon there's little chance of that."

"I'm serious. And you said, 'little chance,' but not, no chance."

Then I'll correct myself. There's no chance the world will be destroyed by fire tomorrow or the next day, whenever it was."

Johnny was quiet for a spell, then said, 'Sean do you think the stewpot will fit my head?"

"Like a helmet, you mean?"

"Yeah, a helmet, like them Romans used to wear."

"Well, first off, there isn't a stewpot in Texas big enough to go over your noggin, and secondly, the fire will come at you from all directions, so you'd need a suit of armor, and the Running-S doesn't have one of them. Anyway, the flames would just cook you inside the suit like one of Maria's roasts."

"You're not taking this seriously."

"Of course, I am. Saving you from the wrath of God isn't easy, you know."

"Well, by this time day after tomorrow we'll know for sure, won't we?"

"And, Johnny, if we're getting scorched by fire, you

can say, 'I told you so.' Say extra prayers tonight if you're worried."

"I will," Johnny O'Neil said. "Trust me, I will."

That night before bed, Johnny O'Neil kneeled in prayer for quite a long time before finally collapsing into his bed with a smile.

CHAPTER 39

At sunrise the next morning, while civilized folk were frying up eggs and drinking their morning coffee, a cold wind rushed into the town of Mustang Flat. It came on the heels of a tall, handsome, man, riding a black thoroughbred with all the imperial elegance of a great king. Beneath his black overcoat he wore the regalia of a gambler, highlighted by a silver signet ring set with a dazzling sapphire on his pinky. The ladies about their town business stopped to gossip about the tall rider's fierce good looks and resemblance to noble Custer, found in his long blond locks and impeccable dragoon mustache. The man tipped his hat at them as he passed, smiling warmly, and showing bright white teeth that enhanced the glint of his cornflower eyes. They rewarded him with giggles, and one daring young maid blew a kiss.

He made his way to old John Baxter's livery, dropping off his horse and paying for oats and hay, then set off for the Crystal Palace. Lucas Battles took one look at the refined gentleman and knew that he'd spell trouble. If Lucas had any idea how much trouble, or how many lives would be lost thanks to the arrival of this man, he would have sounded an alarm. For now, he just kept a wary eye on him and after providing the bottle of whiskey and glass the man ordered he made light conversation about the unseasonably warm weather. Battles' main concern was what would happen when Black John and his men wound their way to the saloon, and what kind of gunfight that may entail. He would soon realize that those were the least of his concerns.

CHAPTER 40

As the stranger settled in for an early drink at the Crystal Palace, people were stirring in the doomed wagon circle. Silas Booker sat on the buckboard of his covered wagon, coffee in hand. A light breeze sent his fine silver hair out in every which way, but at his age there was no desire for vanity left in him. He watched the frayed tatters of the cobalt night sky dissolve into a brilliant pink and red of a prairie sunrise and thought upon the glory of God who created such scenes. Silas missed his wife Goldie most in the dawn hour. They'd woken up before the sun together since he was just a young man claiming the territories of his providence with rows of corn and wheat. Calico Farm, they'd called it, and Silas hated the cutesy nature of the name, but it was Goldie's idea, and his heart broke at the thought of displeasing her, so Calico it was.

The old man took a sip of his coffee and wrapped his hands around the tin cup to transfer the soothing warmth to his arthritic fingers. As the sun continued to push its way up into the sky he reflected upon happier times. He'd give up anything to have his Goldie beside him, to brush away the stubborn curl that always fell across her forehead, to catch a touch of her fragrance on the air and enchanted by it lean in for a kiss. But those times were long past. Goldie had borne him three children, only one of whom lived and now slept in the wagon behind him. There had been hope of a fourth child, but it was not to be. Then during a particularly harsh winter, Goldie fell ill, and the doctors said there was nothing for it but to make her comfortable. Oh, Silas had raged against God then, he'd fallen to his knees in the snow, in the howling wind, the very storm that seemed to gather strength with each of Goldie's labored breaths. He'd blasphemed, God forgive him, and as he unleashed his fury at the sky, he was Job and Jonah and David, and yet God carried on his merry way and took Silas's wife.

He set the coffee cup down and stood with a sharp exhale of breath, stretching out his sore spots best he could. The rheumatisms were certainly upon him today. A quiet rustle from within the wagon, and soon Rebecca, the only child the Lord saw fit to let him keep on earth, poked her head out and yawned.

"Mornin', Pa, is there coffee?" As she spoke a stubborn curl bounced down onto her forehead and she tried to brush it away.

Silas smiled. Goldie wasn't truly gone if he had Becca. "Of course, darlin', come get a cup."

CHAPTER 41

Standing outside his surgery sipping his own morning coffee, watching the comings and goings of Mustang Flat, Dr. Grant knew that within a few moments one of his two gunshot patients would be ready for Clem Milk. The undertaker had been skulking in and out to check a few times already. Elliot Flint at first seemed to be the better off of the pair, but infection had sunk in and none of Grant's remedies were making a difference. The doctor had considered amputation, but after the infection spread into Flint's pelvis all hope was lost. Now Grant just made him as comfortable as possible with copious amounts of morphine and whiskey, and he knew the man's heart would beat its last any minute now.

As for Tommy Holton, he was sitting upright and eating, still on morphine and content to read through the children's books Doc Grant kept on hand for young patients. It seemed that Mr. Holton was not very smart, but that was a blessing as far as Grant was concerned, because the young man was easy enough to keep calm. He'd even given the young gunfighter a bottle of sarsaparilla and packet of pear drops which had cheered him greatly.

Holton would make a full recovery, but never regain

normal use of his arm. There was nothing to be done about it, and Grant felt a twinge of pity as the lad had clearly fallen into a life of crime due to being too unintelligent for most honest jobs.

Finally a loud and slow groan emitted from Elliot Flint, and Doc Grant checked his pulse, then noted his time of death down as ten a.m.

"Mrs. Pierson, can you please fetch Mr. Milk at once. We've lost our patient. Better see if John Hannah is around, too. He may take the news better coming from a lady."

Mrs. Pierson clucked a sad noise. "Right away, Doctor."

Black John Hannah had indeed taken the news better than expected and arrived alongside Sheriff Bob Beason to meet with the undertaker Clem Milk. The three men stood in the surgery over the still form of Elliot Flint, who looked peaceful and almost boyish in death. Adam Curtis played cards in the background with Tommy Holton, who kept telling him about some legendary boots he was going to sell "for hunnerds of dollars" when he was well again. Curtis assumed it was a morphine dream and feigned polite interest.

"I'll pay for his burial, Milk," Hannah said, "Give him a stone too, make it nice enough, but, keep in mind you don't charge much since I'm paying for Stern and Ransom, too. I should get a package deal—seems I'm keeping you in business, you old ghoul."

"Of course, right away, Mr. Hannah," Milk said before setting about his business.

Black John made his way over to where Curtis and Holton sat and pulled up a chair. "Well, boys, it's just the three of us now."

Tommy Holton laid down his cards, "Sorry boss, but

I'm out of it." Holton kept his eyes downcast and spoke in a timid voice. "I am real sorry, I mean it, but my gun arm is never gone be right again, and the doc says it'll take six weeks afore I can even get out of this here cast. It sure do itch, too."

Black John nodded, "Well, I'm right sorry about it, Tommy, but we'll get your revenge soon enough."

Adam Curtis shifted in his seat, "Don't you think killing our men, the rubes, the woman, all of them . . . wasn't that enough revenge for a man?"

Black John stared hard at the pistolero padre, noticing the dark halfmoons under his eyes and worry lines creasing his handsome face. John chose his words carefully and they simmered with malice.

"Curtis? I'll ask one last time, you still for me or you agin me?"

Adam Curtis tightened his grip on the ever-present rosary. The garnet beads left impressions deep in the flesh of his palm. "I already told you I'm for you, John. Quit trying to make me change my mind," he said grimly.

Sheriff Bob Beason wobbled over to where the tattered remnants of Black John's fearsome gang now sat and loudly proclaimed, "Well, I have decided to be benevolent of heart, for the law is always fair and just. That means I won't charge you boys with a crime even though you disobeyed my orders. All that dying, John, you think it was worth it?"

Rage filled Hannah's face, and he dug his fingernails into his thighs but didn't say a word. Minutes ticked past, and finally Beason spoke again, "Next time we do it proper, orderly like and calm, you hear?"

"There ain't gonna be a next time, sheriff. Them pilgrims aren't worth dying for. Their foolishness will come clear once they see the world doesn't end in fire and brimstone,"

Hannah said, surprising Curtis who whipped his head up to watch the gunfighter speaking, searching for sarcasm. "Beason, I suggest you leave it alone from here on out."

Black John Hannah had no intention of leaving the pilgrims be, but he was putting together in mind how it could be done. He adjusted his shiny new ring and found his mind filled with evil thoughts, many, too many to sort out quickly but something would come to him soon. The last thing he wanted when it came time to collect from those murderous rubes was a meddlesome, stupid sheriff standing in his way.

CHAPTER 42

As the sun began its descent across the cloudless sky, Dallas Hamer left the Crystal Palace, and was quietly making his way through Little Sonora where many of the residents were snoozing in afternoon siestas or away at work, ensuring he attracted little notice. Prior to making his grand entrance into Mustang Flat that morning he'd hidden a prized possession just outside of town and then circled back so that no one saw what direction he'd arrived from.

The telegram that had drawn him to the dull little town had given him a good reason to use his newly acquired toy, a treasure he had gained on the road between Fort Concho and Fort Bliss thanks to the hand of fate. Tucked into a small limestone cave hidden behind a pile of saguaro cactus and brush, Dallas had stowed away an infernal killing machine stolen from the U.S. Army, and he was gleeful with pride over his accomplishment.

The way it come up, about a week earlier, he'd been riding the trail between the forts in a torrential downpour. Sheeting gray-steel rain dropped the visibility to only a few feet and booming roars of thunder shook the muddy ground.

The sound of men shouting rose above the storm's din, and the flashing light of swinging lanterns drew his eye to a half-sunken flatbed wagon sucked down into the quickly rising mud. Grinning like he was visiting kinfolk, Dallas halted ten feet away and bellowed, "Hallo, the wagon!" sending the three young buffalo soldiers scurrying for their guns.

"Whoa now, fellas, I mean you no harm. Looks like you've run into a spot of trouble and what a night for it!" The men cautiously lowered their rifles and peered through the darkness at him, blinded by their own lantern light.

"Identify yourself, stranger, you're speaking to soldiers of the 10th Calvary unit of the United States Army. Come on, step into this light a little." The man talking held his lantern aloft and it swung and sputtered in the rain. Dallas obliged and with his hands raised in a gesture of peace, approached.

"Close enough," the solider said. A knot of fear tightened in the young man's belly—the sense of being hunted by a predator swept through him the moment he looked into the stranger's cold blue eyes. He searched the darkness behind Dallas as if expecting an ambush but saw nothing but the vague outline of a solitary horse and the miles of empty road they'd traveled before getting bogged down. An older, more experienced soldier may have listened to his gut and told the man to scat, but Dubois Brown was just twenty-three years old and by nature friendly, so to his later regret he let himself relax instead. "Didn't mean to be short with you, sir, but we are having a heck of a time as you can plainly see." Brown gestured to their predicament with his light. A flatbed wagon was half sunk into mud at a sharp angle, on the back a canvas tarp whipping in the strong wind revealed cargo that was shaped like a small cannon, and Dallas was immediately intrigued. "You three hauling a cannon clear across Texas tonight?" he asked.

Dubois laughed softly, "No sir. This is a Gatling gun, you ever heard of one?" The two soldiers accompanying him were busy unharnessing the struggling horse before it ended up trapped, and the big grey fought and nipped at them, cantankerous about the predicament.

Dallas lit up, "Why, sure I've heard of them, I've never seen one before. Mighty impressive looking gun, I'd love to see it in action. You ever get to use it?"

Dubois nodded, "They trained us up on them, now the war is over the Army sends them out for Apache trouble. It only takes two men to operate and fires two hundred rounds a minute. Makes it easy to defend against even dozens of warriors."

The horse was freed, and in a flash of lightning Dallas saw that the canvas had come all the way off the gun, and the soldiers had hurriedly worked to get the wheels un-strapped before the wagon tipped all the way over. The smaller of the pair was knee deep in mud and floundering but still managed to get the gun rolled off the wagon by pushing the back while his teammate pulled from the front.

"What the heck are you doing with it out here?" Dallas asked. "Haven't heard of any recent Apache troubles 'round here." As he spoke with the man, he'd been inching his way closer, and stood only a foot away from Dubois who hadn't noticed his approach.

"Well," Dubois said, "We were moving it up to Fort Bliss, but this storm whipped up so fast it—" He never saw the strike coming. Dallas pistol-whipped him with such velocity that the soldier's skull made an audible crack, and he dropped like a lead-filled gunny sack facedown into the mud.

The young soldier who had been pulling the Gatling went wide-eyed with fear, and as he fumbled for his pistol, a red blossom opened in the center of his forehead, and all the life in him fled as he died on his feet. The small solider, who had just met his fifteenth birthday but lied to the recruiters in his bid to join the army, froze in fear. The kid willed his arm to move for his rifle but his body's only response was to let warm urine spread over his crotch. Dallas fired a shot into the boy's belly with a grin and watched him fall to the earth.

"You know, they say being gut shot is one of the most painful ways to die." He crouched beside the writhing and terrified solider and took the pistol off his belt, weighing it in his palm. "It can take days, and the smell, woo-boy, disgusting." Dallas tossed the gun, and it landed ten yards away in a patch of roadside weeds.

The solider gasped, blood trickling from his mouth, "Puh—puh—." His dusky skin had turned gray, and his eyes bulged with terror.

Dallas patted him on his head like a dog, "Puh-puh? Puh-leaze? Don't beg, boy, only cowards beg. I have been kind enough to leave you with choices. You can wait for the vultures and coyotes to come tear you apart, or you can crawl over to that nice army-issued pistol and blow your brains out." He shrugged. "Maybe you'll get lucky, and a good Samaritan will come along and put you out of your misery, since suicide is a mortal sin. Did you know that men who kill themselves burn for all eternity? The preacher told me that after my father shot himself. Say, if you see the old weasel down there, tell him I said Howdy." The rain had begun to ease, and the red and brown gore leaking out of the young soldier's belly started to stink. Dallas wrinkled his nose in disgust and stood. The last thing the solider saw before the pain made him lose consciousness was the stranger dragging the Gatling gun away behind his horse as lightning crackled across the black sky.

CHAPTER 43

Black John Hannah headed to the Crystal Palace early, hoping whiskey would open his mind to a clear battle plan. The moment he entered the door, all eyes turned to him in a way that set him instantly on edge. A tall blond man with a magnificent mustache stood at once, approaching Black John with easy familiarity.

"My old friend, how happy I am to find you here," he said in a voice loud enough for the entire saloon to hear. His smile was warm, but anyone paying attention would notice it never reached his eyes.

Black John Hannah stood rigid and unsmiling, and then at last said, "Why, if it isn't Dallas Hamer as I live and breathe. Murder any innocent schoolchildren recently?"

Immediately the saloon grew silent, the other patrons pausing their conversations and watching the two men with interest. After long moments, Hannah and Dallas studying each other head to toe, finally Dallas reached over and threw one arm around the rigid John Hannah's shoulder. Into his ear he whispered, "Why, Johnny, I heard about what happened to your legendary gang. Taken out by pumpkin rollers, eh? I think I may have a solution that will help. Something glorious and beyond your wildest dreams. Now, won't you pretend to be my friend today? If not, you'll be dead before you hit this filthy saloon floor." Still smiling, Dallas Hamer withdrew his arm, gestured at a table and sat down. Another long moment, and Hannah joined him. He knew as gunfighters went Dallas Hamer was possessed of an almost supernatural speed, and though Black John was seething, he didn't dare draw down on the man.

"Two glasses and a bottle of your finest whiskey, barkeep, for me and my friend here. Heck, give the whole saloon a round on me!"

The small smattering of saloon patrons cheered, and Lucas Battles was soon busy, serving the gunfighters first. "Enjoy, gentlemen." Battles said before scurrying away, although he was desperate to eavesdrop.

Dallas kicked a chair out to rest his heels on. "Forgive me, old friend, I walked quite a piece, and my dogs are barking." He yipped like a coyote so loud that even Black John cracked a smile, and from his vest pocket he withdrew a brown tincture bottle marked as a cure-all and dropped a capful into his whiskey glass. He offered a sip to Black John who politely declined. "Hard getting old, John, ain't it?" He flipped open an ornately tooled silver case and selected a tailor-made cigarette, lit it with a Lucifer match and then settled back against his chair.

Hannah smirked, "Speak for yourself, I'm still a virile young man as the whores in town can tell you."

"I suppose that means you've stopped killing them all, then. How many was it at last count?"

"Only two, I'm a Christian man now that the padre travels with me."

Dallas smiled mirthlessly. "I bet. So, tell me, John, how you've ended up in your current predicament even with God on your side."

Black John Hannah said, "Well, how it come up . . ."

CHAPTER 44

For over an hour Black John Hannah sipped whiskey and told Dallas Hamer the tale of the unsuccessful rush at the circled wagons, with a great deal of embellishment about his own brave part in the fray.

"I want them all dead, Dallas. Every one of the prairie rats, lock, stock, and barrel, especially that one calls himself a prophet. I don't trust you worth a darn, but if you want to throw in with me and swear on your mother's soul to not shoot me in the back I'll split the treasure with you, fifty-fifty. That'll be a loss on my side since Adam Curtis is going to want his share, too, but I'm willing to compromise for the sake of vengeance." Black John slumped in his chair, whiskey, rage, and exhaustion catching up to him all at once. Dallas remained ever cool and calm, enjoying hearing about another man's misery as was his nature.

"I ain't going to shoot you in the back, but my mother's soul is not a thing worth swearing on. Did I ever tell you how I came by my name?"

"No, although I've heard a rumor or two."

Dallas lit a cigarette and fiddled with his ring. He knew that Black John didn't give a darn about the story he was about to tell but enjoyed drawing it out, forcing the man to sit and listen to him talk.

"When I was born, my mother was thirty-eight years old and thought she was barren. My father had bought her off a hog farmer when she was thirteen and he was thirty. He paid five dollars for her because she was too ugly to be profitable even by the hog farm crib standards. By the time he got ahold of her she'd already caught syphilis and of course he got it, too, which gave him an added enthusiasm for knocking her around every day of their miserable lives together. By the time I turned up, she had found the Lord, and the old cow named me Heaven Sent Hamer."

Black John snorted out a laugh, and Dallas smiled grimly before continuing. "I guess she changed her mind about me being heavenly not long after, because she was a cruel old hag. After my father hung himself, she was worse. So, one day when I was sixteen and going hungry in the Dallas whorehouse where she worked because she'd spent her housekeeper wage on opium, I slit her throat."

Black John startled at that. Even a man of his depravity had a low opinion on matricide.

Dallas grinned, "I enjoyed it so much that I kept the name of the city I killed her in, and it's stuck ever since." A moment of tense silence hung in the air as Dallas stared down the man across from him with flinty malice. "I ain't gonna shoot you in the back, John, but you ever mention my mother again, I'll cut your throat, too."

CHAPTER 45

Dallas Hamer rolled the Gatling gun out of the lime-stone cave he had hidden it in, revealing it to Black John Hannah under a cloudless sky painted bright with turquoise and red.

"It's a bringer of death," he said. "Lethal at a hundred yards."

"I'm listening," said Hannah. "Tell me more."

"See here, the Gatling has six barrels arranged in a circle and they fire .45-70 caliber, two hundred rounds a minute. It takes two men to operate it, one cranks this handle here, and the other feeds this hopper. As it turns" —Dallas laid his hand on a brass funnel attached to the gun—"the round is turned to the firing position. After the bullet is fired, the barrel rotates to feed another. It's a fearsome weapon, but I brought it out here with one horse easy enough. It weighs about a hundred and seventy pounds, light for such a big gun."

Black John's excitement grew, but on the surface, he remained calm, vaguely interested. "How long until the Army comes looking for it?"

"Heck if I know, but not before we have a chance to take down those pilgrims like you want."

"Do you have ammunition for it?"

"Some. I was going to scope out the mercantile in town and see what they've got."

"Well, that's crucial," Black John said.

"Maybe we have enough to get some fun in with what I have and can pick off stragglers if we need to."

Black John considered. "All right, I can talk to Luke Lawson and see if he's got ammo on hand. The man is a packrat. His store is stuffed to the rafters with all sorts of odd finds." He spun the ring on his finger as he spoke, and the red gem cast off what looked like blood splatter across the barrel of the Gatling.

"We should get a wagon, it was slow going on the wheels alone, and if we hit muddy terrain it could be a hindrance."

"John Baxter over to the livery probably has a flat wagon with a ramp and if he does I'm sure he'll be glad to let you rent it. Here, grab a wheel and we'll lift it together, I want to see what it weighs."

Dallas and Black John easily lifted the Gatling six inches off the ground. "See, not bad at all. What do you say, John, do we have us a deal?"

Black John Hannah only grinned in reply.

"Sure, I can rent you a flat wagon with a ramp," said John Baxter, a broken-nosed man with a lively smile that he kept at the ready. "What are you hauling, lumber?"

"No, a Gatling gun," Black John Hannah said.

"A what?"

"You heard me," said Hannah.

"What are you planning to do with a Gatling gun?"

"Have you ever seen one?"

"Only once during the siege of Petersburg in the spring

of 1865. The Gatling was a widow-maker. Cut down more than its share of Rebs, I can tell you that."

"Me and my hunting buddy plan to take it out on the prairie and shoot us some jackrabbits."

Baxter's face showed concern. "Mister, there are cattle out there. Shoot a cow and you could end up swinging from a rope."

"That is not our intention," Black John said. "If we see some jackrabbits, we'll make sure there are no cows, or ranchers, in the vicinity."

"A tad over-gunned ain't you?"

"That's the whole point. When will we ever get a chance to hunt with a Gatling gun again?"

"You bought that big gun at Luke Lawson's place, didn't you? He had one over there for years, I think."

"No, the Gatling belongs to the army. My friend is borrowing it for a while. He helped them transport it and they were . . . called off elsewhere."

John Baxter took this at face value but shook his head. "Folks are mighty notional, and I'm not going to stand in your way," he said. "My rate for the flat wagon and a horse to pull it for a day will cost you three dollars, and I'll throw in rope to tie down the Gatling's wheels. It's not a one-way rental, so you must return the wagon here. Extry charge for any damages."

"Seems fair," Black John said.

"Do you and your hunting companions have riding horses?"

"Yeah. We're staying at the Red Dust Inn, and they have stalls out back."

"I know," Baxter said. "It's something new they've started and it's already hurting my business."

"Sorry to hear that," Black John said. "Next time we're

in town we'll give you our business. Depend on that. Have the wagon ready in an hour."

"You're planning to hunt in the dark?"

"No, we want set up at dusk when the jackrabbits come out to eat."

"Mister, how are you gonna see rabbits in the dark? And have you studied on the fact that the flames from six gatling barrels will blind you?"

Black John Hannah's smile was not friendly. "Baxter, you're a questioning man, ain't you?"

"Yes, I am," the old man said. He put a finger on his mashed nose. "Why do you think I got this?" Then he offered a ready smile and said, "I'll have the wagon ready before the shank of the day. Good luck with the hunt."

"Thank you," Black John said. "I'm kinda looking forward to it."

"Gatling ammo? What are you going to do with it?" Luke Lawson asked, bewildered.

"Nothing if you don't have any," Black John said, tamping down his rising irritability. A hangover was creeping on him, but the thrill of the Gatling gun was keeping the worst at bay.

"Well, funny thing, we had some Apache trouble here about four years ago, and the Army left us a Gatling for a while. I hung onto it here until they came and took it back last year, but they left about two thousand rounds for the thing in my storeroom. Guess they just forgot. Comes in metal boxes so it can be poured into the hopper, like."

Black John Hannah grinned. "Luke Lawson you are true blue. I knew if anyone would have it in this town, you'd be the very man."

Lawson's cheeks pinked and he smiled. "I'll give you a

real fair price for it if you'd like. What are you going to shoot at?"

"We're hoping to find some jackrabbits for target practice," said Hannah.

"Jackrabbits! That sounds like fun, although I wonder if you'll have any meat left on'em after firing a . . ."

He frowned. "Say, where did you get the gun from, Mr. Hannah? There aren't many Gatlings just sitting around, and I don't want to get in trouble with the army or nothing."

Black John smiled reassuringly, "Well, Luke, how it come up was . . ."

CHAPTER 46

"You plan to use the Gatling gun against the pilgrims in the wagon circle?" Adam Curtis's face revealed his consternation.

"Yeah, we set the gun at a hundred yards and then start chopping them up. They'll run for their lives, and we can walk in and take the money."

"They may not run, John."

"Then they'll all die."

"I don't like it, John. Those wagons are on the O'Neil range, make enough racket and cowboys could swing by to see what all the firing is about."

"And by then we'll have loaded the treasure chest in the wagon and made our getaway. Those rubes won't stand up to a Gatling, I guarantee it." Black John saw the objection forming on Curtis's lips and said, "Sure we're taking a chance, Adam, a big chance, but that's what men in our line of business do. It could be we've spent our lives preparing for this, the biggest score we'll ever make. Heck man, it's our destiny."

"Still, gunning down innocent people like that, it's . . ."

Curtis said, the sentence dying on his lips as Black John interrupted him.

"It takes two men to operate the Gatling, and I'll do the gunning. I'll turn the crank that fires the piece and you feed shells into the hopper. Dallas Hamer is so fired up for murder, heck, you probably won't even have to lift a finger and do that. I don't trust him and need you there, Adam. But the killing will be on my conscience, not yours, preacher man."

"John, you don't have a conscience."

"Probably not, so what? Conscience is a dog that can't bite but never stops barking. I just ignore it. Listen, Adam, I can't do this thing without you. When we attacked the wagons, you fired your pistol. Heck, you might have killed one or two of them already."

"Still, a Gatling gun . . . we could kill women and children."

Long John said, "Adam, I'm offering you a chance to get rich. Don't turn your back on me now."

After a long moment, Curtis groaned and said, "When do we leave?"

"Tonight, couple hours after sundown. I don't want anyone seeing us go, especially that interfering sheriff. Before then, we pick up the flat wagon at Baxter's livery and then load the Gatling."

"You sure Baxter and Lawson don't suspect anything?"

"Those rubes? They think we're hunting jackrabbits." Black John read the doubt on Curtis's face and said, "I've met Lawson's kind before. He's a towny. He believes civilization stops at the city limits, and he doesn't give a hoot about what happens out there on the range. Sure, the ranches help keep him in business, but they're a necessary evil. He didn't ask too many questions. John Baxter did, but they were all about hunting jackrabbits."

"We're hunting people," Curtis said, his face in his hands.

"No, we're not," Black John said. He grinned. "Cheer up, Adam, we're just conducting business."

CHAPTER 47

"Hunting jackrabbits with a Gatling gun sounds like a whole lot of fun. I wish I could go with you, but I can't leave the store," Luke Lawson said. "Your best chance for jacks is at dusk and first light," he added. He reached out and tugged at the Gatling gun wheels, making sure they were securely lashed to the back of the flat wagon.

"That's what I reckon," Black John Hannah said. "I sure hope to kill us a few."

Lawson beamed. "And I'll pay you a nickel for every jack you bring in, so long as it's not mangled too badly."

Black John turned to Adam Curtis. "A man can't say squarer than that, can he Mr. Curtis?" Hannah said.

"No sir, he can't," Curtis said.

For some reason, Lawson felt himself flattered. He said, "Well, listen up, Mr. Hannah, you might want to try this when you get back or have the Red Dust Inn's cook whip it up for you."

"What is it?"

"Why jackrabbit stew of course."

"Of course," Black John said as he and Curtis exchanged glances.

"It's an easy dish to cook and right tasty," Lawson said.

"Then give us the recipe when we get back," Curtis said.

"But it's easy," Lawson protested.

Black John glanced at a cobalt blue sky heralding the coming night and said, "All right, we're listening."

"Good! Now, when you get back, put a four-pound jack in the pot, then add peeled and sliced carrots, two stalks of celery, one large onion, chopped, six cloves of minced garlic, a half a cup of white wine . . ."

"And cook until tender," Black John said with an air of finality. "Now we have to go."

"Wait, there's a dozen more ingredients," Lawson said.

The wagon swayed as Curtis climbed into the driver's seat, and Black John said, "Tell us later."

He slapped the reins, the gray in the shafts lurched into motion, and he swung into his saddle to ride alongside. Behind them, Lawson called out in a forlorn tone. "And don't forget the vinegar . . ."

"You know something, I've shot a man for less than that," Black John said as they headed into the darkening distance. "Don't forget the vinegar, he says, as though it mattered."

"Come to think on it, so have I," Curtis said. "I can't abide a preaching man."

"The seminary did that to you," Black John said. "All them yacking sin busters."

"Probably," Curtis said.

CHAPTER 48

"We go at first light," Charlie Wade said. "Sneak out of here while the rubes are still asleep, and the going is good."

"How come?" Ben Gallagher said. Then after a pause, "Micah."

"I don't know how come. It's just a feeling that things ain't right."

"You had one of them visions of yours?" Gallagher said.

"Visions? I don't have visions, but I can sense when something big is coming down. It's a sense I learned to heed years ago when I was long riding with Jesse and Frank and them. May good 'ol Jesse rest in peace."

Gallagher's dull features showed a flash of alarm. "Here, you don't think that fire and brimstone stuff is true, do ye?" he said.

Wade's irritation showed. "Of course, it ain't true. I made the whole thing up to fleece the rubes, so how can a made-up story be true?"

"I was just asking, Charlie," Gallagher said.

"Then no more stupid questions, and call me Micah within the circle." He glanced at the sky to the east . . .

frosted glass interrupted by bright forks of lightning. "Goddarn storm better pass, at least it'll make the fools more convinced about the end arriving. Wish we had a few trumpets!" Wade cackled.

Gallagher wasn't learned enough on Biblical texts to get the joke but offered a smile in reply, just to appease.

The two men fell silent and listened to the hushed noises of the camp around them, and as the gloom gathered and thunder rose, Charlie Wade started to feel an inexplicable sense of doom rising in his belly.

Nervous, he thought, why, just as jumpy as a maiden aunt in a cathouse. He'd pulled off bigger stunts against much sharper men than these skinny farmers. It was his most elaborate plot but not the most dangerous.

Still, he couldn't shake off the feeling, a sense of something dark and predatory lurking outside on the prairie. Something that smelled like decay and smoke and wouldn't give up until it died. No, Charlie Wade thought, whatever is coming, I don't like it one bit. He retreated into the warm lights of his tent and drew the flap closed against the coming night.

CHAPTER 49

Thoughts of murder and gold had Black John Hannah downright giddy as he led the Gatling gun procession across the prairie, the horses kicking up the rich black soil, filling the air with a pleasant earthy fragrance. Occasionally a prairie dog would scurry between its den holes, and Black John would fire potshots at the critter and yell, "You better run little dog!"—delighted by their fear of the flatbed wagon's racket. The full moon was rising, a glowing pearl in the sky paired by the effervescent light of Venus, and Dallas Hamer, who had met up with the wagon outside of Mustang Flat, rode alongside atop his black thoroughbred. He had his own plans in mind and wanted a fast escape and few witnesses to his role in the proceedings.

Black John drew his horse up alongside Curtis who handled the wagon reins with surprising skill. "Give us a song, Padre, I'm feeling festive like," he commanded.

"I don't know any festive songs," Adam replied.

"Well then, sing us a sad one."

Curtis shifted uncomfortably in his seat. He didn't celebrate death the way Black John Hannah did and had misgivings about the potential for murder ahead. The addition of Dallas Hamer made him unnerved, and the

minute the gunfighter had joined them his gut had filled
with a sense of impending doom. But he squeezed his iron
rosary and began to sing in a smooth, beautiful tenor.

We're tenting to-night on the old camp ground,

Give us a song to cheer

Our weary hearts, a song of home,

And friends we love so dear.

Many are the hearts that are weary tonight,

Wishing for the war to cease;

Many are the hearts looking for the right,

To see the dawn of peace.

Tenting to-night,

Tenting to-night,

Tenting on the old camp ground,

We've been fighting to-day on the old camp ground,

Many are lying near;

Some are dead and some are dying,

Many are in tears.

Many are the hearts that are weary tonight,

Wishing for the war to cease;

Many are the hearts looking for the right,

To see the dawn of peace.

Dying to-night,

Dying to-night,

Dying on the old camp ground.

Black John wiped away an imaginary tear and smiled. "Why, Adam that'd bring tears to a stone. You are a mighty fine singer for a man who almost took a vow of silence."

"Priests don't take a vow of silence, John, you're thinking of monks."

CHAPTER 50

"Pa, do you think it'll hurt?" Rebecca asked. The wagon circle was alight with campfires, and she stirred watery stew in a beat-up tin pot over their own fire.

"Will what hurt, punkin?" Silas asked.

"The end when it comes. Micah says it'll be a great fire and . . . well, I'm afraid of burning is all. I ain't afraid to die but I don't want to burn up, neither."

Silas shifted awkwardly on his seat next to the fire, and Becca knew his arthritis was bothering him fiercely tonight. She was worried by how thin he'd become in the six weeks or so it took them to travel from Kansas out to this patch of prairie where Micah had led them to wait for the end times. He thought a spell and then looked up to meet her gaze. Once, she thought, his blue eyes would have sparkled with mirth and jollity, but tonight they were sad and dull. Her heart twinged, and she once again questioned if selling off the farm to follow the prophet was a mistake.

"Well," he began, choosing his words carefully, "we are chosen by God to ascend to heaven. The Bible tells us that

Jesus died on the cross to pay for our sins, so I reckon God won't be too hard on us true believers when the time comes."

Becca nodded, she sipped a spoonful of stew and grimaced at the gamey jackrabbit meat. If only they'd a little salt and pepper, but they'd finished that weeks ago.

She poured the meager supper into their two canteen cups with a sigh. It felt like years had passed since she last enjoyed a fine, juicy steak and potatoes. Silas immediately poured part of his stew into her cup as he always did, despite her protests.

"Don't worry, Becca, our suffering is almost at an end. God sees our meekness and won't let us burn up. Now, will you say the blessing over our generous supper?"

"Pass me the salt, Ben. This steak is tougher than shoe leather and about as tasty." Charlie Wade tucked into his steak and eggs; the steak was courtesy of the O'Neils' stolen Hereford and the eggs had been brought by the lone remaining Gallagher twin. Ben passed the saltshaker and then returned to his post, peering out the tent flap in an agitated state. Charlie glared at him and slammed his fist on the table, making Ben jump six inches in fright.

"Jesus, Charlie, what'd you do that for?" Ben said, wheedling.

"Because your yellow bellied peeping is gonna spook the rubes if you don't quit it. A man can't even enjoy his supper with you hanging about like a wraith," Charlie said. Truth be told, he hadn't much appetite as the sense of doom he'd felt at twilight had increased ten-fold in the hour and a half since. Truth was not a thing Charlie cottoned to, so he continued chastising Ben to distract himself. "If you're gonna become a sniveling schoolboy then maybe I don't need you to tag along with me in the morning, after all. You might chicken out and blow the whole endeavor, which I have worked very hard to organize." He shoved a forkful of fried egg into his mouth and nearly gagged from his sour stomach. Something was afoot. He knew it as he knew the sun rose in the east.

Ben flushed and wheeled on him, suddenly his whining voice menacing. "You listen to me, you scrawny cuss, I lost my brother to this 'endeavor' of yours, and I ain't going to lose my cut of the gold, too. I could shoot you right where you sit and keep it all to myself, you ever think of that, Charlie?" His hand dropped to his gun and at the same moment he heard the unmistakable click of a hammer being cocked beneath the camp table.

"You ever wonder what it'd feel like to have your balls shot off, Ben? You ever think of that?" Wade's voice was smooth and calm, but his eyes sparkled with malice.

"Listen to me, son, I've dealt with bigger, tougher villains than you and your dearly departed brother. There ain't a thing I need you for now besides carrying the riches out of this godforsaken prairie land, but I'm sure I could bribe one of the pumpkin rollers out there to help." Ben stood stock still, the blood drained from his face. Charlie continued, "The minute we reach El Paso, I'll pay you a fair share and then we will go our separate ways. We ride at dawn, and we will be rid of each other soon enough."

Ben slowly moved his hand away from the gun at his hip. Charlie smiled and released the hammer of his Derringer. "See, now we can be friends again. Isn't that better? Sit down and have something to eat, you'll need plenty of grub in your belly for tomorrow's traveling."

As Wade watched Ben Gallagher sit down and pick up a fork, he held onto the truth, that the man would never reach El Paso, not even close. That had never been part of the plan.

CHAPTER 51

Adam Curtis pulled the wagon to a stop shortly after the midnight hour, only two hundred yards away from the ill-fated sleepers of the wagon circle. Curtis took out the makings and rolled a cigarette, wishing for coffee but knowing a fire would attract attention. He slipped out a flask instead and took a long pull before passing it to Black John, who waved it away.

"I need a sharp mind for the task ahead, Curtis. Heck, you shouldn't be guzzling firewater either. Rots your insides, you know," Black John said, busily unstrapping the Gatling gun from the wagon so they could get things assembled.

Curtis rolled his eyes, took another swig, and offered it to Dallas, who accepted. "Thanks, padre. Unlike your boss, I find my insides prefer whiskey to water. Keeps a man healthy and wise."

Curtis hopped down from the seat to help unload the Gatling. "John, you're going to give them a chance to surrender, right? I ain't in the mind of killing these men purely on account of them being foolish enough to follow a false prophet. If they have the sense God gave a fly, they'll take one look at the Gatling and flee . . . won't they?"

Black John became still and significant and stared hard at Adam Curtis, darkly sizing him up. "Why, Adam, what kind of man do you think I am?" His words were quiet, but his voice held menace. "We will let the rubes surrender their gold to us before a single shot is fired. I am above all else a gentleman. Wouldn't you agree, Padre?"

His smile was terrible to behold, and the scar that ran along his cheek looked ghoulish in the light of the small lantern. Curtis knew that the scar was physical confirmation that Black John was the furthest thing from a gentleman. He drank again before returning the flask to his pocket but found the whiskey did little to ease the sinking feeling in his gut.

"Sure, John, if you say so," Curtis said and began unloading the bags of ammunition, piling them beside the wagon. He felt Black John shooting daggers at him as he worked and was alert for any sign of the threatening gunman reaching for iron. The moment passed, and Black John set back to unstrapping the Gatling gun and wheeling it off the flatbed into position. Dallas Hamer sat and watched his companions work, lighting a cigarette and watching the blue smoke swirl into the sky. His meditations before murder were a sacred ritual and besides, his labors were the sole reason Black John had been given the fine weapon at all.

"All right, we attack . . . sorry, Adam, we negotiate, at dawn. How about we get a few winks in until then, tomorrow is bound to be a long and exciting day."

The two men wrapped themselves in blankets and sat beside the wagon and horses, but Dallas didn't move, and his stone stillness gave Curtis a chill. He knew that his boss was making a mistake in trusting the gunslinger just as he knew the sun would rise in the east, but to mention it would be both dangerous and pointless, so he kept his thoughts to himself.

Black John pulled out a bottle of rum to celebrate the morning ahead. "I thought you said booze rots the brain?" Curtis said, shivering despite being tightly bundled inside the wool blanket and smoking with one hand and eating beef jerky with the other. Black John grinned, "Ah, come on Padre, I say all sorts of things I don't mean. Now have a drink to help you sleep. Stop looking so darn worried and relax."

Curtis knew that Black John did indeed say all sorts of things he didn't mean. That was in fact why he was worried.

CHAPTER 52

As the first rays of dawn broke across the prairie and bathed the earth in shimmering gold, Charlie Wade was in a state of panic. "Saddle the horses. It's time," he called over his shoulder as he rushed to the treasure tent. But Ben Gallagher wasn't listening, his eyes fixed on the scene unfolding about a hundred yards north of the circle.

"What is that?" he said. Then his voice rising in notes of alarm. "Charlie! What . . . what the heck is that . . . thing?"

The prophet, rapidly transforming back into plain ol' Charlie Wade, knew exactly what the heck that thing was the minute he'd heard it approaching the circle. He'd seen one of them chop up a Cheyenne village on the Red River until the water ran red and the ground blazed with fire.

"Quick, let's load up the gold and get out of here!" Wade yelled, no longer concerned about the pilgrims who were now crawling out of their wagons and shouting in terror.

"What is it?" Gallagher said, his voice edged with tension.

"It's a Gatling gun. And if we don't hightail it, the damned thing will kill us all."

* * *

The Gatling gun had a unique, rattling sound, like a brass bed pulled across a floor of knotty timber, and when a gleeful Black John Hannah cranked the gun's handle that morning, it's believed to be the first time a Gatling had been fired in anger in West Texas.

As Dallas Hamer fed the hopper, Hannah's opening barrage hammered a two hundred round a minute firestorm into the circle, killing men, women, children, and horses, sheets of blood splashing as high as the top of the wagons, staining their canvases red. Adam Curtis stood ashen and slack jawed as he watched the massacre unfold. Despite Black John Hannah's promises, there had been no attempt at negotiation. There hadn't even been a warning issued to the circle. The pilgrims were being slaughtered without mercy, the circle becoming an inferno as the canvas wagons were set ablaze. Black John had opened fire without a word the moment the sun broke over the prairie.

There was a pause as Dallas tossed aside an empty ammunition box and retrieved another, and several riflemen attempted to leave the circle and rush the Gatling, but all of them were cut down within seconds as the grass around them burst into flames.

Black John Hannah paused his dreadful fusillade, tossed back his head, and bellowed a maniacal laugh, "Heck, Adam, we're cutting them up!"

"Boss, they've had enough," Curtis yelled. "Let them be."

"They haven't had enough until they're all dead and we have the money," Black John said. "Load the darned hopper."

Curtis reached for his gun, and then instead put his hands on his head with despair. Screaming with all his strength he implored the dying pilgrims, "Run! Run away!"

Dallas Hamer turned and glared at him, and then shook his head and poured cartridges into the hopper. Reloaded yet again, the Gatling resumed its death rattle.

As the big gun chewed up the milling people, men, women and children, now reduced to a score or less, Charlie Wade and Gallagher rushed to the far end of the circle where their horses were tied to a wagon, the terrified beasts lathering at the mouth and fighting to break free. The men struggled but managed to load the sacked gold as bullets buzzed around them like angry hornets.

"For God's sake hurry," Wade said, passing a sack to Gallagher. "Or we'll both be dead men. All this work and now we must leave so much behind. Mark my words, Ben, I'll kill the men responsible for this the first chance I get."

As Gallagher fought to tie a sack to his saddle horn atop his agitated horse, he said, "Someone coming."

"It's Jim Petite. What does he want?" Wade said.

"He's got something on his mind, fer sure," Gallagher said.

Petite hurried toward them, a big, florid-faced man with bushy side whiskers, wearing mule-eared boots and baggy pants. He carried a Sharps .50 with a chip out of the stock, a near miss by the Gatling.

"Wait, what are you doing?" he said. "What's going on here?"

"God's work, brother," Charlie Wade said. "We're securing His treasure."

"These are the same men who killed my Emma, Prophet! Is this the work of God, have we been forsaken? You gotta help me. There are still some alive and—"

Petite did a double take when he saw Charlie Wade's getup. He'd never seen the chosen one in anything but the scarlet robe. "Prophet . . . how come you . . ."

"I'm dressed as the Lord would expect to see me, in the garb of a common man," Wade said. "Now help get us loaded."

Petite didn't move. "Prophet . . ." he said again, confusion mounting on his face and unable to believe that this shabby little man was his revered, red-robed prophet.

All three men ducked as Gatling rounds buzz-sawed their way across the top of nearby wagons and tore the canvases into shreds.

"Ben, there are loose coins in the treasure box," Wade yelled. "Fill your pockets."

"Wait," Petite said. "This isn't right."

"What ain't right?" Charlie Wade said.

"That's God's money," Petite said. "It's not yours."

"Come with us or die with us," Wade said. "Saddle a horse and fill your pockets."

Yelling over the relentless racket of gunfire, Petite said, "No, people around us are dying, I think they're dying over that money. Leave it!" His face purpled. "The Good Lord will find it soon enough."

Then Petite signed his own death warrant. He made a slight motion with the Sharps, small, almost imperceptible, but enough to alarm the sharp-eyed Wade who'd gunned five men in face-to-face shooting scrapes and knew the moves. Charlie was fast. His gun hand streaked for the pocket of his high-button coat and he palmed a Remington .41 derringer and fired. One shot in the middle of Petite's chest, and the angry expression on the man's face changed to a look of horror as he dropped. Never one to do things by half, Wade fired a second bullet into Petite's forehead and sealed the deal. As a row of shots from the Gatling kicked up exclamation points of dirt close to Wade's feet, he yelled, "Right, Ben, saddle up and let's get out of here. Follow me. We'll loop wide and then head north. Got that?"

"Let's go," Gallagher said. "My horse's nose will be an inch from your horse's butt. Heck, I can't believe we're still alive."

"We ain't still alive," Charlie Wade said. "That Gatling could be the death of us yet."

Black John saw the riders leave the circled wagons at a gallop, but he couldn't redeploy the Gatling in time and when his hand finally reached the cranking handle, Charlie Wade and Ben Gallagher were far out of range, trailing dust.

CHAPTER 53

Dallas Hamer saw the two men ride out with what he had considered to be his treasure since the moment he received that fateful telegram and immediately mounted his horse. He stopped only long enough to stare down Black John Hannah with a wide grin. Satisfied immensely by the massacre though he was, he was disappointed that there was no time now to shoot both Hannah and his soft-hearted little priest friend the way he'd planned. At least he'd have something to look forward to, he thought. With a sweep of his hat and a wink, he waved goodbye to the two men before picking his way through the parade grounds of death and taking off after Charlie Wade and his gold.

"John, I never thought that madman would leave you alive," Curtis said, his voice hoarse and tired.

"He went after those boys who were carrying sacks," Black John said. "Dang it, Adam, they've taken the money with them."

"Your horse is still around somewhere, and the pilgrims have horses, too," Adam Curtis said. "If you haven't shot them all."

Black John spun on Curtis, red with rage, "You and I

got business to attend thanks to you being a yellowbellied betrayer and lowdown, but right now ain't the time, Curtis. Don't go thinking I'm done with you." He turned back to the riders who were becoming distant black specks against the dazzling sunrise. "Heck, look at them go, even loaded down with gold, we'd never catch them, not now," Black John said. "But they've headed north. I'll drive back to Mustang Flat in the wagon and pick up fresh horses. Two men riding heavily loaded mounts cut an easily followed trail."

"It's worth a try," Curtis said. He knew that disobeying Black John Hannah had been as good as signing his own death warrant, but he also knew that Black John would keep him around long enough to retrieve the gold. Curtis knew, and that's why he would kill him before that time came.

"What about these people?"

"What about them?"

"They'll need medical care."

"We ain't doctors, and they ain't any of my concern."

"Some of them are running away," Curtis said, his gaze following the panicked progress of a dozen men, women, and children, all of them heading south, away from the nightmare Gatling.

"They got no fight left in them," Black John Hannah said.

"The big gun saw to that," Curtis said.

Then from Hannah, his eyes fixed on the southern range, "Riders coming. This could be trouble."

"There's only two of them," Curtis said.

"One of them could be that interfering sheriff."

"I don't think so. The sheriff sits his horse like a sack of corncobs. Those two men are riders," Black John said.

"Maybe just punchers . . . that rancher, O'Neil, and a hand."

"Well, loosen your iron in the holster," Black John said. "You might need it."

"More killing, John?" Curtis said quietly.

"It's shaping up that way," Hannah said.

CHAPTER 54

A demanding knock at the door halted Sean O'Neil's breakfast eggs midway between his plate and mouth. "Just open it, don't knock it down," he yelled

Sean's foreman Joe Dean rushed inside, letting the door slam shut behind. "Boss, there's a war going on . . . out on our range, maybe hundreds of guns firing."

Sean smiled. "Maybe Bob Beason has himself an army."

"Boss, this is no joke," Dean said.

"No, but it could be distant thunder," Sean said.

"The thunder of guns, boss. That's what it is."

Maria Perez stood at the stove, frying bacon as she sang a plaintive Mexican love song, the baby was fussing loudly in the bedroom, and Johnny, always loud, was bellowing at himself over a lost sock.

"Boss, come outside," Dean pleaded. "You can hear the gunfire. It sounds like a battle."

Sean threw down his napkin and yelled, "Johnny, look under your bed. Your socks have a habit of wandering under there." Without waiting for an answer, he said to Dean, "All right, Joe, I'll come listen to your war."

Dean led the way outside, into the newborn day, the

sky a thin blue, furrowed with wispy bands of white cloud, the breeze smelling of grass, cattle, horses . . . and something else.

"What the heck?" Sean said.

"Told you so," Dean said.

"That's gunsmoke, a lot of it," Sean said.

"And listen, boss. How many men firing rifles?"

"Judging by the racket, everybody and the dog," Sean said.

"I saddled your hoss," Dean said.

"Where are the rest of the hands?"

"Fencing the west pasture. I sent them out early, remember?"

"Then it's you and me, Joe." Sean swung into the saddle. "Let's go stop a war."

"Or start one," Dean said. By nature, a cheerful, sunny man, but now his homely, bronzed face clouded into a worried frown.

"Sean, where are you headed?" Johnny said from the cabin doorway. And what's all that shooting?"

"Probably Bob Beason and his posse," Sean said.

"Mighty big posse," Johnny said.

"Stay with Maria and the baby," Sean said. "I don't know how this thing will end."

"Sean, I wish you hadn't said that," Johnny said.

"Don't worry. I'll be back before you know it," Sean said.

He and Dean kicked their horses into motion, leaving Johnny to fret, worry chilling his belly like blue ice.

"Black John we got some explaining to do," Adam Curtis said as his troubled eyes watched the riders grow nearer.

"How much explaining do drovers need?" Black John

said. "We uncovered a plot by the pilgrims to raid and burn all the local ranches as a sacrifice to their god."

"It's mighty thin," Curtis said.

"And I don't give a darn how thin it is," Black John said. "They can take it or leave it."

Sean O'Neil took in the destruction—and mass murder—at a glance. Beside him Joe Dean looked stunned and horrified, like a man just awakened by a night terror.

"What in God's name is this?" Sean said.

"We'd information that the rubes planned to attack and burn all the local ranches and enslave the women and children they aimed to take as prisoners. My name is John Hannah and this is Adam Curtis. We beat them to it, hit them earlier this morning with the Gatling. Now the darned scum are all dead or running for their lives and you have me to thank for it."

"The children were scum?"

Hannah shrugged. "You can't make an omelet without cracking a few eggs."

Sean swung out of the saddle in one graceful, easy motion. "Walk with me, Hannah," Sean said. "Let's see if we can discover who the real scum are."

"I hope you're not implying that I'm the guilty party," Black John said. "I'm a red-blooded patriot who saved this range from an orgy of burning, killing, and rape by a bunch of fanatical lunatics."

Sean O'Neil was aware of two things: Joe Dean had dismounted and stood with his hand within drawing distance of his gun. The second was that the man called Curtis had gradually cleared a space between himself and Hannah. Whether he was trying to disassociate himself from the man or opening a clear field of fire, he could not guess.

"Walk with me, Hannah," Sean said again.

"Sure, but there's nothing to see except dead criminals."

"Where's the treasure?" Sean said.

"It's a myth, it doesn't exist," Hannah said. "Why, Luke Lawson over to the mercantile, told me the very same thing when we were loading the gun yesterday evening. 'There is no treasure and never was,' he said."

Surprised, Sean placed a hand on the still hot gun. "Luke sold you this killing machine? Did he know how you intended to use it?"

"He didn't sell me the gun, only the ammunition. The gun came courtesy of an old friend who borrowed it from the U.S. army to aid in my noble cause. Of course, Lawson knew, and he approved. 'John,' he said, 'take that instrument of destruction and use it well. Clear the range of those murdering fiends and once again make West Texas a haven for civilized, Christian people."

Sean said, "You're a liar, Hannah. It doesn't sound like Luke Lawson had any . . ." and then his voice faltered. They'd walked inside the now-abandoned wagon circle, a charnel house clogged with gore, corpses chewed up by a weapon of a deadliness few of them could ever have imagined. The fires had mostly petered out in the light rain that had begun to fall, but the charred remains of both people and covered wagons were emitting a malodorous steam. Crafty-eyed buzzards were already in place on the outskirts of the massacre site, patiently squatting on the top of shot-torn canvases and in the tall prairie grass.

No hurry . . . take your time . . . we can wait . . .

Sean stumbled out of the slaughterhouse, gagging and taking vast gulps of fresh air as soon he was free of the suffocating stench.

A massacre had been committed on the Running-S, a bloodbath that would live in the minds of Texans and on the lips or pages of storytellers for a long time. Sean knew that there had to be a showdown, and it was a responsibility that fell on his shoulders.

To a man like Black John Hannah, Sean O'Neil was a minor inconvenience, a pesky fly to be swatted. He and Adam Curtis stood about seven yards from Sean, but Curtis had considerably increased his separation from Hannah.

Sean gathered his strength and said, "John Hannah, my name is Sean O'Neil, this is my range and you're on it. I'm arresting you for the murders of the people who died here today."

Hannah laughed. "Cowboy, you don't have the authority to arrest anybody. So now it seems you face a choice, don't it?"

"And that is?"

"Go away and round up some cows . . ."

"Or?"

A smile from Hannah. "Or die on your own ground, right where you stand."

"No, John, there's been enough killing," Adam Curtis said. "Too many doors have banged here this morning. Let it be."

"Adam, are you stepping aside?" Black John said. "Are you afraid of banging doors?"

"That's what the gun sounded like, just like we heard it in the Red Dust Inn, and like it sounded when Legion took control of Father O'Rourke. That sound foretells an evil thing. John Hannah, you've become a demonic man, and I will not stand for more killing!"

"Then stay right where you are and keep your mouth shut." Black John jabbed his finger as he spoke, and the sun caught the red ring and cast an infernal red light across his face. Curtis saw a mask of hatred and greed beneath the scarlet tint and felt the claw marks that scarred his flesh begin to burn.

"John . . . you are lost to the Devil, and you have to stop this now. Haven't we spilled enough blood this day?"

"Yeah, we've spilled blood, so much a little more here and there ain't going to make a hill of beans of difference, to us or the dead folks, or God and the Devil. And I did the killing, Adam, me, and Dallas. You're not wearing the collar, but you're still a priest and you only betrayed me and got in my way. You get out of my way this time. This ain't your fight anymore."

Sean took note of the name Dallas. He had only seen the two men when he and Joe had ridden up. If there was another man involved, then he had to hunt him down. Later, he saw where the confrontation with John Hannah was headed and knew that there was little chance they'd both make it out of the conflict alive.

"Hannah, listen to your friend. Unbuckle your gun belt and let it drop, nice and slow," Sean said. "You claim to have saved Texas civilization so now you can take your chances with the law."

"I'd rather take my chances with you, cowboy." Black John grinned maniacally. "You're heeled, so have at it. Skin the iron."

Black John Hannah was fast on the Texas draw, lightning fast, but one man there that morning was even faster. Sean's Colt had barely cleared leather when he heard a shot and saw Hannah stagger, crimson rose blossoming in the middle of his forehead. The man died, surprised at the time and manner of his death, and when he hit the ground, Black John Hannah was as dead as he was ever going to be. Adam Curtis had drawn his gun but aimed it at the ground and stared at the body of his former companion, a man he now regretted ever meeting.

"You making a play . . . Father?" Joe Dean said.

Shocked into silence, Sean couldn't find the words as his foreman stepped beside him.

Adam Curtis looked up and saw the ice in Dean's eyes. He holstered the gun and smiled, "Against you, Joe? God, no." Seeing the confusion on Sean's face, Curtis realized that the rancher had no idea about his trusted cowboy's history.

"O'Neil, this here is Joe Dean, named pistolero out of Galveston. Black John makes for your tenth kill, don't he, Joe?"

"I suppose I should give a confessional, Father. Thirteen dead men. But times have changed and so have I. Never thought I'd need to draw on a man again like I did today." He holstered his Colt and relaxed his posture, but Sean O'Neil was still frozen with shock beside him.

"Joe is the man who done for Johnny Potts, the Dallas shootist. Folks figured Johnny would never get shaded on the draw because he'd made a pact with the devil. That is until a stranger in town put two in his brisket before Johnny boy had even cleared leather. The local lawmen covered the holes in Johnny's chest with a silver dollar. You shot well that day, Joe."

"Glad our paths never crossed, Father," Dean said. "I mean, back in the day before you met up with Black John Hannah when you were the Pistolero Padre."

"I studied for the priesthood, but I was never ordained," Curtis said.

"Then I could've shot you with a clear conscience," Dean said. "You sure you don't aim to try me, Adam?"

"Nope," Curtis said. He smiled, unbuckled his gun, and let it drop. "But I'll say a novena for you tonight, Joe."

"And say one for yourself. I guess we're both on the atonement trail, huh?" Dean turned to Sean. "Sorry, Mr. O'Neil. As soon as we get back, I'll pick up my gear and be on my way."

"Why?" Sean said. "Where are you going?"

"Wherever washed-up gunmen go."

Sean shook his head. "And that's the Running-S where you belong. You're a first-rate foreman, and you saved my life today."

"Yes, he did. Boss man, you weren't even close," Curtis said. He looked down at Hannah's sprawled body. "John, you never expected to meet a man faster that you. That must've been a big disappointment."

"Yep, the Gatling gun man, he was good," Joe Dean said. "Fast on the draw and shoot. Not sure if he'd be faster than you though, padre."

"You called it, Joe, and I'm not going to argue with you," Curtis said. "But you shot him first."

Sean was getting over his shock, "Say, what is your name again. Curtis, was it?"

"Adam Curtis. I'm the last man standing out of what used to be Black John Hannah's gang. Well, Tommy Holton is still alive, but he's back in Mustang Flat recovering from a gunshot that happened during our first confrontation with the pilgrims when the sheriff asked us to help clear 'em off your land. John was a fool and rushed them and got his men killed." He shook his head, "And I was a fool to think we were only coming out here to rob them, this time."

"Joe, will you get back to the ranch and tell Johnny what's happened here, and tell him I'll probably be late for supper," Sean said. "He will be worried sick by now, and he can get mighty notional when he is upset. The last thing I want is him having to see this . . . horror."

Joe Dean nodded, "Sure thing, boss." He went to his horse but didn't take off, not trusting Adam Curtis alone with Sean just yet.

A keening wail rose from the wagon circle as the people who'd fled started drifting back in search of their loved ones. The sound hit Sean in the gut, and he looked over to see a silver haired man cradling a burnt, broken form and rocking on the ground. Feet away from the man, a young woman beat the ground with her fists and screamed in anguish. There would be a time to grieve for these people, but justice had to be served first, and steeling himself, he looked away.

"Curtis, when Hannah was talking about firing the Gatling he said the name Dallas. What was he talking about?"

"Dallas Hamer, you ever heard the name?"

Sean shook his head, "Can't say I have."

"He's a named gunfighter. I can't say how many he's gunned because the man is ruthless and without morals. There's a rumor that he murdered a pair of schoolboys a few years back in Louisiana, just for sport. I've no doubt the sheriff has his name on flyers all over his office, but he probably just wasn't in town long enough to be noticed. Although, maybe I just ain't seen the best of him yet, but I can't say that your town sheriff is . . . the sharpest."

"I'd tend to agree with that," Sean said.

"Hamer is the one who brought the Gatling to town. I have no idea how, or where, he got it, but I'm sure that whatever happened someone will be looking for it. What John told you was true, Luke Lawson did have the ammunition, but he thought we were hunting jackrabbits out here."

"Jackrabbits? He believed that?"

Curtis shrugged. "Seemed to."

"This Dallas Hamer, where is he now?"

"He took off after the two men who fled with the treasure. O'Neil, I know you'll want to bring him to justice, but you are outgunned by a lot when it comes to that demon. To be frank, me and Joe Dean are probably outgunned by him, too. There's a reason why he hasn't been hanged yet for all that he has done."

"I see," Sean said. "Curtis, I heard what Hannah said to you, and I don't believe that you fired on these people. But is a man who helped other men set up for a massacre as guilty as the one who cranked the handle and loaded the hopper? I'll have to leave that decision to Bob Beason, and I need to take you into Mustang Flat."

"I'll give you no problem," Curtis said. "I'm done. I've got a lot to atone for, O'Neil."

"I've got a lot to atone for myself. Killing Hamer is just another thing on the list I suppose," Joe Dean said. "Boss, thanks for the second chance."

Sean said, "Joe, we may not get everything right the first time, the third time or the fourth or the hundredth time." He smiled. "That's why second chances are so important. Now get back to the ranch like I told you before my brother either has a heart attack or does a foolish thing like try to ride a horse."

Joe Dean's face lit up in an untroubled grin. "Sure thing, boss."

After Dean rode away, Sean said, "Curtis, get up on the wagon. I'll join you when I tie my horse to the back. Leave your gun rig where it lays, I'll carry it for you."

"Anything you say, boss man," Curtis said.

As they rode away from the terrible scene, the rain began to fall in earnest as though God himself wept for the souls lying motionless in the swaying prairie grass and the forever broken people they had left behind.

CHAPTER 55

Silas Booker sat in the middle of Hell on earth and cradled the charred and blood-soaked form of his daughter. A keening wail rose from his chest and echoed across the prairie, a ghostly sound that no human should ever produce. "My girl, my girl," Silas sobbed into Rebecca's beautiful hair that was so like his beloved Goldie's. "I failed you, I'm so sorry, Becca, I have failed you. I promised you . . ." He choked on a sob. "I promised you that God wouldn't let you burn up . . . Oh my God, Becca, it should have been me. Why didn't he take me?" Rebecca's blue calico dress had caught fire and burned into her skin, and her glazed eyes stared skyward from under a mask of drying blood. The carnage made it impossible to say if she'd died from a bullet or the blaze, but Silas felt as though he'd set the fire that marred her once porcelain skin with his own hands. Losing a child is a pain that can never be overcome, and a piece of the once faithful man's soul broke off and withered, never to be retrieved again. All that was left now was vengeance, and as Silas sat drenched in rain and feeling the agonies of loss mingle with the physical pains brought by his age, he swore to himself, and his daughter, that he would kill the

false prophet with his bare hands. Even if he lost his own
life in the process.

The cold October rain was soaking through the clothing
of the survivors of what would come to be known as the
West Texas Devil's Massacre, but none of them felt a chill
or even knew that they were wet. A few yards beside Silas
Booker, a young woman named Laura Smith lay prostrate
over the bodies of her twin girls, who'd just passed their
third birthdays days before. Laura's husband Michael had
died trying to protect his girls and lay sprawled out beside
them with bullet wounds peppering his broad chest. The
Smith family's wagon was nothing but a burnt husk, and
the little girls' rag dollies were piles of ash that lay
crumbled under Laura's fingertips. The only memento the
young wife and mother may have had left was her golden
wedding ring, but she'd gladly handed it over to the
prophet Micah, who she now knew to be nothing but an
evil man. Overwhelmed by grief, Laura slipped into un-
consciousness where she remained for a very long time.

As the survivors continued to gather, a happy reunion
took place amongst the Douglas family, who'd run off
when the shooting had first started and escaped unscathed.
"Was it the army, Papa?" Alice Douglas asked her father,
Dan, who held his children close and did his best to keep
them from seeing the terrible field of death. "No, honey, I
don't think so. Why would the army come after pilgrims?"

"It sounded like the army," his son Rodger said, frowning as he tried to see around his father's broad arms.
Despite the grim surroundings, his parents smiled. His
mother, Louise, patted him gently on the head, "Rodger,
you don't know what an army sounds like."

"Yes, I do."

"No, you don't," Alice scolded.

"I do, too! I'm six, I know what an army sounds like for sure!"

"Do not!"

"All right, all right, that's enough. Be quiet, people are sad, and you must be mindful of their feelings. Come on, let's see if we can find some wildflowers to pick." Louise met her husband's eyes and smiled sadly. He nodded and returned her smile, both thankful to be alive.

"Can we give them to the sad people?" Rodger asked.

"Sure, honey, that would be nice. Now come along."

CHAPTER 56

"A massacree?" Sheriff Bob Beason said, his normally florid face ashen as he flopped into his office chair. "O'Neil, are you talking about a massacree?"

"Most of the wagon people are dead," Sean said. "Only a few escaped, and their leader and another man made off with the treasure."

"Prophet Micah . . . his real name is Charlie Wade . . . and the other man is Ben Gallagher, a small-time crook," Beason said. "So they made away with the money?"

"And left at least thirty dead behind them," Sean said.

"But . . . how?"

"Black John Hannah and a man named Dallas Hamer cut them up with a Gatling gun. Adam Curtis, this feller here, was with them but I don't think he fired on them."

"A Gatling gun," Beason said. "The town used to have one of them. Luke Lawson had it for a while, but I think it's long gone. Where did they get a Gatling gun?"

"Lawson sold them the ammunition, but the gun that was used in the massacre was brought in by the Dallas Hamer character. We don't know where he found it."

Beason looked stricken. "Luke Lawson . . . I can't believe . . ."

"Beason, pay attention, Lawson only sold them the ammunition," Sean said. "Hannah and Hamer did the shooting. For what it's worth, Curtis helped them carry the gun out there and set it up but as far as I can tell he didn't crank the handle or load the hopper."

"Guilty and guiltier!" Beason yelled, thumping his fist on his desk. "Forget about Hannah. He's dead," Sean said.

"How?"

"My foreman shot him."

"In the back."

"In the front. He outdrew Hannah and dropped him."

"That's hard to believe," Beason said.

"Believe it, lawman," Curtis said. "It happened. The name Joe Dean ring a bell with you?"

"Yeah, a gunman, ran with John Wesley Hardin and them for a spell. Some say he was faster than Wes."

"Dean is O'Neil's foreman," Curtis said.

"Small world," Beason said. Beason called over a young redheaded boy who was sweeping the floor. "Jack, did you hear what's happened out at the wagon circle?"

The little boy nodded enthusiastically.

"Then go get Doc Grant, tell him what you heard, and say I want him here," Beason said. "Tell him to harness up his surrey and bring medical supplies. He might be gone for a spell." Jack nodded again and set his broom back in the corner before hurrying out the door.

Sean said, looking at the young girl who lay on a blanket spread in a corner, "Is she the wife of the man Johnny had the fight with?"

"Yeah, she was his child bride. Her name is Liza, and I don't know what do with her," Beason said. "I've offered her bacon and beans, but she won't eat, even though she's fat."

Sean rose from his chair and stepped to the girl who was as a pale as death. Her forehead was contracted in pain so biting that her eyebrows formed a single, black line and she breathed in short, uneasy gasps. "This child isn't fat, she's pregnant and she's ill."

"Hold on there, O'Neil, let me lock up my prisoner," the sheriff said. He took a set of clanking keys from the wall, selected one, and locked a compliant Adam Curtis in the cell.

"Rule one of this establishment, no sass or backtalk, and rule two no complaints about the food or coffee. Comprende?"

"I hear you loud and clear, lawman," Curtis said. "I'll be a model prisoner and you'll be right proud of me."

"I doubt that," Beason said.

He crossed the floor and stood over the girl. After a while he said, "I guess she could be a little bit with child. Come to think, I suppose someone may have mentioned that after Johnny killed her husband."

"Beason, she's a lot with child," Sean said. "I want Dr. Grant to see her."

"He'll be here for me to tell him about the wagon train," Beason said. He shook his head. "I don't know what to do with a pregnant girl."

"The Mexicans will probably have midwives," Sean said. "They could take care of her."

"That's a good plan, O'Neil. I'll mention it to the doctor."

When Dr. Grant arrived, Mrs. Pierson in tow, Beason filled him in on the details of the wagon massacre. "There may be wounded," he said.

Grant was horrified. "I'll leave right away," he said.

"Doc, can you take a look at this girl before you leave," Beason said. "She's pregnant."

Wearing the frustrated expression of a man who had bigger and better things to do, Grant briefly examined Liza and said, "She'll give birth soon, but she'll be fine."

"I had the idea of bringing in a Mexican midwife," Beason said.

"Crackerjack!" Grant said. "The very thing. Now I must leave. Mr. O'Neil, I'll be trespassing on your range."

"Feel free, Doc," Sean said. "If you need help, you know where my cabin is."

Grant nodded. "That offer is much appreciated." Then he and Mrs. Pierson left.

In the corner, Liza Hart, pregnant and a widow alone, groaned.

CHAPTER 57

Although a wanderer by nature and occupation, peddler Solomon Cohen was a man with a strong sense of civic duty. His meeting with two men on the trail north disturbed him so much he returned to Mustang Flat to report what he'd seen.

"Sheriff, it was their horses that troubled me," Cohen said. "They were both loaded down with sacks of something."

"Gold, maybe?" Sean O'Neil said.

"That's what I thought, so I hailed them and asked what they carried in their pokes and if they'd care to do some honest trading," Cohen said.

"And what did they say?" Bob Beason asked.

"The smaller man said only one word, 'Git.'"

"And you got," Beason said.

"I got because the little man pointed a belly gun at my head. I wasn't much inclined to do any trading after that, sheriff," said Cohen.

"Sol, the other man, was he big, wearing city slicker duds?" Beason said.

"Yes, he was. He carried a gun but didn't look like a Western man."

Sean and Beason exchanged glances and then the sheriff said, "It's got to be them, Charlie Wade and Ben Gallagher making off with the treasure."

"Sounds like," Sean said.

"What's going on in Mustang Flat?" Cohen said.

"When did you meet these men, Sol?" Beason said.

"Just this morning, why?"

"Then you haven't heard?" Beason said.

"Heard what?"

The sheriff told him about the Gatling gun and the wagon circle massacre. "That's one of the killers in my cell," he said. "The other is dead and another one was . . . say, did you see another man? Fella on a black horse who looks like Custer?" Cohen shrugged, "Nope," he said, "Well, I'm right sorry to hear it. Them wagon folks never bought anything." His eye widened and he clapped a hand to his mouth. "I shouldn't have said that. May God forgive me."

Sean smiled. "You're a businessman, Sol. I'm sure God will understand."

"I hope so," the peddler said. But he looked worried.

The old grandfather clock in Beason's office struck four when the office door opened and an Old Testament prophet stepped inside, a man almost seven-foot-tall with wild silver hair, fire in his eyes and a 10-gauge Greener cradled in his arms.

"My name is Silas Booker, and I'm here to see the sheriff," the man said. His voice matched his size, booming but edgy, possibly a tad nervous.

Beason seemed taken aback by the man's towering presence to say nothing of the scattergun. He said, "I am he. What can I do for you, stranger?"

"I managed to get away from the massacre today at the wagon circle. I thought my beloved daughter Rebecca was behind me but somehow, we were separated and when I got back"—the man had lost some of the strength from his voice—"she was dead." As though reciting from a prepared speech, he continued, "I met your doctor on the way here and I told him he was wasting his time. Except for the few who escaped, they're all dead. Shot many times by the same gun or burnt up in the fires from it. Every last one, including my daughter. I'm here because I want to help bring the men responsible to justice, and I won't take no for an answer."

O'Neil studied the man and realized that he was rail thin and old, his hands gnarled with arthritis and his skin stretched like rawhide over the protruding tendons in his arms. Grief and rage had made a giant of him, but he was not a man fit to lead a posse.

"Mr. Booker, we have reason to believe that the man you and the other pilgrims followed, the prophet, his real name was Charlie Wade, accompanied by a man named Ben Gallagher, were seen riding north this morning. It is my opinion that they're headed for El Paso."

"Was the money once reserved for the Lord with them?" Booker said.

"That's highly probable. They were carrying sacks that could've contained gold coins."

"Then I'm going after them," Booker said. "Back in Kansas I knew everyone who sold a farm and I'll see that the money is distributed to their surviving kinfolk who chose not to chase a mad dream."

"You can't hunt down two gunmen by yourself, Mr. Booker," Beason said.

"Three," O'Neil said. "They're being chased by a deadly gunfighter by the name of Dallas Hamer. This isn't a fight you can win alone, sir. Hamer is the one who brought the

Gatling gun to town and, accompanied by a man who is now dead, murdered your daughter and the rest."

"I'd like to say that the Lord will protect me, but I won't. I put my faith in this Greener shotgun."

"This is a task for the law," Beason said.

"But will the law act?" Booker said.

Then, surprising the heck out of Sean, Beason said, "Yes, by God, in this case it will. I hold Wade and Gallagher equally responsible for what happened this morning. That Hamer feller, too. So many dead, guilty and guilty . . . I'll hang them all."

"Sheriff, you've got a prisoner to feed and a pregnant girl to care for," Sean said.

"I'll arrange for the Red Dust Inn to feed my prisoner, and I'll have Mexican midwives care for the girl. Mr. Booker, give me time to do all that and then saddle my horse. We've got some daylight left."

"I have supplies from the wagons," Booker said. "Enough jerky and canned peaches to last a few days." Then a rare smile from Silas Booker. "You're a brave man, sheriff."

"No, I'm not, but there are some crimes any lawman worth his salt can't ignore, and this is one of them."

Sean O'Neil slowly shook his head and then said, "I can't believe I'm hearing myself say this, but I'll come with you."

"You reckon you've got a stake in this, O'Neil?" Beason said.

"The massacre happened on my range, that's stake enough. And I can't let the likes of Charlie Wade go unpunished. If there's no law in Texas, the result is anarchy, and there's no greater evil than that." Sean smiled. "And besides, where you're going, an extra gun could come in handy."

"Then I'm glad you'll be with us, O'Neil," Beason said. "Just remember, as an officer of the law I'm in charge, and I call the shots."

"You're the boss, sheriff," Sean said.

"Good. Just remember that."

Adam Curtis had been listening intently and called out from his cell, "Hey, sheriff?"

"What do you want, you scoundrel?" Beason snapped.

"Listen, I know you want to hang me, and I suppose you probably will, but O'Neil is right about you needing an extra gun. Now, remember that I didn't fire on them pilgrims."

"So, what's your point?"

"The men you're after, the one who looks like General Custer. Take a look at your wanted flyers a moment, look for Dallas Hamer."

Beason grumbled but obliged and rummaged through his office pigsty, pulling out documents splattered with food and coffee. He found what he was looking for and laid it on the desk, and then found another, and another . . . the sheriff began to pale. "Oh, my God. O'Neil, did you know about this?"

Sean pressed the heel of his hand to his forehead and sighed, "Did I know about your collection of wanted flyers? Yes, Beason, I sneak in here at night and do clerical work just for fun."

Beason glared at him. "You are sassing an officer of the law, and it has been duly noted. This man Hamer is a menace, I don't think there is a state he is not being sought in, wanted dead or alive and bounties on his head. Why was I not notified that he was in town?"

"Sheriff, if you'd tried to arrest him, you'd already be planted in the Mustang Flat cemetery. So, I'd wager it's just as well you didn't know," Curtis said.

"Well, thank you for informing me. I'm glad someone around here thinks it important to keep the law up-to-date."

"The reason I brought it up, is because you, O'Neil, and that old man, no offense to you, sir, are no match for the likes of Dallas Hamer. Me now, I'm a named gunfighter, they used to call me the Pistolero Padre. Still do, I guess. The only other man I'm aware of who could take on Hamer and stand a chance is O'Neil's foreman, Joe Dean. Either let me help or see if you can convince him to come along, but if you don't . . ."

"My foreman is not putting his ass on the line again, Curtis, and no one is asking since he'd feel obligated to agree. This isn't his battle," Sean O'Neil said sharply.

"Then convince the sheriff to let me help you. If I die, then that's the hand of God. If I live you can march me right back to this cell, on my word. I accept my fate either way."

The room fell silent for a spell as the three men contemplated the best path ahead. Liza, suffering and sweaty, rolled on her cot with a groan, and Silas leaned over to pat her back in a fatherly way.

"Do I have a say, Sheriff?" Booker asked.

Beason sat with his head in his hands and spoke without looking up. "I suppose so. What say you, Mr. Booker?"

"I'm old, and I was never much of a marksman even in my younger days. My intent is to kill the false prophet, but I have no chance of standing against this Hamer fellow. Curtis speaks the full truth, I believe, that he didn't fire upon us in the wagons. I heard him yelling for us to run for our lives, and I saw him draw no weapon against us. I reckon I've proven myself to be a poor judge of character by following the feverish prophecies of a conman, but I can trust what I saw with my own eyes and heard with my own ears, sure enough. Let this man come so that I have the chance to avenge Rebecca and all the others who were lost today. Please, Sheriff, it is an old man's last wish to see this thing through to the end."

Beason sighed deeply. "O'Neil, you want to weigh in?"

"I think we need all the help we can get. If the padre wants to be our fast gun, then you should allow it. I'll be personally responsible for what happens if he turns against us."

"All right." Beason stood and walked to the cell, unlocking it with only a slight hesitation. "I'm going on the record now to say this is a terrible idea, and I don't trust him, but I'll hold you accountable to supervise him, O'Neil."

Sean O'Neil nodded, and prayed that this was not to be one of the worst mistakes he'd ever made.

CHAPTER 58

The redheaded kid who'd gone for Dr. Grant was still hanging around, and Sean said, "What's your name, boy?"

"His name is Jack, and he can hear but he don't talk none. Mute, they call it, but he can write pretty well when he has something to say. One of Bill Campbell, the blacksmith's brood," Beason said. "Seven kids and all of them redheaded boys." He sighed. "Poor Mrs. Campbell. She has a time with them."

"Jack, can you ride a horse?" Sean said.

The boy nodded and whipped out a small notebook and stub of pencil, scribbled something and showed it to Sean.

"Course I can."

"Do you know where my ranch is?"

Jack nodded and grinned, the new note said:

"I know it. I like to go see Maria and Billy!"

"How on earth do you know . . . never mind, tell me later. I want you to take my horse, he's the paint at the hitching rail, and ride out to the Running-S," Sean said. "Tell my brother Johnny . . ."

Jack's face lit up and he scribbled "The champ?"

"Yes, the champ. Tell him I'll be gone for a few days

and not to worry." Sean waited for the note, which read, "O.K. Mr. O'Neil. I'm on it."

"Make sure you tell your parents where you're going," Sean said.

Jack scowled and scribbled, "They don't care."

"Tell them anyway, Jack," Beason said.

"Yes, sir," the boy wrote. Sean was impressed by how fast the kid's hand moved, sharp as a whip he thought, and wondered why it was a child so bright couldn't speak. Then looking out the window, he mouthed the word "WOW!" and wrote his longest note yet: "That's a right pretty paint. What's his name?"

Sean said, "Rocky. Be careful, by times he can be a handful."

"By times, so can Jack," Beason said.

The boy grinned and shot out the door to begin his adventure.

CHAPTER 59

Once the cussing and discussin' over the posse had been settled the men began their preparations with haste, wanting to lose no time in tracking down their quarry. Sheriff Bob Beason made arrangements with the Red Dust Inn to feed the pregnant girl in his absence and stopped to inquire about finding her a Mexican midwife. Sean O'Neil crossed the street to buy a box of .44-40 cartridges for his Winchester.

"Mrs. Lawson, you're in charge today, huh?" he said to the woman behind the counter. "Has Luke gone riding?"

Alice Lawson, pretty and pleasingly plump, looked at Sean with damp, worried eyes that signaled an alarm of some kind.

"Luke has taken to his bed," she said.

"I'm sorry to hear that. Is he sick?"

"You could say that, but he's sick at heart. Luke sold the ammunition for the Gatling gun to the men who murdered all those people at the wagon circle."

"Yes, I heard that. They told him . . ."

"That they were hunting jackrabbits," Alice said. A tear formed in her left eye and dropped on her tanned cheek, as alarming as a knife scar. "Who hunts rabbits with a Gatling

gun? By times, Luke can be so gullible, and now he
blames himself for the slaughter. He's lying in bed, staring
at the ceiling and he won't talk to me . . . as though he's
struck dumb."

"I'm sorry, Mrs. Lawson," Sean said. "Perhaps he made
a mistake, and we all make mistakes, but he's not responsible for what happened this morning. It took two men
to fire the gun, but Luke wasn't one of them." He placed
his hand over hers. "He'll get over it, Alice. Luke is a
strong man."

"Or he may never get over it," the woman said.

The bell above the door jangled and another customer
came in, loudly demanding six yards of calico cloth and
pearl buttons. Alice left to attend to the woman, and Sean
picked up his box of cartridges and placed some coins on
the counter.

He stepped to the door, grabbed the handle . . . and then
froze. Some call it the Irish gift, others the Celtic curse, the
icy feeling in the spine and the churning of the belly that
tells you all is not as it should be.

Lawson!

Sean turned, hurried past the two startled women at the
counter and into the back of the store where the Lawsons
had their living quarters. Luke Lawson's bedroom was to
the right of the hallway, its door slightly ajar. Alarm clam-
ored at Sean as he burst into the room.

Luke Lawson, his face gray as pine ash, sat up in a
brass bed, the muzzle of a .44 British Bulldog revolver
pressed against his right temple.

"Nooo!"

Sean's long strides quickly covered the distance between him and the bed and he dived on Lawson with such
force that the frame collapsed, slamming both men onto
the wood floor. It gave Sean the time he needed to reach

out, grab the revolver and wrench it from Lawson's hand. He rolled, sprang to his feet, and stood, looking down at the man's sprawled body. Lawson ripped at his hair with despair and let out an angry wail.

"Luke, if you'd pulled the trigger, you'd be stone-cold dead by now, this very instant," Sean said. "Alice would be a widow, your sons orphans, and the death of hope would blight this house forever. And where would you be . . . eaten up by eternal guilt, you'd watch from the special Hell reserved for cowards and suicides. Killing yourself is not an answer, it's a cry of despair."

"All those people," Lawson said. His eyes welled. "I'm as guilty of murder as the men who fired the big gun."

"You're guilty of being a gullible because your heart is big, and of being a trader trying to make a profit, that's all. Luke, your guilt is unearned, and that's the worst kind there is."

"Oh, my God!" Alice Lawson brushed past Sean and threw herself on her husband. "Luke, what did you try to do?" she said.

Being deliberately frank, Sean said, "Out of a false sense of guilt, he was going to shoot himself. I stopped him."

"Luke, don't leave us," Alice said. "Don't you dare leave us. We . . . I . . . need you."

"Alice . . . all those people . . . the children . . ." Lawson said.

"Oh, Luke, can't you see they were a star-crossed group who would've perished anyway," Alice said, cradling Lawson's head in her arm. "You did nothing wrong, Luke, except listen to violent men who lied to you."

"Listen to Alice, Luke," Sean said. "She's talking sense."

"What would have become of our boy, do you know what it does to a son when his father kills himself? What if he'd been the one to find you here?" Alice had shifted her tone slightly from compassion to anger as the reality of what her husband had tried to do settled into her mind.

"I'd be dead now. Oh my God, Alice. I'd be dead here on the floor right now," Luke said. "Sean, you saved my life."

"Just don't try it again," Sean said.

"I won't. Alice, I promise to you I won't. I'm so ashamed of myself, it was a cowardly act, please forgive me Alice." He kissed her hand. "Somehow, I'll find a way to shed the guilt and find forgiveness for what I done to those people and what I almost done to you."

"Forgive yourself first, Luke," Sean said. "You were led astray as many men before you and many will after. It hurts to make a mistake, but now you must learn to live with it. Any merchant in your position would've done the same."

The doorbell jangled, followed by Bob Beason's booming voice. "Is Sean O'Neil here?"

"I'll be right with you, sheriff," Sean said. "Just after I pick up the cartridges I scattered across the floor." He smiled at Alice. "The box burst when I jumped on your husband."

"I'll get them later," Alice said. "In the meantime, I'll find you a fresh box." She took Sean's hand. "I don't have the words . . . but thank you. I'll be forever in your debt."

"I'm glad I was here," Sean said. "I'm sorry about the bedframe, but I imagine you'll forgive me."

Beason's spurs chimed as he crossed the floor. "We're moving out, O'Neil, and I don't want to lose any more daylight," he said.

"I'll get your cartridges," Alice said. "God bless you, Sean O'Neil for what you did here today."

"I'm glad I was around," Sean said.

"Mr. O'Neil, how did you know?"

"Irish intuition, that was all. Maybe divine intervention. Luke is a good man, Alice. No matter how he feels about himself now, he will come to remember that again."

"Do you . . . do you think Luke would have pulled the trigger?"

"It was a split-second decision, and it only takes another split second to fire a gun," Sean said. "Yes, I think he would've shot himself. Alice, keep an eye on him. He isn't out of this struggle just yet."

"I will and thank you once again." She smiled. "You saved both our lives."

CHAPTER 60

Maria was soothing Billy in the cabin kitchen, dancing and singing with the little boy's head resting familiarly against her shoulder, nuzzling her neck with his soft face. In truth, little Billy was perfectly calm. It was his mother who needed comfort. The endless banging of gunfire had ceased, but the acrid smoke still came on the breeze, and Maria found herself weeping in fits and starts at the thought of the doomed pilgrims. Children are innocent, she thought, stroking Billy's back gently, and should never suffer cruelty born from the avarice of evil adults. "Don't worry." She pressed a gentle kiss upon Billy's forehead, and he giggled, making his fond mama smile. A sharp rap-tap-tap at the door, and Maria jumped with fright. She clutched Billy tighter and crept to the window. Seeing Sean's beautiful paint pony outside, she threw open the door but was surprised to see not Sean, but the little redheaded boy Jack Campbell who called now and then.

"Jack! What a pleasant surprise! How are you, little one?" Jack beamed with delight and scribbled quickly on his notepad, "Hi Miss Maria, Mr. Sean sent me with a message for the champ! Is he here? May I hold Billy?"

Jack was the youngest of seven brothers, and though he

could hear just fine he'd never spoken a word out loud despite everyone's best efforts. Occasionally he'd form a word with his mouth but no sound would come out. His parents had taken him to a specialist doctor in El Paso, and then to another one in Dallas, but they had no answers within the medical knowledge of the time and eventually told them they would have to hope his education and wits would carry him through life well and that someday maybe he would find a way to talk. He could write with an impressive speed and read voraciously, borrowing books from neighbors all around Mustang Flat and often memorizing them. Scary stories were his favorite, although he also absorbed history texts with great fascination and enjoyed reading about the exploits of gunfighters in dime novels.

Being only eight and mute, his older brothers never paid him much mind, and though he prayed every night, God hadn't yet brought him a baby brother. Then one day he'd been tasked with delivering a box of fencing nails to the Running-S for his father, and met Miss Maria and little Billy, the baby brother he'd always dreamed of. Maria was a kind lady, and she always had sweet treats on hand, or books to borrow, and most important, let him play with Billy. Even though he was just a baby and couldn't do much yet, they'd watch the sunshine or bees in the flower fields, and Jack was trying to teach him how to play pattycake. Maria, for her part, adored little Jack.

Johnny O'Neil was loudly thumping in his room and turning the air blue with his curses, furious about the murder that had taken place on his land and even madder that he was stuck here.

Maria looked toward the room, and handing Billy to Jack said, "The champ is a little out of sorts, Jack. Let me go settle him down and then I'll bring him out, okay?" Jack nodded with a grin.

"Knock-knock," Maria called softly at Johnny's door. "Johnny, little Jack is here to see you. Sean sent him."

The door swung open with a bang that made Billy start yowling. Johnny flushed, "Sorry, I didn't mean to." Maria waved off his apology and steered his giant frame toward Jack, who stood staring up at the Champ in awe, oblivious to the crying babe in his arms. Maria gently took Billy and went outside so Jack could deliver his message in peace.

Johnny knelt so Jack could look him in the eyes and extended a hand. "Hello, Jack, I've heard so much about you, pleased to meetcha. You have a message from my brother?" Jack nodded and after shaking Johnny's giant mitt with his own tiny paw, scribbled a note.

"Mr. Sean sent me to tell you that he's off to help the sheriff, and won't be back home for a few days." He paused and then added, "But to not worry."

Johnny rubbed his face with his palm, there was not a chance he'd not worry until Sean was back on the Running-S range safe and sound.

The boy made a face of consternation, clearly deciding if he should share some more news. Johnny stood up and said, "What's on your mind, son, go ahead and tell me."

Jack scribbled a lengthy note and tore it off, handing it over shyly. Johnny read it and his eyes went big as saucers.

"A baby! Maria, Maria, get back in here, there's a baby being born to that little girl I saved in town. Jack says the doctor left her alone with Mexican midwives, and I think you're needed!" Johnny quickly said a silent prayer for his brother's safe return and an easy birth for this baby soon to arrive, then hurried out to get the surrey ready for the trip.

Maria rushed inside and reappeared with Billy tied to

her back and a heavy case filled with medical supplies. She'd often found herself playing field nurse to the ranch hands and was well-equipped for all sorts of emergencies. "A baby?! Jack, did the doctor just leave the mother?"

Jack nodded and scribbled another note: "Doc is at the wagons, the sheriff said he'd send for someone else, but the doctor wouldn't stay."

Maria tossed her hands in the air "Mios Dios! These men are useless. Okay, let's hurry, you ride back with us in the surrey and the hands will tend to Rocky. Come along Jack, no time to spare. Oh! Hurry, go get some of Billy's blankets from my bedroom, Jack. It doesn't matter which ones."

Minutes later Johnny, Maria, Billy, and Jack, were loaded into the surrey with everything needed to bring a new life into the world. Johnny, who adored babies, was grinning a mile wide as he picked up the reins, setting the surrey at a fast pace toward town.

CHAPTER 61

Charlie Wade turned in the saddle, scowling. "What the heck's the matter?"

"My horse pulled up lame," Ben Gallagher said. He swung out of the saddle, ran his hand over his mount's left foreleg and then looked up at Wade. "He's done. The weight of the gold sacks was too much for him, I reckon."

"Darn it all, I didn't need this," Wade said. "Transfer your sacks to my mount."

The midday sun was bearing down on them, and sweat trickled into Wade's eyes, making them sting. He wiped his forehead with a filthy bandana and just made it worse. Aggravated, he said, "Hurry up, Ben, it's hotter than the devil's pepper patch out here."

"And what about me?" Gallagher said.

"I'll think of something," Wade said. "Now move those sacks."

After Wade's horse was fully loaded, Gallagher said, "Charlie, riding two up is bound to lame your mount, as well. We'll be stuck miles from El Paso without horses."

"That's not gonna happen," Wade said.

"We can lead him, I guess."

"That's not gonna happen either, Ben."

"Then what is gonna happen, Wade?"

Wade pulled his derringer from his pocket. "Sorry, but this is the parting of the ways, Ben."

The writing on the wall was plain to see, and Gallagher didn't try to argue the point. His hand dropped for his gun.

Even as he drew the Remington, Charlie Wade made a calculation . . . one in the belly to shock and slow Gallagher and the second to the center chest.

His *triggerometry* paid off.

Knowing he was already a dead man, Ben Gallagher took the gut shot badly. The .41 caliber round staggered him, pained him terribly, and slowed his draw. When his gun came up, Wade's second bullet hit, center chest as he'd planned. Gallagher's legs buckled and he thumbed off a wild shot that went nowhere. He fell on his back, the belly wound punishing him, but fast as a pouncing hawk, Wade was on him, the heel of his boot grinding the wrist of his gun hand into the dirt. Gallagher's fingers opened and Wade grabbed the man's Colt. He thumbed back the hammer, shoved the muzzle between Gallagher's eyes and pulled the trigger.

Lights out . . . Ben Gallagher was as dead as he was ever going to be.

At heart, Charlie Wade was a petty, avaricious man. Despite a fortune in gold slung on his horse, he studied Gallagher's fancy, engraved Colt, and shoved it in his waistband. The pistol was worth at least twenty dollars in El Paso, maybe more.

Now wary of the specter of lameness, Charlie Wade led his mount north through the heat of the day. He couldn't shake the feeling that someone was watching him, making the back of his neck tingle. Yet he had checked his back trail many times and saw nothing move on the wagon road, but that didn't surprise him. Who would come after him? The yokel lawman from Mustang Flat? Hardly likely. The farmers from the wagon circle? No, they were all dead or on the run. Only the men who'd brought down the wrath of that infernal Gatling gun concerned him, but he'd been watching over his shoulder for hours, and there was no one. It was just the leftover fear of the morning he supposed, or a lingering memory of chasing off that meddling peddler who'd had the nerve to question him early that morning. Convinced that he was free as a ship sailing for a safe harbor, Charlie Wade set his course for El Paso, picturing the rich and exciting new life that lay just ahead for him.

CHAPTER 62

Dallas Hamer saw the wiry little man shoot his traveling companion in the belly. It was a cruel play that he admired, and he'd smiled as he watched the proceedings through his brass naval telescope from several hundred yards away and off the trail. He knew that a nervous man was a deadly man, and the old conman constantly looked over his shoulder to check his back trail. Adept at stalking his quarry, Dallas Hamer had evaded detection even after catching up to the pair ten miles back. He planned to wait until after sundown when the old man was sleeping to make his move, grab the treasure, and then drift off to the east. Black John Hannah and his pet priest hadn't made an appearance yet, and Dallas wondered at what that meant. He let the false prophet gain some headway and then collapsed the telescope and heeled his black into an easy walk.

CHAPTER 63

At the same moment Ben Gallagher drew his last breath on the dusty trail to El Paso, new life was preparing to take its first back in Mustang Flat. Johnny O'Neil brought the surrey to a halt in front of the sheriff's office where a small crowd had gathered, drawn by the shrieking cries of young Liza Hart in the throes of her labors.

Maria rushed inside, clutching blankets to her chest and her medical bag at her side. "Get out of the way!" she cried, shoving the onlookers who were gossiping amongst each other. Inside the dim room, Liza lay drenched in sweat on a cot, teary eyed and wailing in anguish as her contractions came on. A handsome young man with dark skin and a heavy white bandage wrapped around his head knelt beside the girl and clutched her hand.

Maria looked around the office and saw only the man, who wore the trappings of a U.S. Cavalry soldier and no one else. "Where are the midwives?" she asked him, shouting to be heard over Liza's screams.

The soldier shook his head, "They wouldn't stay, said it was bad luck to deliver a baby in a jail. I got here at the same time they did and begged them to help but had no luck. They fogged it out of here in a hurry."

Maria scowled. "And who are you?"

"Lieutenant Dubois Brown, ma'am, 10th Cavalry. I came to see the sheriff, but I found this young lady instead."

Maria had left Billy with Johnny outside, but young Jack accompanied her and stood frozen at the proceedings. She snapped her fingers in front of his face. "Jack, listen up, go fetch me fresh water from the pump. Now, Jack!" The boy quickly grabbed the water pail and ran to his task.

"Liza, darling, I know it hurts. My name is Maria Perez. Young Mr. Campbell said you needed my help. How long have you been laboring?"

Liza writhed in pain as she spoke, "Thu—teh . . ." she tried before letting out a wild scream. Dubois answered for her, "She's been like this for three hours now, since I arrived."

Maria tsk'd and rummaged through her medical supplies. "Lieutenant, please look away while I check how far along she is now. It's bad enough to deliver a baby in a jailhouse, she doesn't need gawkers." She smiled kindly, realizing her tone had been sharp.

Dubois immediately turned his back, staring out the window at the gathered townsfolk, and Maria examined the girl. Then with a stiff smile she offered a comforting lie to the terrified girl. "Almost there, Liza! It's almost over, you're doing so well!" Although it was true that she was nearly ready to deliver, Maria had seen an alarming amount of blood and felt an icicle of dread run down her spine. Childbirth in the Wild West was often fatal for mothers and more often for the babies they delivered. Maria was no stranger to the pain and fright the girl was feeling and had no wish to add to it by sharing her own fears.

Dubois Brown studied Maria's face and knew something was amiss. "Ma'am?" he said, softly.

"Oh, please, call me Maria. This is no time for formalities."

Dubois smiled, revealing straight white teeth. His left eye was swollen shut and the bandage that wrapped most of his head was edged in blood, but despite the grisly injuries he exuded a warmth that set Maria at ease.

"All right, Maria," he said. "I know that it may be improper for a man who isn't a doctor to assist in delivering a baby, but I have three sisters all older than me and I was there while each of my nieces and nephews were born. I'd like it if you'd let me stay and help you, especially if . . ." He trailed off and shot a pointed glance at Liza, who was chalk white and drenched in sweat. "Well, if you think an extra hand may be needed."

Maria placed her tiny hand on the man's broad shoulder, "Thank you, sir, that is very kind. If you can just continue to comfort her, I think that'll be the best help of all. She's a widow and as you can see very young."

Jack Campbell burst through the door toting a pail of water, sloshing it over the floor in his rush. Probably the closest thing to a mop this filthy office has seen in years, Maria thought with a sniff. The morning rain had lifted and the air had become close and humid, the goggling crowd outside the open door making it all the worse. Maria was about to go chase them when she heard Johnny's booming voice approaching the doorway.

"You folks git! Good Christian folk acting like this should be ashamed of themselves." He peered around the doorframe and met eyes with Maria, shaking his head with exasperation. Little Billy cooed and giggled in his arms, doing his best to pull the derby hat off the big man's head. Maria smiled at her two favorite boys and her heart swelled with the knowledge that soon they'd officially be a happy little family for all eternity.

Liza shrieked, and gasped, "I think the baby is coming, what do I do?" Maria returned her attention to the girl and checked her progress, relieved to see the bleeding had eased and the baby was crowning. "You push, Liza! Squeeze Mr. Brown's hand as hard as you need to and push!"

Dubois Brown would later say that he never imagined such a tiny girl could break a grown man's fingers, but it was a small price to pay for witnessing the joy of welcoming new life into the world.

CHAPTER 64

The day had faded into evening as the posse of men following the trail left by Charlie Wade stumbled across the stiffened corpse of Ben Gallagher. The dead man stared into the softening blue and gray of twilight with a face twisted in anguish.

"Is he dead?" Sheriff Bob Beason said. "Sure looks it."

"As dead as a doornail in a parson's parlor," Sean O'Neil said. "It looks like it took three shots to kill him."

"Charlie Wade?" Beason said.

"Who else?" Sean dismounted and approached the gray horse who lazily munched on grass near the body, favoring its left foreleg as though pained by it. Sean gently ran his hand down the horse thigh to fetlock and winced at the heat coming off the poor beast.

"Inflamed real bad, poor old fellow. Seems Gallagher's horse went lame, and they shifted the gold to Wade's mount. Two men and one overloaded horse, you think Charlie would be agreeable to that? Must have gunned down Gallagher and made off with the treasure alone."

"Where is Hamer?" Beason said, looking to Adam Curtis.

"Somewhere ahead of us and behind Wade." He shrugged. "We'll find out soon enough."

282 William W. Johnstone and J.A. Johnstone

"How close are we?" Beason said.

"I'd say by now he's no more than a day ahead. If he's leading his horse, and judging by the tracks he is, we can make up time on him and press him close."

Sean stripped the lame horse of its saddle and bridle, then slapped its rump. "Time will heal you, old fellow, now move on. You don't want to hang around a dead man." Another slap and the horse moved away, then found a patch of brush and bunch grass where it dipped its head to graze. "Maybe we can pick him up on the way back," Sean said. "He's a good-lookin' gray."

Beason stood in his stirrups, shaded his eyes from the sun glare with a bladed hand, and said, "I see no dust."

"A lone man walking a horse won't raise dust," Sean said. "Besides, he's still too far ahead of us."

"But he'll see ours," Beason said.

"When that time comes it won't matter, we'll be as close as kissing cousins," Sean said.

"Close enough to grab him," Beason said.

"That's the plan," Sean said.

"Your plan, Mr. O'Neil," Silas Booker said. "It's not mine."

"What do you have in mind?" Sean said.

Silas slipped from his saddle and stretched his back with a wince. He took out the makings and rolled a cigarette, taking his time before answering. "I want to rid the world of Charlie Wade's shadow. You know what he did, Mr. O'Neil, all the innocent deaths that are of his causing. Am I right or wrong to think this way?"

"A man's got to choose what's right for him," Sean said.

"And right with the law," Beason said. "It's my duty to bring Charlie Wade to justice and see him hang."

"Then I won't argue with you, sheriff," Booker said.

"What happens, happens, and we'll soon see how it all ends."

"Yes, we will," Beason said. "And I'm the man who will write the ending."

Sean O'Neil studied Booker's face and thought that when the time came for writing an ending for Charlie Wade, Silas would be the one holding the pen.

Darkness was fast encroaching, and Silas was moving as though fiercely pained, but Sean had no desire to sleep beside a dead man. "Come on boys, let's carry on away from this vulture bait and bed down for a few hours. I could do for some coffee."

The four men set back on the trail and left Ben Gallagher to his roadside rest.

CHAPTER 65

That night Sean O'Neil and the others made camp beside the old wagon road, ate some jerky and shared a can of peaches. The mesquite fire cast a ruddy glow over the three men but beyond, under a moonless sky, the darkness was endless and kept its mysteries. Adam Curtis was quiet, lost in his own thoughts and watching the fire, wondering if this would be his last night on earth.

"Think we gained on them?" Sheriff Bob Beason said. "I set us a fast pace."

"Hard to say," Sean O'Neil said. "Come first light their tracks will tell the tale."

"If they're even headed this way," Beason said.

"If they're headed for El Paso, this is the way they'd go," Sean said.

"O'Neil, you ever been in El Paso?" Beason said.

"No, I haven't had that pleasure."

"I was a deputy there for six months, my first job as a lawman."

"When was that?" Sean said.

"Eighty-two, a year after the Southern Pacific, Texas and Pacific and the Atchison, Topeka and Santa Fe railroads arrived in town and helped turn the place into what the newspapers called The Six-shooter Capital."

"Pretty wild, huh?" Sean said.

"El Paso had become a boom town and boom towns are wild all right. If you discount hangings, I've only killed one man in a gunfight in my life, and that was in 3rd Street in El Paso."

Sean was surprised. "Beason, I never pegged you as a pistolero."

"I'm not. But on that day, I still recall it was a Sunday and the church bells were ringing, I was forced to draw down on a man."

"How did it happen?" Sean said.

"You sure you want to hear this?"

"I'm not ready for my blankets yet, so I have nothing better to do, and I love a good yarn. Tell your story. What say you, gentlemen?"

"I'm sure it's a violent tale, but I'm listening with bated breath," Silas said.

Beason hesitated as in the distance an owl asked its question of the night and then said, "How it come up . . ."

"That's a good start, go on," Sean said.

"There was a piece of coyote dung by the name of Willie Hands who was well known in El Paso as a liar and a thief. He was a suspect in the rape and death of a Mexican woman, but nothing could be proved, and he never stood trial. Then, about a month after Hands was released from jail, another woman was found dead in her home. Like in the previous case, she'd been raped and murdered, and suspicion again fell on Hands, but again there was no proof, and he walked free."

"Too bad," Sean said.

"Yeah, it was. Especially since I knew he was guilty as sin and so did my fellow peace officers, but suspecting and proving are two different things. For a few weeks Willie Hands strutted around El Paso as though he was the cock o' the walk. I even heard he boasted in a tavern that he'd fooled the lawmen twice and aimed to fool us again. It was about that time I made a pledge to myself that I'd do all in my power to bring him to justice. And then . . ."

"And then, what?" Sean prompted as Beason hesitated.

"And then I got a break. A man I knew, a street peddler by the name of Juan Ramirez, told me he saw Willie Hands hanging around the front of a Mexican church in 3rd Street. Now, his two previous victims were middle-aged, church-going women, and I headed for 3rd with the intention of foiling his plans. And sure enough he was there, watching the women come out of church."

"God bless them," Silas Booker said.

"He did that day, I guess, because mistakes began to be made," Beason said.

"What kind of mistakes?" Sean said.

"The kind that get you killed. And the first mistake Hands made was that he didn't run away when he saw me walk toward him. To this day I don't understand it."

Sean said, "He'd gotten away with murder twice and was a tad overconfident."

"Maybe, because when I ordered him to move on, he told me to go to blazes. He said he knew his rights and was entitled to stand at a church door if he felt like it. 'Then I'm arresting you for trespass and loitering with intent,'" I said.

"'You're arresting no one, star-strutter,' Hands said. 'Move on and be about your business.'"

Beason shook his head at the memory of it all. "'Hands, right now, you are my business,' I said. Well, he glared at me and made the second and final mistake of his miserable life. I didn't see it until the last minute, but he had a small

pistol in his waistband, and he proceeded to reach for it."
Beason looked across the campfire at Sean. "Now why did
he do a thing like that?"

"Maybe he was afraid if you arrested him, your loitering
charge would stick and give the law an excuse to resurrect
the murder charges," Sean said.

"Could be. But the next thing I knew my gun was in my
fist, and I triggered two shots into Hands' head, scattered
his blood and brains all over the front door of the Church
of Our Lady of Guadalupe." Beason paused and then said,
"I've never pulled a trigger on a man since."

"You did what you had to do," Sean said. "You're not
to blame." A wisp of a smile, then, "You're the second
man I've said that to today. But to set your mind at rest, I
reckon we can bring in Charlie Wade without shooting."

Firelight flickering amber on his face, Silas Booker
stared at Sean O'Neil as though he was a madman.

CHAPTER 66

A primal drumbeat seeped into Charlie Wade's consciousness, and he untangled himself from the Mexican blanket he'd fallen asleep in beside the fire.

He stood slowly, cautious of the pounding drums that now filled the prairie around him like the heartbeat of a great beast. Flickering fires in the distance illuminated the gray shapes of many people swaying in a great circle, and Charlie's belly filled with despair. Something terrible was happening, and though he fought to stay still he found himself dropping the blanket and approaching the shadowy dancers. As he neared the circle, he saw that the fires came from the canvas of many wagons alight, and flames rose unnaturally high into a black sky that held no starshine.

"No," he said aloud, "No, I won't go," yet his feet carried him forward. "I can't bear to look!" he bellowed, but he could neither force his eyes shut or turn away. Finally, he came to rest at the edge of the decimated wagon circle and saw that the revelers held blood red ribbons that streamed from a pike with a rotting head atop it, a macabre maypole sent from Hades. The stench of decaying flesh and acrid smoke assaulted his nostrils, and his eyes watered from fear. All the while the throbbing drums grew louder, yet he saw no source of the sound. Charlie strained his eyes but couldn't make out the face of the unfortunate soul who had become the maypole's crown. He became aware of a presence to his right, and without turning asked, "Who . . . who is it? Whose head is that?" A rasping voice filled with gravel replied, "Don't you know, Micah?" Charlie turned and stared into the filmy dead eyes of Jim Petite.

"No, I killed you, I killed you dead!" Charlie cried.

Petite grinned and revealed nothing but a clotted, black hole that stood stark against the waxy pallor of his skin. "You sure did, Micah, you killed us all."

He gestured toward the circle where the demented dance had stopped. Every figure now turned to face Charlie, and even the drumming did little to blot out the sound of slopping flesh and creaking tendons. Men, women, and children who he had once called rubes and pumpkin rollers now terrified him to the very core of his being. Some were burned black, others stared from empty eye sockets, and all were putrefying as he watched. "My, my name isn't Micah, stop calling me that," Charlie stammered, desperate to run but frozen in place.

"You told me to always call you Micah in the circle, remember Charlie?" said a voice to his left. Ben Gallagher placed a putrid hand on Charlie's shoulder and leaned to whisper in his ear with fetid breath. "Do you recognize the head now, Micah?" Fat, writhing maggots fell onto Charlie's shoulder and he wanted to scream but couldn't open his mouth. Gallagher chuckled, "Why, Charlie, can't you see? That's you!"

As the risen dead began to close in on him, Charlie screamed, and screamed, and . . . He woke up and bolted upright, brushing at his shoulders, and drenched in sweat that the cool night air turned to ice on his skin. Charlie looked around for the drumming and quickly realized it was the sound of his own heart, his pulse pounding in his ears. The trembling man struggled with shaking hands to light a rolled cigarette and inhaled with short, gasping breaths. He clutched his Derringer tightly with his right hand and smoked with his left, frantically scanning the dark night around him. When he'd calmed his breathing, he retrieved a bottle of rum from his bag and drank deeply. The fire was dying out, and Charlie built it up, suddenly very afraid of the dark. Then, for the very first time in his adult life, Charlie Wade sat and wept.

CHAPTER 67

Bob Beason had awoken just before the dawn, convinced he heard a man's terrified scream echoing through the chilled night air. He listened but heard only the soft snores of Sean and Silas and the quiet whickering of the horses. Beason built a fire up and set the coffee onto a boil, eager to get the day started and his quarry captured. After a moment, he realized that Adam Curtis was missing, and Beason immediately thought the worst, but then the gunslinger returned to the fireside and gave the sheriff a curt nod, which was met with a scowl. Soon the first pink and orange rays of sunshine peeked out across the rocky terrain, and the birds began their morning songs. Silas groaned as he pulled up to sit near the fire and poured himself a cup, taking out his tobacco and lighting his first cigarette of the day. Sean staggered a decent distance away to relieve himself and then retrieved his own coffee. The men sat in silence, sharing two cans of peaches and a dozen crumbly biscuits sent with them courtesy of the Red Dust Inn.

Silas spoke first, his voice gravelly and pained, "Could a'sworn I heard something last night. Screaming, wild screaming like a man being skinned by Apaches. Gave me shivers but then it just . . . stopped."

Sean sat to attention, "I heard it, too! Boogered me something fierce, like something out of a nightmare. I didn't wake anyone because it stopped so suddenly, I thought I dreamt it."

Adam chimed in, "Navajo say that there are creatures in the night called skin walkers. Powerful shamans who've betrayed their tribe and turned evil . . . shapeshifters. That was what it sounded like to me, a man who'd sold his soul and was no longer human."

Bob Beason felt a chill run up his spine. "Just nightmares and nonsense, that's all it is. You lot are too old to get spooked by a bogeyman. Besides, no need to worry when the law is with you." He tapped the star pinned to his vest. Adam shared a look and sly smile with Sean.

"I reckon you're right, Sheriff. You're all the protection we need out here," Silas said.

"Exactly right, Mr. Booker," Beason said.

Sean O'Neil tried to choke down a chuckle but failed, and soon Silas and Adam were laughing, too. Bob Beason was not amused.

CHAPTER 68

It was a long walk to El Paso, and Charlie Wade felt every step of it. His heavily loaded horse set a slow pace, and several times Charlie led his sweating mount off the trail into patches of creosote, tarbrush, and acacia in search of meagre shade.

It was during one of those forays he discovered a crater filled with the blackened remains of what looked to be a stage, judging by blackened wheel rims and other debris. Wade had no idea what had happened to the coach, nor did he care, but if there were remains of a stage, there might also be the remains of people . . . and people carry money and valuables. It was worth a short search. Perhaps he could add a few more dollars to his wealth.

While his horse grazed on a patch of sparse bluegrass, Wade found a charred spar and began to poke around in the ashes. His efforts were rewarded almost immediately when he uncovered a scorched pocket watch that looked to be gold and then a man's expensive signet ring. A few minutes of further searching yielded nothing of value, but Wade was mighty pleased. It seemed that money just flew into his hands like a golden goose, and he realized then that his future was destined to be paved with gold . . . and French champagne and glossy whores.

He straightened, turned, and in that instant his bright window to the future shattered and crashed around his feet in countless shards.

Charlie Wade recognized the grim men facing him . . . Bob Beason, the sheriff and pompous idiot . . . Sean O'Neil, a drover . . . the handsome young gunslinger who had been part of both the attacks on the wagon circle . . . what was his name? Curt or something like that he thought . . . and Silas Booker, hollow eyed and cadaverous, one of the faithful . . .

One of the faithful. Darn it all, there was hope yet.

"What can I do for you boys?" Wade said.

"You can come along with us, face murder charges in Mustang Flat, and suffer the full penalty of the law," Beason said. "Let your guns drop to the ground."

"I murdered no one," Wade said.

"Ben Gallagher was no one?" Sean O'Neil said.

"It was self-defense, cowboy. He tried to kill me and rob"—he looked at Booker—"the Lord's gold."

"You are the one who stole the gold," Booker said. "You and your confederate." Silas had leveled his Greener at Wade's gut, and the conman watched with eagle-eyed awareness, but the old man's gnarled hands looked incapable of pulling the trigger—at least not with any speed.

"No, I was carrying it to a secure place I know of near El Paso," Wade said. "I planned to bring the treasure back to Mustang Flat to be distributed among the survivors of the terrible massacre. The Lord revealed the very morning of the attack that the Gatling gun men were planning to rob us, and it was upon me to keep the Lord's treasure safe. Silas, you know my heart is good."

"You are Micah," Booker said. "And the world is not burning."

"A small miscalculation, Silas. But the day of the terrible fires from heaven is close." Wade's hand slid into his pants pocket. "Silas, join me in saving the Lord's treasure. Put your shotgun to good use and destroy our enemies." He pointed with his left hand. "The Lord sent me a vision as I slept, and He warned me that these men you travel with are our mortal foes."

"Where will we take the fortune?" Silas Booker said.

"El Paso first, my friend. Perhaps Mustang Flat again after a time, if the Lord smites these men and they are no longer a threat. From there we can carry it back to Kansas and I will wait for the Lord to send me a vision. I suspect in due time He will tell me to organize another wagon train. He will make his wishes clear because I am The Chosen Prophet Micah and his voice here on earth."

Like a man in a trance, Booker muttered, "You are Micah, the prophet."

"Yes, Silas, I am. Now kill our enemies."

Sean O'Neil's hand dropped to his gun.

"But you are Micah the false prophet," Booker said. "The blood of men, women, and children who believed in you stains your hands."

"Silas!" A yelp of desperation. "I am the prophet. Do as I tell you."

"I know exactly who you are," Silas said and, then in a whisper so faint only Adam Curtis who stood nearest caught his words, added, "Judas."

"Yes, Silas, of course you know who I am! I am the prophet of God," Wade said, smiling.

The shotgun blast came at the same time as Silas Booker's

roaring declaration in a voice that boomed like thunder. "JUDAS! You are Judas Iscariot and have betrayed all that is sacred for pieces of coin!"

The effect of two barrels of buckshot on Wade's small, slim body was devastating. His rib cage was almost blown wide open, and a scarlet mist of blood and bone fanned above his head. He struggled to speak and managed, "But . . . but I'm rich . . ."

"No, Charlie, you're dying," Silas said.

Wade bared his teeth in a snarl. "You . . . you . . . son of a . . ."

"Bitch," Bob Beason said, robbing Wade of the last word he ever planned to say. The sheriff moved his gaze from Wade's mangled body to Booker, who had sunk to the ground and sat shaking and exhausted, the Greener cast aside and the man massaging his hands together with a wince.

"This could be a case of murder," Beason said.

"This was a case of justice," Adam Curtis said.

"Murder is hard to prove without a body," Sean said.

"We could take him back to Mustang Flat," Beason said.

"What's left of him," Sean said. "He'll stink."

"Well, maybe it's not such a good idea," the sheriff said.

"He's a coyote," Sean said, looking without sympathy at Wade's contorted face. "His kin will look after him." Irritated, O'Neil couldn't bite his tongue, "And honestly, Beason, even if he'd died in the middle of Mustang Flat, do you really think it would be right to hang a grieving old father for the sake of a vile conman with blood on his hands? I could have had Charlie Wade strung up just for stealing and butchering my cow. He got what he deserved. Leave it at that."

Beason looked at Sean sheepishly, and after a pause

changed the subject. "Well, I guess now we can split the gold among the horses and take it back to town," Beason said.

"I'm sure there will be survivors waiting for us in Mustang Flat," Booker said. "They will help me get the money back to Kansas."

"I'm leaving all that up to you, Booker," the sheriff said. "Of course, I'll have to investigate the matter, make sure everything is on the square."

"It will be," Booker said. "But I'll welcome your investigation, sheriff. And I appreciate you speaking on my behalf, Sean, but I would also welcome it if you three would quit referring to me as 'old,' I don't need a reminder." Much needed laughter broke some of the tension, and Silas grinned.

Beason said, "Say, O'Neil, let's take a minute and I'll show you what's left of the Tucker and Scott stage I found. It's over here a ways."

"Isn't there a reward for finding that stage?" Sean said.

"Yes, but I was told that it was only a reward for the safe return of the stage and its passengers, not ashes and bones. Jim Tucker and Dave Scott are darned crooks."

Sean and Beason walked through brush to the crater. "There it is," the sheriff said. "What's left of it."

Sean was stunned. "What happened?"

"Something fell from the sky and landed on it," Beason said. "At least, that's the most likely story."

Sean said, "One time I saw the body of a puncher who got struck by lightning, but he looked nothing like this."

"I think the stage was hit by a falling star," Beason said. "The coach destroyed and everybody on it killed in an instant."

"What kind of luck do you need to have to get hit by a falling star?" Sean said.

"The bad kind," Beason said. "Seen enough?"

"More than enough," Sean said. "You know when I'm out on the range I see falling stars all the time."

"Makes a man think, don't it?" Beason said.

"It surely does," Sean said, glancing up at the sky.

CHAPTER 69

O'Neil and Beason were making their way back from the site of the doomed stage, eager to start loading up the gold. Sean had broken the happy news of his brother's upcoming marriage and the two men were cheerfully discussing the upcoming wedding plans—now to include Beason's fiddling talent—when they stopped dead in their tracks. A tall, beautifully dressed man who bore a striking resemblance to General Custer stood ten feet away from Adam Curtis, who'd positioned himself protectively in front of the still seated Silas.

"That Hamer?" Beason whispered.

"Must be," Sean said.

If the outlaw had seen their approach, he hadn't acknowledged it, and though Adam was facing them he was careful to not glance in their direction and give them away. Slowly and quietly, Sean pressed the sheriff back and to the right where the path to the wagon had curved behind a low acacia tree that provided meagre camouflage.

"Well, if it isn't my old friend the priest. Save any souls today, father, or you only in the business of sending them to hell?" Dallas said, pointing to the sprawled corpse of Charlie Wade with his chin. Adam Curtis made no reply and began to calm his breathing, readying himself for the impending showdown. He'd seen Beason and O'Neil inch back and silently willed them to stay there and not decide to enter the fray.

"I appreciate you killing him for me, Adam. That was true blue of you. But now I need another favor before you and that old man die, tell me where I can find Black John?"

"He's dead," Curtis replied, voice emotionless.

"You plug him?"

"Nope. Joe Dean did, about half an hour after you fled the scene yesterday morning."

Dallas barked out a laugh, "Joe Dean! How did the legendary Mr. Dean end up in the middle of all of this, hunting John I suppose."

"Nope, seems he gave up drawfighting to become a puncher."

"Well, I'll be. Unfortunately for him, Black John Hannah was a prize I've been waiting on for quite a while. Sometimes a man must savor the hunt to make it worthwhile. Dean'll have to repay me for that and won't be punching cows much longer."

"My God, Dallas, do you ever shut up," Adam Curtis said. "We both know how this is gonna end. Playing the madman may amuse yourself but it's nothing but tiresome and boring for me." Curtis was aiming to provoke the draw only because he'd caught movement out of the corner of his eye. Behind him, Silas was slowly crawling his fingers towards the Greener and about to make a deadly mistake. Sean noticed the old farmer's movement, too, and dropped his hand to his gun, and then all hell broke loose.

CHAPTER 70

Dallas Hamer's eyes flashed with rage and his hand became a white blur of movement as he cleared leather. Silas Booker grabbed the Greener and rolled onto his belly in one smooth movement that belied his age, while Sean O'Neil drew his Colt. Bob Beason saw the imminent gunfight and likelihood for crossfire and bellowed, "Nooo!" while charging into the open, waving his hands above his head.

But the gunfight was over before the sound passed his lips. One man was faster than all the rest that day. Before Sean O'Neil's Colt cleared leather or Silas brought his Greener to bear, a crimson blossom opened in the center of Dallas Hamer's forehead at the same time as a trio of matching blooms appeared over the gunslinger's heart. As Adam Curtis watched the life drain from his adversary's face, he saw the gates of Hell reflected in the man's blue eyes. A violent howling wind whirled up dust devils in the road as Dallas hit the ground, and he died staring into nothing, his face a frozen mask of abject terror. The wind stopped fast as it had begun, and silence fell across the trail once more.

CHAPTER 71

Sheriff Bob Beason returned to Mustang Flat to find a squalling, blanket-wrapped newborn in a box on his office floor, a wounded buffalo soldier sprawled out on the cell bunk napping, and a crowd of loud women fussing over the little pregnant girl who he reckoned wasn't pregnant anymore but remained on his cot reveling in the attention like a queen on a litter. After standing, stunned, for long moments, he flopped into his chair and muttered, "Oh my God."

Maria Perez fussed with the baby and smiled. "Last night Liza gave birth to a beautiful little girl," Maria said. "Isn't that wonderful?"

His face like thunder, Beason hollered at the women to stop clucking like hens and quiet down and then said, "Why is there a solider in my jail cell?"

"Oh, he helped deliver the baby, isn't that so kind of him?" Maria said, beaming.

"What . . . O'Neil, are you listening to this?"

Sean O'Neil nodded, "Every word." He shook his head. "I swear girl babies yell louder than boys."

"I'm not talking about babies. I'm asking why there is a solider of the United States army in my cell and why the jailhouse is being treated like a manger in Bethlehem. It has been a long couple of days O'Neil, and I'm not one to be trifled with."

"No indeed, sheriff," Sean said. Then to Maria, "How did the buffalo soldier come to be the deliverer of babies in Mustang Flat?"

"What, who? Oh, his name is Dubois Brown, and he's a Lieutenant with the 10th Cavalry. He was a perfect gentleman, and I told him he could stay here until the sheriff returned."

"But why is he here, Maria? And all bandaged up, at that." Sean smiled, he was on to Maria and knew she was being obtuse about the story purely to irritate Beason.

"He was here when I arrived to help Liza, since a certain doctor and sheriff decided to abandon her in her hour of need."

Beason was confused and held his face in his hands. When he reappeared, he said, "I sent midwives for the girl. Did they disobey the law?"

Maria said, "They did, but it all worked out in the end I suppose. Dr. Grant looked over her and the baby and they'll be just fine. He bandaged Mr. Brown's hand, too."

"I'll just have to wake him up," Beason said. "This is getting me nowhere. O'Neil, help me get the crowd out of here before I lose my mind."

Sean politely greeted Liza and offered her congratulations and then asked the ladies to come back and visit another time. "I'm sorry, we have some official business to tend to, and it's getting a bit crowded in here." The handsome young rancher smiled and winked at the eldest member of the group, who blushed. After hugs and kisses were given to the new mother, the giggling and tittering women went off on their way. "He's so handsome, and

304 William W. Johnstone and J.A. Johnstone

single you know . . ." Sean heard as the last of them trailed out the door.

"I wish you wouldn't wake him, he has a terrible head injury, and Dr. Grant said he really must rest." Maria said curtly.

"Darn it, woman, I'm not running an inn."

"Oh, don't you dare raise your voice at me, sheriff. While you were off doing God knows what, I've been here holding down the fort and making sure that no one got up to trouble in your office," Maria said.

"Doing God knows what?" Beason sputtered, "I— we've—O'Neil, help me with this woman!"

"Nope," Sean said, "You got yourself into this mess, Beason. You're on your own."

Adam Curtis made his way into the office, having dropped Silas Booker off at the Red Dust Inn and then stopping by the surgery to ask Dr. Grant if he'd head over to the inn and give the old man a look over. When he entered the room, he took in Sean grinning like a 'possum, Beason red faced and sputtering, and a beautiful Mexican woman glaring at the sheriff like she was on the verge of murder.

"What did I miss?"

CHAPTER 72

Adam shocked Beason and Sean by breaking into a wide smile and rushing to fuss over the newborn. Then he took the rosary from his pocket and said prayers for the baby and her mother. "What have you named her?" he asked, still smiling. Watching the slick, handsome gunfighter turning goofy over a newborn baby, Sean O'Neil realized that his judgment of the man had likely been correct. Bad choices don't always create an evil man, just as he'd told Luke Lawson.

"Liza wants to call her Alma, but I guess we'll have to talk about that," Maria said.

Liza turned the babe in her arms toward the three tall men crowding into the office and said, "Do you want to see her?"

"Sure thing," Sean said. And then a small lie. "I like babies." The men made the appropriate fuss and then Beason pulled Sean aside.

"O'Neil, if you're through kissing babies, we have to talk about Curtis," he said, quietly.

"What about him?" Sean said.

"You're still deputized. Once we get the buffalo soldier

out of my cell, we have to break it to Curtis that he'll be locked up again."

Sean sat in the chair opposite the sheriff and said, "A feller who made a grave mistake . . . and then saved our hides, kept his promise to return with us, tended to an old man like he was his own father . . . kisses babies . . . and you want to lock him up?"

"You're slick with a gun yourself, O'Neil," Beason said. "If he hadn't been there, I've no doubt that the outcome would have been the same."

"If you truly believe that I'm in the same class of gunmen as Adam Curtis, or Dallas Hamer, you're a fool." He jabbed his finger on the desk to emphasize his point and said, "Let. It. Go."

"The law demands justice!" Beason cried.

"What are you two over here whispering about?" Adam Curtis asked, having a feeling he knew.

"The sheriff thinks you should be brought in front of the court," Sean said.

"And what do you think, O'Neil."

"I think that you'll suffer enough from the role you played in the massacre, and that much like Luke Lawson selling the ammunition for the big gun, you made poor choices but didn't pull the trigger."

"I'll be atoning for helping to bring that Gatling gun out there for the rest of my life. Joe Dean started fresh with you, O'Neil, and I could make a new start, as well. The seminary is not closed to me forever, even though I drifted from God for a spell."

Before the conversation could continue, Dubois Brown staggered out of the cell with a yawn and caught the men's attention.

Beason stood and looked the man up and down with a

frown, "Some solider you are, there's been enough noise in here to wake the dead for gone three-quarter of an hour now. I'm Sheriff Bob Beason and this is my jailhouse, and my town." Stunned by the rude tone of the very man he'd come to see, Dubois offered a sheepish smile and squinted against the light to take a better look at the portly, florid-faced man who sported a golden star pinned to a leather vest. Dubois took in the other two men at the desk and thought that they looked exhausted and wrung out. He smiled and offered them an acknowledging nod, which he immediately regretted as it made his head ring with fresh pain.

The bandages around his head had been freshened by Dr. Grant, but blood was once again seeping around the edge nearest the eye that was swollen shut. The ring and pinky finger of his right hand now sported a splinted bandage, too, courtesy of Liza Hart.

"Forgive me, Sheriff. I'm afraid I traveled without rest for quite a distance to get here, and all with this bump on my noggin. The doctor here in town offered me something for the pain—made worse when this young mother broke my hand." He turned to Liza and grinned, and the girl flushed bright pink. "I guess the medicine knocked me out good."

"I'm still so very sorry about it, Mr. Brown, I didn't mean to." Liza said.

He laughed, "It's quite all right, ma'am. I've been through worse. Which brings me to the reason I'm here. Sheriff, I am Lieutenant Dubois Brown, and I was responsible for transferring an expensive piece of ordinance between Fort Concho and Fort Bliss. My men and I were ambushed, and I was the only survivor. I have reason to believe that the man brought the stolen army property to this town. He left quite a trail to follow."

Beason plopped back down in his chair, already knowing the answer before he asked, "What was the ordinance, Mr. Brown?"

"A Gatling gun."

CHAPTER 73

Dubois Brown filled the other men in on how the Gatling had been stolen, and they shared what had resulted from the theft, embellishments to both stories being thrown in with great enthusiasm from all.

Liza had fallen asleep, and Maria tried to interest the baby in milk from a pap boat, making little cooing noises.

The baby drank milk and, with the stories told, a silence fell on the office. "Sheriff," Sean said, "the army will get their gun back, and the men who committed the atrocity are dead. Is the matter settled because I'd like to end my deputization and go home. I am bone tired, and I'm sure everyone else is, too."

"They aren't all dead. I'm looking at one of them right now," Beason said.

"He's a religious man at heart, and he's now seeking God's forgiveness for a terrible crime. He has earned my forgiveness, and I imagine Silas Booker feels the same. Please, I'm asking you not as your deputy but as your friend to let this matter drop."

"I can't let the law drop," Beason said.

"Then find another deputy. I have no interest in helping you prosecute Adam Curtis."

"O'Neil, he drove the wagon."

"Yes, he did, and he'll spend the rest of his life atoning for it."

"Mr. Brown, what do you say?" Beason said.

Dubois moved to Beason's side. "It sounds like Mr. Curtis avenged my dead, and yours got their justice with the death of Charlie Wade and that John Hannah fella. I've no quarrel with this man, and I say neither do you."

"He's near as guilty as Wade, but in a different way," Beason said.

Brown said, "And now he'll live with it. Sheriff, have you ever heard the verse John 8:7, about casting the first stone. Jesus Christ said, 'He that is without sin among you, let him first cast a stone.' Can you honestly say that you can cast stones, because I cannot."

"So because of my own errors, the law is just kicked aside," Beason said.

"No, like a great tower of rock, the law remains, sheriff," Adam Curtis said. "You know, I could have run off a dozen times, and I haven't. That ought to count for something."

"Yes, it does." Sean said. "But we're talking in circles here. You're outnumbered Beason, and I wish that you'd give up."

Beason sighed and scrubbed his face with his hand. "Fine. But mark down my words, Mr. Curtis, if I ever catch you stepping outside the lines of the law again, I'll pull the lever to hang you myself."

"I don't think you can say fairer than that, Sheriff," Curtis replied.

The office door opened, and Johnny O'Neil stepped inside. With much backslapping, he and Sean embraced and then Sean answered the question his brother was about to ask.

"Charlie Wade is dead," he said. "The men who fired the Gatling are dead, too." He nodded to the piled-up money sacks in a corner of the room and added, "We recovered the treasure."

"And I'm going to make sure Liza gets her fair share of it," Maria said.

Bob Beason smiled. "And she will. I've left Silas Booker in charge of that and he is a fine man, young lady. You have no worries on that score."

"And there are other survivors," Johnny O'Neil said. "The Red Dust Inn is sheltering about a dozen people and the proprietor says he's willing to accept a dozen more if they show up."

"Booker said he'd take the survivors back to Kansas if they want to go," Sean O'Neil said. "Perhaps they can buy back their farms and put this terrible time behind them."

"I sure hope so," Beason said.

Johnny clasped his brother in another bearhug. "I was worried sick about you."

"I'll tell you all about it when we get back to the ranch," Sean said. "Why are you here?"

"To pick up Maria and the baby in the surrey," Johnny said. "Maria asked John Baxter to stop by the house before he went looking for his flat wagon." He looked at Beason. "Baxter is outside, sheriff. He wants to talk to you. I would guess it's about the Gatling gun since I helped him load it onto the back of his wagon."

Beason was shocked. "I don't want the Gatling gun."

"Well, the army will want it back," Dubois Brown said with a yawn. "But it'll take some paperwork on your end to have them come collect it, I imagine. And on mine."

Beason rose to his feet, pushed back his chair, and said, "Darn it, it seems there's always a problem."

"Goes with the job, sheriff," Johnny said.

"True champ, very true, but why are there so many of them?" Beason said.

Johnny grinned. "Because this is the Wild West, old fellow."

Beason sighed and left, leaving Sean in a state of some distress. "Johnny, you said you came here to pick up Maria and the baby."

"And Liza," Maria said.

As though he hadn't heard, Sean said, "After you pick them up, where do you plan to drop them off?"

Again, Maria spoke up. "At the Running-S, of course. We can't leave Liza and her baby here in a jailhouse, and she has nowhere else to go."

"You mean"—Sean swallowed hard—"we're going to have not one, but two squalling babies under my roof."

"Not for long, Sean," Maria said. "Just until Liza gets settled."

"Johnny, wake me up," Sean said. "I think I'm in the middle of a bad dream."

Johnny smiled. "Brother, you'll get used to it. You might even come to like babies."

"Like babies? Oh, my God." Sean held his head in his hands and groaned.

CHAPTER 74

"What do you want to do with it, sheriff?" John Baxter said.

"How did you get it up there?" Beason said, a question answering a question.

"Johnny O'Neil helped me. Big feller. Strong as an ox. I swear he could tie a bowknot in an iron horseshoe."

"I don't want the gun," Beason said.

"You'd only be storing it until the army comes for it. I see you have a shed back there."

"Evidence. It's full of evidence."

Baxter jerked a thumb over his shoulder. "And this ain't evidence?"

"John, store it in your barn," Beason said.

"I don't want it. I don't need any more bad luck."

Beason turned to Dubois Brown, "When will the army come for it?"

"I'll send the report, but they will come when they feel like it, and it better be here, or you could be charged with theft of army property. That's ten years in the pen."

Beason's voice rose in a whine. "Why does this stuff always happen to me?"

"Because you're the law, and the law takes care of these

things. Now where do you want to store the Gatling? I'll need to mark down the exact location in my reports."

Beason thought about it, shrugged, and said, "In the shed, I guess. We'll cover it up."

"Ask Johnny O'Neil to lend you a hand, sheriff. No point in giving yourself a hernia," Baxter said.

CHAPTER 75

Three weeks before the wedding, Sean O'Neil and his brother Johnny sat in rockers on the front porch of the Running-S ranch cabin and watched the sun go down.

"Right purty, ain't it?" Sean said.

"It sure is," Johnny said, his words tangled in a cloud of cigar smoke.

The sky spread a cloak of red over the declining sun, and the air smelled fresh, the dust of the day long settled. Sean's Hereford bull grazed close, marking out the limits of its territory, and he raised his head every now and then to glare at the humans on the porch as though they'd no right to be there.

Johnny said, "I still can't believe Bob Beason had the wagons towed away. How did he organize that?"

"Beats me. I didn't think he had the smarts," Sean said.

"Or the inclination. He has no love for you, brother."

"There must've been money in it. The wagons can be repaired and sold."

"I think that's probably the case. By rights, they were yours since they were on your range."

"I wanted nothing more to do with them. Let Beason make a profit. He probably deserves it."

"Probably," Johnny said.

"Ye gods, what one is that?" Sean said, shaking his head.

"That's Liza's. The kid's got a pair of lungs on her."

"Maria said Liza is using Silas Booker's money to build a house in Mustang Flat," Sean said. "Tell me I heard right."

"Yeah, it's true," Johnny said. "She set herself up as an apprentice seamstress with Alice Wings."

"Thank God for that," Sean said.

"Oh, I don't know, having babies in the house livens things up, don't you think?"

"No, I don't think," Sean said. "When they were both caterwauling last night, I wrote the same entry in a ledger three times."

Johnny laughed, "Well, you'll have a break from us while Maria and I are on our honeymoon in Boston. Then it won't be long until our cabin is built, I'm glad I held off on selling the tavern until I heard the right price because the man who bought it is giving me a bit more than it's worth. Maria has expensive tastes, as Sol Cohen can tell you."

Johnny shook his head and smiled, then his eyes searched into the distance, and he said, "Rider coming."

"I know," Sean said. "Let him come."

The visitor was a tall, lean man with a long, taut face bisected by heavy eyebrows and a trimmed mustache. His eyes were hazel, his hair black, and he dressed like a somewhat seedy preacher. If he carried a gun, it was hidden, but he did carry a Bible with a gold stamped cross on the cover.

"Good evening, my friends," he said, leaning forward on his scrawny black horse.

"Right back at ya," Sean said. "What can I do for you, stranger?"

"No, ask what I can do for you."

"All right," Sean said amicably. "What can you do for me?"

"I bring good tidings."

"Then lay them on me," Sean said. "I could use some."

"The end of all things is nigh, and I am here to save your immortal souls," the man said.

Sean smiled. "How do you aim to do that?"

"With a passport." He reached into his coat and produced a long, white envelope. "Within this envelope is a passport to paradise. When the Lord comes to destroy the earth, and it will happen within a twelve-month, you will show him this passport and it will save your life. Do not scoff, gentlemen. What I tell you is the truth."

"Where did you get the passports, preacher?" Johnny said.

"From the Lord himself. I am sworn not to disclose how."

"And how much is God charging for his passports?" Sean said.

"Nothing, not a penny. But he told me I should make a small charge to cover my expenses."

"How much?" Johnny said.

"Fifty dollars to pay my expenses and help me continue with my great missionary work."

"What are you called?" Sean said.

"Malachi is my name."

Sean and Johnny exchanged a glance, then Sean said, "Johnny, do you want to shoot Malachi or will I?"

The man's face showed his alarm. "No guns!"

"Johnny, get the shotgun," Sean said.

Johnny stood and revealed his giant frame, "All right,

but I kinda want to shoot him so how about a coin toss to decide?"

Malachi didn't hang around. He turned his scarecrow horse and hightailed it, Sean and Johnny's laughter following him.

When the man was out of sight, Johnny said, "Now where were we?"

"Watching the sunset," San said.

"Ah, so we were. It sure is purty."

CHAPTER 76

The splendor and fun of Johnny and Maria's wedding was spoken about for months afterward. The town of Mustang Flat pulled together for the occasion, eager to celebrate and forget the doomed wagon train. Alice Wings had come to learn from her apprentice Liza Hart that Maria's son Billy was her lost love, Lance Kincaid's grandson, and she surprised everyone by changing overnight from a cranky spinster to a loving mother figure. Alice was the very model of Victorian propriety and helped Maria with the etiquettes and fashions of the day.

Young Queen Victoria had made it fashionable for brides to wear elaborate white dresses when she'd chosen such a gown for her own wedding to her beloved Prince Albert. It took many late nights of stitching and beading to create a gown for Maria that put even the queen's to shame, and the young woman had squealed and wept in equal measure when Alice and Liza revealed the finished masterpiece. A mantilla lace veil special ordered by Luke Lawson was held in place by the beautiful Parisian comb the groom had proposed with as the crowning touch to Maria's cascading tumble of black hair. Jack Campbell picked a bouquet of wildflowers for the bride to carry, and those were tied together with pink roses pruned from Mrs. Campbell's own garden. Little Jack was given the role of ring-bearer and though he protested being dressed up in the outfit Alice Wings had chosen—complete with a white crepe bow around his neck—he couldn't stop grinning.

During the ceremony, Liza Hart stood as Maria's bridesmaid and Sean O'Neil as his brother Johnny's groomsman, and in a touching gesture of fatherly love, Silas Booker had asked Maria for the honor of walking her down the aisle and giving her away. To the slight chagrin of Bob Beason but pleasure of everyone else, Adam Curtis performed the ceremony beneath a beautiful oak on the Oaktree Ranch, where Dick Peterson had graciously agreed to the request of Alice Wings that the wedding stage should be set.

Johnny and Maria said their vows under a spectacular sunset sky, and when Adam Curtis declared, "You may now kiss your bride," the whoops and cheers of the guests could be heard from miles away.

The fiddler, even after he got drunk, played into the night, and the sheriff joined in with his own fiddle while Sandy McPhee strummed a guitar and washboard in alternating turns.

The evening before the wedding Dubois Brown had returned to Mustang Flat with another detachment of soldiers to retrieve the Gatling gun, much to the relief of Bob Beason and the entire town. The sheriff insisted the soldier come to the event as a surprise for Maria and Liza who were elated to see him again.

Dubois borrowed a banjo that was collecting dust in the evidence shed for a reason Beason had long forgotten and played rousing versions of "Red River Valley" and "Turkey in the Straw" with fast finger-picking that received enthusiastic applause. The handsome young soldier soon found himself swept away to dance with the ladies of the town and smiled so much his cheeks were sore. As the whiskey flowed, Johnny even managed an Irish jig before he fell on his butt and Sean made him stop, the brothers laughing to tears as the chair he'd planted the big pug in broke beneath him and he fell on his butt again.

Surprising everyone, most of all the bride and groom, Dick Peterson sang the old Irish wedding song "The Rose of Mooncoin" in a fine baritone voice despite his claims of being heartbroken being a popular topic of town gossip. And even Sean made a stab at singing "She Walked Through the Fair" to great applause.

Later, when Dick Peterson asked Liza Hart to dance, it was apparent to everyone why his heart had healed. Maria whispered into Johnny's ear, and he looked upon the dancing pair, both shy and pink cheeked but alight with the glow only new love can bring. Johnny clapped and cheered until a giggling Maria made him shush.

The Red Dust Inn had brought wagonloads of food with the help of John Baxter, and Lucas Battles had ordered the list of Irish whiskeys provided to him by the O'Neil brothers and a variety of liquor, beer, and even French champagne. The bill was staggering, but that was Sean's wedding gift to the happy couple and he didn't mind one bit. Alice Wings had ordered a special wedding cake that was a towering display of fluffy white frosting and sugar that glittered beneath the oil lamps that lit the Oaktree barn where the party had moved after the ceremony.

Sheriff Bob Beason, in his usual impeccable good taste presented his wedding gift to Johnny and Maria, a blue and white chamber pot that had sat on a mercantile shelf for a six-month. He was rewarded by a kiss from Maria that made him blush. The couple received a silver serving set from the Lawson family, a wreath of dried flowers from the Campbells, and many other Victorian dainties that Maria was already envisioning places for in the new home her husband was having built on the Running-S range.

Finally, just before the witching hour, Johnny and Maria left in a surrey decorated with crepe ribbons and flowers to spend their wedding night at the Red Dust Inn, from where they'd leave the next day to begin their trip east to a Boston honeymoon. Before she stepped into the surrey, Maria handed her bridal bouquet to a starry-eyed Liza for luck in love, yet another Victorian tradition handed down from Alice Wings, who was also taking charge of young Billy while the young couple traveled back East.

The crowd gathered round to see husband and wife off, and one young rooster fired his Colt in the air to give the departing couple a six-gun salute. The festivities at the Oaktree Ranch continued well into the wee hours of the morning, until the guests were finally spent and dispersed to their homes.

Dr. Grant would later say that he spent the morning after the wedding dispensing hangover cures by the dozen, and the very first one had been administered to himself.

EPILOGUE

It was a new emotion to Sean O'Neil and for a while it puzzled him until he identified it . . . loneliness. His cabin, that he'd once thought cramped, now seemed large and empty, echoing with the love and laughter of people who were now moved away.

Johnny and Maria had built their cozy little house on the Running-S nearly a full two acres away from Sean's cabin and at first, he'd found relief to lay down at night without needing to pull a pillow over his ears to drown out the caterwauling baby. Now he found that silence could be deafening and would often sit up reading until the small hours while waiting for sleep to claim him.

It wasn't the bittersweet memories or eerie quiet that troubled him now, he realized, rather a growing sense of unease. He stepped out of the cabin, built a cigarette, and studied the vast land around him. The sky had been the color of raw iron since morning but was now splashed with billowing red clouds, like blood on a sword blade.

What did it portend?

The Irish gift of foresight was strong in him, and he wondered if the violent sky was a warning. He felt it was, but a warning of what? Hard times to come?

Bloodshed on the range again . . . or worse bloodshed of his family.

Sean shook his head and ground out the cigarette butt under his heel. If Johnny was here, he'd laugh and tell him that he was acting like an old maiden aunt who hears a rustle in every bush.

The evening passed without trouble, and Sean tucked into a hearty supper before surveying his land from the porch one last time before settling in for the night. Coyotes yipped at the moon, and a gentle breeze swept through the prairie grass but nothing else stirred in the dark night. Still, as he lay in his bed, the feeling of foreboding remained, and he fell into a troubled sleep until a nightmare filled with gunsmoke and blood woke him with a start and left his heart racing.

Sean gave up on rest and sat at his kitchen table, sipping a glass of whiskey, and attempting to shake off the dream. Half an hour later, he forced himself to admit that the Celtic curse of clairvoyance had never failed him before and it was time to pay it heed. He'd dreamt of destruction after seeing blood and iron in the sky and that could mean only one thing . . . the Running-S would soon be plunged into danger worse that any he'd ever known.

TURN THE PAGE FOR AN EXCITING PREVIEW!

Before the Sugarloaf Ranch became legendary across the western frontier, the Jensens had to survive a Wild West infested with barbaric men who sought fortune and glory while killing with violent glee.

JOHNSTONE COUNTRY.
WHERE DYING AIN'T MUCH OF A LIVING.

Building a ranch takes heart and grit. Smoke and Sally Jensen are more than capable of meeting the challenges of shaping the land, raising the livestock, and establishing their brand. But Smoke wasn't always an entrepreneur. He's more apt to settle accounts with a fast draw than a checkbook. And when he learns his old friend Preacher has been ambushed by outlaws, he wastes no time saddling up and hitting the vengeance trail with his fellow mountain men Audie and Nighthawk.

Preacher's attackers have taken over the town of Desolation Creek deep in Montana Territory. Their scurrilous leader, Vernon "Venom" McFadden, has his men harrassing terrified homesteaders and townsfolk to get his hands on nearby property that's rumored to be rich with gold. Smoke and his helpmates drift into town one by one with a plan to root out Venom's gang of prairie rats and put the big blast on each and every one.

National Bestselling Authors
William W. Johnstone and J.A. Johnstone

DESOLATION CREEK
A SMOKE JENSEN NOVEL OF THE WEST

On sale June 2023 wherever Pinnacle books are sold!

Live Free. Read Hard.
www.williamjohnstone.net

Visit us at www.kensingtonbooks.com

CHAPTER 1

When a bullet zipped past Smoke Jensen's ear, leaving a hot, crimson streak in its wake, he had a realization.

Trouble sure had a way of following him.

He hadn't come to Big Rock with anything on his mind other than taking care of his business, maybe saying hello to a few friends, chief among them Sheriff Monte Carson and Louis Longmont, and then getting on back to the Sugarloaf.

Of course, his wife, Sally, had it in mind to do some shopping, but that was harmless enough, except for the damage it did to his pocketbook. So, no reasonable explanation existed as to why he found himself smack-dab in the middle of a shooting scrape.

Or rather, *another* shooting scrape.

The last thing he wanted was trouble. He wasn't the type to just stand idly by when bullets were flying, though. He might catch one of them. Or worse, innocent folks might get shot. So, he drew his Colt with lightning speed and took aim at the man who had just emerged from the general store.

A wisp of powder smoke still curled up from the muzzle

of the gun in the man's fist. He had already shifted his focus elsewhere after firing that first round. Evidently, he caught Smoke's movement in his peripheral vision and turned his attention back in that direction. He leveled his weapon and sneered.

"I wouldn't," Smoke said.

The warning fell on deaf ears, and the man's finger twitched, ready to squeeze off another shot. Smoke's keen eyes saw that, and his gun roared first.

The bullet hammered into the fella's chest, sending him backward as his feet flew from beneath him. He landed flat on his back. His fingers went slack, and he released the revolver. Smoke ran to the gun and kicked it away. One quick glance told him the gesture hadn't been necessary, although erring on the side of caution was always better.

A scarlet ring was spreading on the man's dirty, tattered shirt. Dull, glassy eyes, with the life fading from them, stared up at Smoke.

"Who in the—" Smoke began, wanting to know who he had just shot, and why.

He didn't have time to finish the question as another shot rang out from inside the general store.

"Sally," he said, working to rein in the worry he felt rising in his chest. He swung his gun up, while quickly stepping away from the dead hombre, who lay sprawled out in the middle of the street. Eager to check on his wife, who'd gone inside the store a few minutes earlier, Smoke was about to close the gap between himself and the structure, when the door flew open again.

Another gunman burst onto the store's porch, spinning wildly as if trying to assess his surroundings, but not moving cautiously enough to gain a true lay of the land. This gave Smoke all the time he needed to dive behind a water trough. He reached the cover just in time as the panic-stricken gunman sent two wild shots into the air. As far as Smoke could tell, no one was hit. Most of the folks who had been on the boardwalks or in the street had scrambled for cover when the shooting started.

Just who was this fella and what was he all fired up about? Maybe, Smoke thought, he could end this without any more bloodshed. He didn't care for the fact that a fresh corpse was only a few feet away. Smoke didn't hesitate to kill when necessary, but he didn't take any pleasure in it. If he had his way, he'd never be mixed up in gunplay again.

Smoke rested his arm on the trough and drew a bead, his hand steady, his aim sure.

"Put that gun down!" he called. "No one else has to get hurt. Or worse."

A few townspeople were hustling around, trying to get out of the line of fire. Two old men who'd been sitting on a bench, enjoying the shade the boardwalk's overhanging roof offered, dove off the side and onto the ground. Smoke had to chuckle, realizing the impact had probably jarred the old-timers. They were in one piece, though, and didn't have any bullets in them as they crawled beneath the porch. Thankfully, it seemed as if everyone was out of harm's way.

Until the little girl dashed past.

Smoke hadn't even noticed her before now. She couldn't be any older than six, but might have been as young as four. She was a little thing, and scared, as she screamed for her ma. She tried to make it off the porch, but the gun-wielding hombre extended his free arm and scooped up the child, jerking her back onto the porch before Smoke could react.

The man held on to the girl tightly, using her as a shield as he swept his gun from side to side. She squirmed and kicked her legs as she continued screaming, but she had no chance of escaping the man's brutal grip.

Smoke regretted not having put a bullet into the wild-eyed varmint as soon as he laid eyes on the man. That would have ended this before he had a chance to grab that poor child.

"I'm gonna get out of here!" he yelled. "You all hear me?"

Smoke caught a glimpse of movement up the street and swiveled his head to see Sheriff Monte Carson hurrying toward the scene, with two deputies following him. Unfortunately, the crazed gunman on the porch noticed them, too, and sent a shot in their direction. Monte and the deputies instinctively split up as the bullet whistled between them. Monte took cover in one of the alcoves along the boardwalk, while the two deputies crouched behind a parked wagon.

The little girl screamed even louder after the shot, but her captor only tightened the arm he had looped around her body under her arms.

"Shut up!" he snarled at the girl. He turned his attention back to the sheriff and yelled, "Stay back! I swear I'll put a bullet in this here child's brain!"

Smoke's blood was boiling. He'd encountered some low-down, prairie scum in his day, but anyone who would hurt a child was the worst of the worst. He had to smile, though, when the girl started writhing even harder beneath the man's arm. She tried throwing her elbows back and even sent a few more kicks toward him, but his strength put an end to the struggle quickly. Still, Smoke admired her fighting spirit. He aimed to tell her as much, too. He'd get a chance, since he would never let that little girl die.

"What is it you want?" Smoke called.

He wasn't the law in Big Rock, but with the sheriff and

his deputies pinned down and unable to get closer, he was in the best position to act.

"I want out of here," the gunman said. "I want to make it to my horse down yonder, climb in the saddle, and get out of town without any trouble!"

"Sure, friend," Smoke replied in an affable tone. "Just let the young'un go and you can mosey on out of here. No one will stop you."

The man's lips curled back, revealing jagged yellow teeth. "That ain't how this works. She comes with me. I'll leave her down the trail when I'm free and clear."

Smoke's back stiffened. He couldn't let the hard case ride out of town with that little girl. If she was carried off by him, she was probably as good as dead.

"My daughter!" a loud, terror-stricken voice screamed. "He has my daughter!"

The hard case swung his gun hand around to cover the panicking woman who ran out of the store next door, holding her dress up as she sprinted. Her feet kicked up gravel and dust, but she didn't slow down any, until the man jabbed his gun toward her.

"Don't come any closer! I'll shoot her!" He jammed the hard barrel back against the child's skull, causing her to cry out. She tried reaching for her mother, the gesture causing the woman to cry even louder and stretch her arms out, too, as she skidded to a stop in the road.

Smoke had seen more than enough. He couldn't get a shot off, though. He was good—probably one of the best there was—but even he couldn't guarantee a clean shot under these circumstances. It was just too risky. And he'd be damned if any harm came to a child because of him.

But he couldn't *not act,* either.

The street was eerily silent. Smoke could see the two old-timers crawling quietly beneath the porch, headed toward the gunman, obviously intent on intervening. There was an opening where they could get out, not far behind the man. Smoke hoped it wouldn't spook the varmint, causing him to shoot the child.

Smoke cast his eyes toward the sheriff. Monte Carson peered around the corner of the alcove where he had taken cover, but he made no move toward the gunman. His deputies stood motionless behind the wagon, following his example.

The tension was thick. Normally, Smoke was as calm as could be in situations like this, but now his heart felt as if it might beat right out of his chest. Perhaps the child's presence did it. Or maybe his not knowing what had happened to Sally. Had that shot he'd heard earlier hit her? Was she okay? Heaven help that crazed outlaw if she wasn't. Whatever the reason, his nerves were a bit more frayed than usual.

He fought hard to control his emotions. He needed to proceed with a clear head. He didn't give a damn about his own life.

Right now, that little girl was all that mattered.

And Sally.

Smoke drew a deep breath, exhaled slowly, and fought down his anger. Now wasn't the time to be blinded by rage. A wry smile tugged at his lips as a plan began to take shape inside his mind. What he needed was a distraction. Maybe those two old-timers would give it to him. They were edging closer, shifting beneath the porch and looking as if they were ready to scramble out and spring up at any moment.

Just like that, though, in the blink of an eye, the old men and Smoke's plan became irrelevant.

The outlaw had taken a few steps back on the porch,

toward the store's door. He never bothered to check behind him.

That had been a mistake.

A bottle broke into a dozen pieces as it crashed against his head. One jagged shard tore into his scalp, slicing away the flesh and leaving a hot, wet, bloody streak.

Out of instinct, he dropped the child. She leaped off the porch as quickly as possible and into her mother's arms. For a moment, Smoke feared the outlaw would trigger his gun, but the man just pawed at his flowing wound. Confusion registered in his eyes as he swayed unsteadily on his feet. His gun slid from his fingers.

"What the—"

He tried spinning around, but didn't have a chance before a second bottle smashed into him, sending him to the ground, out cold.

Smoke was already at the porch now, his gun still drawn, when he realized who had saved the day.

There in the doorway, with the neck of a broken bottle in her hand, stood Sally.

CHAPTER 2

"What on earth is going on here?" Monte Carson asked.

Smoke finished thumbing a fresh cartridge into his walnut-butted Colt and then pouched the iron. "I was wondering that myself." He looked to Sally and arched an eyebrow. "Here I was worried about *you,* and I should have been worried about *him*." He jerked his head toward the unconscious gunman who lay on the porch's puncheon floor.

One of the sheriff's deputies was standing over the downed man, relieving him of his weapons. A small derringer was up his right sleeve, along with a knife in one of his boots. The deputy then rummaged through the man's pockets and pulled out a wad of greenbacks and waved them toward the sheriff.

"Those are mine!" Don Baker said.

He was a large, easygoing man who ran the mercantile, along with help from his clerk, Ike Hairston. Ike was out on the porch now, too, and hurried to the downed brigand. He reared his foot back, but Sheriff Carson stopped him.

"You can't kick him now. He's laid out cold!"

"Well, I oughta," Ike said, and then his voice trailed off

into a consortium of jumbled curse words. "They tried to hold up the store."

"They didn't *try*," his boss corrected him. "They did rob us. Would have gotten away with it, too, if it hadn't been for Jensen."

"Which one?" Smoke said with a smile. His eyes darted to Sally, who was now off the porch and checking on the terrified mother and child.

"Thank God she's okay," Sally said, rubbing the girl's back.

The two old-timers had rolled out from under the porch and, after considerable effort, were finally stumbling to their feet.

"Sheriff, I think Walt done broke his backside," one of them said.

The other groaned as he rubbed his rear end. It took considerable effort for Smoke to control his laughter, and one look at Sally told him she was having the same struggle.

Monte seemed somewhat annoyed when he said, "Will someone just tell me exactly what happened?"

"I'll tell you," Ike said, still red-faced with anger. "Those two no-accounts came in the store, acted like they were shopping, but then drew their pistols and demanded the money from the register. They were also trying to take off with a few supplies, jerky and coffee, mostly." He jabbed a bony finger toward the dead man in the street and said, "He got spooked and told his partner they had to get out of there. That's when he came out shooting!"

"That explains your ear," Monte said, looking at Smoke.

Smoke remembered the close call and touched his ear. It stung a little, but the blood had dried now. He'd had a lot worse done to him over the years.

"Guess I was in the wrong place at the wrong time," Smoke said with a chuckle.

"Or the right place," Monte said. "He may have hit someone with those wild shots, had you not taken him down. Reckon the town is obliged to you for that. Once again."

Smoke nodded.

It seemed as if Monte took every opportunity he could to state how much the town of Big Rock owed Smoke. In fact, Smoke was mostly responsible for the settlement's founding, having led an exodus here of folks escaping from the outlaw town of Fontana, several miles away. They had fled to escape the reign of terror carried out by brutal mine owner Tilden Franklin and his hired guns.

Now, a couple of years later, Franklin was dead, and Fontana was an abandoned town, nothing left but moldering ruins, while Big Rock was growing and thriving. Monte Carson wasn't the only one who gave Smoke a lot of the credit for that happening.

Smoke, however, wasn't interested in accolades. He was thankful when the storekeeper started talking again.

"Anyway," Ike Hairston continued, "that spooked his partner inside the store and he started shooting, too."

"Anyone hit?" the sheriff asked.

"No, but he plugged the dang cracker barrel!" Ike said. He looked as if he wanted to kick the man again. His anger subsiding, he shrugged and said, "That's when he came out onto the porch, and, well, you saw the rest."

Sally was at Smoke's side now. They joined Sheriff Carson in examining the two outlaws. Both wore dirty, torn homespun and it seemed as if neither had bathed in a long while.

Smoke thumbed his curled-brim hat back, revealing more of his ash-blond hair, and scratched his forehead. "Looks like these two had fallen on hard times."

"Explains why they were so desperate," Monte said

with a frown. "Still doesn't give them call to carry on like this."

"Sure doesn't," Smoke agreed. "Reckon they could have gotten a meal just about anywhere here in town."

Smoke wasn't exaggerating. Big Rock was a friendly community, where folks could find plenty of help if they needed it. Smoke might have even given the two work at the Sugarloaf, had they dropped by. Of course, the fact that one had held a little girl hostage showed he was *not* simply a good man who'd fallen on desperate times, so Smoke doubted if they'd had any intent on working for an honest day's wages.

The one Sally had laid out was now starting to groan as he came to.

"Let's get him on down to the jail," Monte told his deputies. "I'll send for Doc Spaulding to patch him up."

"He needs to take a look at my rear, too!" Walt said, still rubbing his derriere.

"Maybe he can get you one of those sittin' pillows," the other old-timer said. "Feels better than resting your cheeks on a hard chair, that's for sure!"

Monte rolled his eyes and mumbled, "Lord help me." He turned his focus to the corpse, which lay in the street, and winced as he saw that flies had already started to gather. "I'll get the undertaker down here, too. I'll look through the wanted dodgers I have back at the office. Could be that you have some reward money coming, Smoke."

Smoke snorted. "A bounty-hunting Jensen? Now that's a thought."

"Don't you go getting any ideas. We don't need any more trouble," Sally said. "Besides, you're a rancher. Remember?"

Smoke held up his hands in mock surrender. "Believe

me, I've had my fill of trouble. I'm not looking for more."
His smile disappeared as he turned his gaze toward the
sheriff. He scratched his strong, angular chin and asked,
"Do I need to stick around and appear before Judge
Proctor?"

"Nah," Monte said. "This is pretty cut-and-dried. The
way I figure it, you did the town a favor. You, too," he said,
smiling at Sally. "Smoke, you sure married one with a bit
of sass in her."

Smoke laughed, nodding in agreement.

He certainly couldn't argue that point.

The ride back to the Sugarloaf was seven miles and
Smoke didn't mind the journey one bit. The country was
mighty pretty, and he had an even prettier woman by his
side. As he guided his black stallion, Drifter, beside the
buckboard Sally drove, he took a moment to soak it all in.

She had an infectious smile, which he never tired of.
Her brown hair hung in bouncing curls. With Sally set
against the backdrop of the rugged Rocky Mountains,
Smoke wondered if he'd indeed been shot back in Big
Rock and was now in heaven.

"What are you looking at?" Sally said, though her smile
hinted that she already knew the answer.

"The woman of my dreams," he said without hesitation.

She smiled even wider. "And what are you thinking
about?"

Smoke laughed. He made a show of looking around and
said, "Well, I suppose I could tell you, since there's no one
else around."

Now Sally laughed loudly. "Easy. We've got a few
miles to go before we're back home."

"Like I said, there's no one else around."

Sally cast him one last devilish grin before turning her attention back to the trail before her. Smoke did the same.

They rode in silence for a few minutes before he said, "That was some stunt you pulled back there, walloping that owlhoot like that. You could've been hurt."

"And that little girl could've been killed."

"True," Smoke admitted. "Reckon I can't be too upset."

"Upset? You knew I was a handful when you put the ring on my finger."

Smoke chuckled. "That I did. And I wouldn't have you any other way. I just want you to be careful, is all. I intend to grow old with you."

"Of course," she said. "I'll be sitting by your side on the porch in our rockers. We can look out over the Sugarloaf. It will be massive by then."

"You have big plans," he said.

"*We* have big plans," she said.

"Yep. And they don't include gunfighting, that's for sure."

She gave him a pointed stare. "It really bothered you, what happened back in town?"

He nodded. Drifter continued to pick his way over the trail, staying beside the buckboard, moving at a measured pace. It seemed as if the horses were just as content to enjoy the pleasant evening as night fell around them as Smoke and Sally were.

The falling sun painted the picturesque landscape in pink and yellow hues. A cloud of gnats hovered just off the road. A few grasshoppers leaped in the brushy grass to Smoke's left. Smoke sucked in a lungful of air and held it a moment, enjoying the smell of the upcoming summer. Something about this time of year called to him. Something peaceful. Thinking about peace, he said, "I just hope this valley is tamed one day, and sooner rather than later. I've had more than enough gunplay to last me a lifetime."

"There will be peace around these parts soon enough," she said. "Men like you and Preacher have worked hard to make this land safe for decent folks. One day, our children will thank you for it."

Smoke smiled once again. He sure liked the sound of that.

Children.

Of course, if they turned out anything like their pa— or ma, for that matter—they'd keep him and Sally on their toes.

They finished their trip in silence, content to simply be in each other's presence. The relaxing ride did wonders in washing away the unpleasantness that had occurred back in town, and by the time they arrived home, it was already nothing but a memory.

That peacefulness didn't last long, though. Upon riding up to the house, Smoke realized they had company. Two saddle mounts he didn't recognize, along with a couple of pack animals, were tied in front of the log ranch house.

Something stirred deep inside his stomach, telling him that all was not well. He remembered that realization he'd had back in town when the shooting had started.

Trouble just had a way of finding him.

CHAPTER 3

Smoke relaxed when he saw the visitors sitting on the porch and realized who they were. His good-natured laugh cut the night silence as he swung down from his horse and started for the steps.

"Audie? Nighthawk? What are you two doing here?"

Some of his excitement faded when his old friends didn't respond with smiles of their own. Even in the fading light, Smoke could see sorrow etched on their weathered faces. Something else was there, too. Something in their eyes.

Something that resembled rage.

"What's going on?" Smoke said.

By now, Sally was off the buckboard and at Smoke's side. Pearlie Fontaine, Smoke's friend and right-hand man on the Sugarloaf, had been waiting on the porch, too. He now stood with the others and spoke first.

"Smoke, I'll take care of the horses and the buckboard. Why don't you head inside. I've got a pot of coffee going. Have some supper left, too, if you're hungry."

"Thanks, Pearlie, but it was getting so late by the time we left town that we grabbed a bite at the café. What's going on here?"

Pearlie looked to Nighthawk and then Audie before heading to the horses. "I'll get these animals squared away."

Smoke handed him Drifter's reins, but kept his eyes on the two visitors.

Age had taken some of Nighthawk's height, but not much. Smoke knew that an enemy only underestimated the deadly and taciturn Crow warrior to their detriment. He was as tough as they came. Smoke doubted anyone would actually take him lightly. Even in his seventies, he was a large, powerfully built man who appeared and moved as if he were twenty years younger.

His close friendship with Audie was a study in contrasts. Audie was a diminutive man, approximately four feet tall, who grew up in the hallowed halls of the prestigious universities back east. Since he had been a professor, many didn't understand why he'd left that life behind so many years ago to head out west and learn the ways of the mountain men.

But that's exactly what he'd done, and now that tough, rough-hewn life was every bit as bred into him as within Preacher himself. Audie had been described as a lot of trouble in a small package. He and Nighthawk were inseparable.

Smoke had had a few adventures with them, back in the old days when he was under the tutelage of Preacher. Now it was great to see them, but one look into their eyes told Smoke it was not under good circumstances. They weren't here simply to pay him and Sally a friendly visit.

Sally interrupted the tense silence and asked, "Are you hungry?"

"No, ma'am," Audie said. "Perhaps we should . . . talk inside."

"Of course," Sally said.

She waited until the two visitors turned to the door

before exchanging a curious glance with her husband. Smoke shrugged as he took her hand and led the way into the main house.

"How about that coffee Pearlie mentioned?" Smoke said.

"No, thank you," Audie said, presumably speaking for Nighthawk, too. "Smoke, it might be best that you sit down for this. You've no doubt already surmised that the news we bring is not pleasant."

Smoke nodded. "Sorta figured that, Audie. Let's sit around the kitchen table." Smoke cut to the front of the procession and swept his hand toward the table. "Make yourselves at home. I think I'll go ahead and have some of that coffee."

"I'll get it," Sally said with a soft smile.

Smoke nodded and then joined his visitors in sitting.

"All right," he said, once situated, "go ahead and speak your piece." He kept his eyes trained on Audie, knowing he would be the one to elaborate. To say Nighthawk was a man of few words was an understatement.

The old professor sighed, looked to Nighthawk, and then back across the table at Smoke. "There is no pleasant way to say this, so I must be blunt. Preacher is dead."

Sally gasped loudly. She dropped the coffeepot, but was able to catch it before it clattered onto the stove top. She forgot about what she was doing, placed it down, and hurried to Smoke's side. "He's d-dead?"

"I'm afraid so, ma'am," Audie said.

Nighthawk offered a simple nod, but his eyes revealed the fact he was contemplating it all and mourning the passing of his old friend.

"Dead? I figured Preacher would outlive us all. Thought he'd see a hundred and maybe more," Smoke said.

"And you might have very well been correct," Audie

said, "had it not been for that murderous bunch that took him out up in Montana."

Smoke's neck muscles tightened. He gritted his teeth and balled his fists. "Are you telling me Preacher was murdered?"

Nighthawk nodded slightly, adding, "Umm."

Sally fell into the chair beside Smoke and wrapped her hands around his arm. Her shoulders shook as her body was wracked with sobs. Smoke pulled free, but only long enough to wrap his arm around her. He held her a moment and let her cry. He understood her sorrow. Perhaps soon he'd feel it, too.

But right now, another emotion had seized him.

Raw, powerful anger.

He knew it wouldn't release its grip, either, until he'd cleared out every last varmint responsible for Preacher's death.

He gave Sally a few minutes and then said, "Might be best you go in there. I have some things I need to discuss with Audie and Nighthawk."

"You mean how you're going to hunt down the guilty and make them pay?" Sally said. Her words were edged in steel. When she ventured a look at Smoke, he realized she wasn't upset about the proposed plan. She wanted justice every bit as much as he did. Even under the grave circumstances, he couldn't help but offer a slight grin.

"That about sums it up," he said.

"I'll stay."

Smoke swallowed the lump in his throat and nodded. There was no sense in arguing with that woman when she'd made up her mind about something.

"All right, Audie. Start at the beginning and tell me everything," Smoke said.

"I wish we had more to tell, but we are still trying to

piece it together ourselves," Audie said. "What we do know—having received word through the usual chain that news travels through on the frontier—is that Preacher had wandered into a settlement called Desolation Creek, up in Montana Territory. We don't believe he had any particular business there. He was simply . . . passing through. But for whatever reason, he ran afoul of a local criminal figure—a Venom McFadden, I believe."

"Venom?" Sally said, jerking her head back. "What kind of name is that?"

"I'm afraid I don't know the details on that, ma'am," Audie said. "Nor do I know the specifics of what happened to Preacher. We've heard tell that this McFadden character has a tight grip on the town and the valley in which it lies. He's exercising control over everything and everyone. A real hard case, it seems."

"The outlaws are in control?" Smoke said, scratching his chin and shaking his head. "I reckon that didn't go over too well with Preacher. He's never been one to sit by and let owlhoots run roughshod over innocent folks."

"Indeed," Audie said.

"Umm," Nighthawk said, his jaw set hard, his hands resting atop the table in tight fists.

"I'm afraid this challenge ultimately proved too much even for Preacher," Audie continued. "He was shot, from what we understand."

"How long ago was this?" Smoke said.

"I'm not certain, but I'd estimate a month, perhaps a little longer," Audie said.

Nausea roiled deep inside Smoke's stomach. He hated to think that Preacher had been gone that long and he hadn't known. Of course, news didn't travel very fast on the frontier, and he understood it had likely occurred even longer ago than a month. The time that had passed didn't change anything, though. He'd ride into Desolation Creek and make McFadden and his men pay. If by chance they'd already bled that town dry and moved on, he'd find them, wherever they'd gone. They could run to the ends of the earth, but they'd never escape Smoke and the retribution he was set to deliver. He had a debt to pay. He'd settle Preacher's account.

In lead.

"I hope you didn't just drop by to give me the news," Smoke said.

Smoke could feel Sally's eyes on him, but he kept his own trained across the table.

For the first time that night, Nighthawk's lips turned upward slightly. A brief twinkle was in his eyes and Smoke realized the old Crow was thinking about the same thing— justice.

"Hardly," Audie confirmed. "We are riding up to Montana Territory just as soon as we leave here.

"And we intend to bring hell down on Venom McFadden."

Visit our website at
KensingtonBooks.com
to sign up for our newsletters, read
more from your favorite authors, see
books by series, view reading group
guides, and more!

Become a Part of Our
Between the Chapters Book Club
Community and Join the Conversation

Betweenthechapters.net